TWO CLASSIC MYTHS, GIVEN

Eve's Daughter's puts a feminist spin on the classic myth of The Fall, times two. Many creation stories depict a cosmic conflict between good and evil. But what if the conflict was something simpler, an earthly divide between men and women? Would things be any different? Book One, based on the Sumerian tale of the goddess Inanna and her lover Dumuzi, takes us back to the Early Copper Age when a matriarchal, agricultural community encounters patriarchal nomads for the first time. Book Two, set in the 20th century, retells Milton's version of the Adam and Eve story, filling in details of what happened after they were thrown out of that famous garden.

Praise for Eve's Daughters

"Pat Valdata has already proven herself a skillful poet. Now she has done it in fiction, with her latest novel. In *Eve's Daughters,* a feminist sexy spin on the Sumerian story of Inanna, and the story of Adam and Eve set in modern times, she explores matriarchal societies using a brilliant inventive structure."—*Lynda Schor, author of five books of short fiction including Sexual Harassment Rules, and the soon-to-be out novel, DEARTH*

"The fall from grace was pinned on Eve in the *Bible* and in *Paradise Lost*. With heartbreaking storytelling, *Eve's Daughters* reminds us of what happens when women are blamed and punished in a patriarchal society. It also examines how peace and hope can be found in matriarchal clans and colonies. A novel I won't soon forget."—*Gail Priest, Author of the Annie Crow Knoll trilogy and Eastern Shore Shorts*

Excerpt

The night before the Sowing Festival, the full moon rose gold and glowing, its light shining like a long torch on the river's calm surface. But when it had risen to almost full height, the moon's face was as dull and red as raw clay…Ana shivered and wrapped her deerskin cloak more tightly around her shoulders. She wasn't cold; the day's warmth was still radiating from the packed dirt beneath her feet. She sat down and waited, awake and troubled, until she saw a sliver of brightness on one side of the moon's face. Every time she looked away and then back again, she saw more light. Perhaps everything would be all right after all.

Eve's Daughters

Pat Valdata

Moonshine Cove Publishing, LLC

Abbeville, South Carolina, U.S.A.
First Moonshine Cove Edition November 2020

ISBN: 978-1-945181-95-5
Library of Congress PCN: 2020921159
Copyright 2020 by Pat Valdata

Cover image used with permission of the author, cover and interior design by Moonshine Cove staff.

Acknowledgments

I am grateful for the support of the following individuals and organizations, without whom this book would not have been completed: the Institute for Contemporary Midrash, especially director Rivkah Walton, workshop leader Alicia Suskin Ostriker, PhD, and the attendees of Ostriker's workshop; the librarians of Sweet Briar College; the staff and fellows at the Virginia Center for the Creative Arts; the extensive Neolithic exhibit at the Magyar Nemzeti Múzeum (Hungarian National Museum) in Budapest; the creative writers and educators on the listserv CREWRT-L, especially Mary Lee Bragg, Fran Claggett, Cher Holt-Fortin, W. Scott Olsen, and David Weinstock, who read all or portions of the manuscript; Lisa Bowden, Natalie Diaz, Mary Heinsohn, Alexis Latner, Jennifer Unter, Amy Williams, and writing group members Patty Adelizzi, Pamela Andrews, Irmgarde Brown, Larry Carmichael, Marie Edmeades, Laura Fox, Bethany Hacker, Cathy Herlinger, David Hoffman, Shirley Horne, Kate Lashley, George Mason, and Michael Venters, who suggested revisions; Cathy Gohlke, who suggested I read *The Red Tent* by Anita Diamant; and Anne DeMott, who suggested I read *Circles of Stone* by Joan Dahr Lambert.

Most of all, I am grateful to my husband, Bob Schreiber, to whom I dedicate this book with love and thanks for your patience—and your superb technical support.

About the Author

Pat Valdata is novelist and poet with an MFA in fiction writing from Goddard College. *Eve's Daughters* is her third novel. Her other novels are *Crosswind* and *The Other Sister,* which won a gold medal from the Árpád Academy of the Hungarian Association. Her poetry book about women aviation pioneers, *Where No Man Can Touch*, won the 2015 Donald Justice Poetry Prize. Pat's other poetry titles are *Inherent Vice* and *Looking for Bivalve.* In 2013, she received a Mid Atlantic Arts Foundation Fellowship to the Virginia Center for the Creative Arts. A native of New Jersey, Pat lives in Crisfield, Maryland, with her husband Bob Schreiber and a rescued miniature poodle.

www.patvaldata.com

EVE'S

DAUGHTERS

BOOK ONE: INTO THE ORCHARD
Old Europe, The Tisza River Valley, Early Copper Age

Part I

The night before the Sowing Festival, the full moon rose gold and glowing, its light shining like a long torch on the river's calm surface. But when it had risen to almost full height, the moon's face was as dull and red as raw clay.

Ana stood outside and looked up at the dimming moon. Why, on the most important night of her life, would the Goddess do this? The last time she had seen the moon like this, one of her cousins had been gored by a stag.

Ana was supposed to be asleep. On this night of all nights she should be well rested. The morning would begin with a long day of preparation for Ana and her cousin Kore, who were going to take part in the sacred sowing ritual for the first time. Ana had been anticipating this day for six cycles of the moon, ever since her flow had started. Tomorrow she and her cousin would be transformed from girls to women. Tomorrow should be a happy, holy day for them. But the moon!

She stood alone in the temple square, staring at the moon as if it would answer her. The night was still—everyone else in the village was sensibly asleep. It was so quiet she could hear the soft stirrings of mice, the hoot of an owl. A bat swooped by, startling her, until she realized it was just the tiny nighttime hunter seeking moths. Ana shivered and wrapped her deerskin cloak more tightly around her shoulders. She wasn't cold; the day's warmth was still radiating from the packed dirt beneath her feet. She sat down and waited, awake and troubled, until she saw a sliver of brightness on one side of the moon's face. Every time she looked away and then back again, she saw more light. Perhaps everything would be all right after all.

Ana stood up stiffly and took a deep breath. She hadn't realized how tense she had become. She exhaled until her shoulders relaxed. Then she went inside her grandmother's house and lay down. She tried to be quiet, but her youngest sister Arina, a light sleeper, woke up and called out. Shela, a very sound sleeper, didn't even stir.

"Don't be afraid, Arina," Ana whispered. She snuggled next to her sister under the fur bedding. "Go back to sleep. Everything is all right."

"Why are you up?"

"I just went outside for a few minutes to look at the moon. Hush. Let's go back to sleep."

"I can't. Tell me a story, Ana."

"All right, a quick one. Promise me you'll go to sleep after that."

"I promise."

Keeping her voice low, and stroking Arina's fine brown hair, Ana recited, "A long, long time ago, the air was very cold, much colder than tonight. Snow fell no matter what the season. People lived on nuts and dried fruits, and if hunters could find no aurochs or boar, the people starved."

"Poor hungry people," Arina said. Ana kissed the top of her head

"Then the Goddess Moon took pity on the hungry people, and asked her sister Sun to move a little closer. The snow stopped, the land thawed, and the Goddess showed the people how to sow grain. They were never hungry again. And ever since that time, we celebrate the sowing and the harvest to thank the Goddess for taking care of our village, just as you and Shela and I thank Grandmother for taking care of us."

Grandmother had been the guiding figure in their lives since their mother had died giving birth to Arina ten summers ago, a long and difficult delivery that left Arina simple. Still, Arina was blessed by the Goddess, for in place of a quick mind, she had a kind heart, and a gentle innocence that made her easy to love. It took her longer than most, but once she learned a task, she did it well.

Their father, too, was dead and buried. He'd let a bad tooth go for too long before asking Grandmother to pull it out, and his face swelled. He could neither eat nor drink, and then he fell into a fever. That had happened almost four winters ago. Ana liked to think that her parents had been reborn as the two wild geese who began nesting in a clump of reeds on the riverbank not long after her father had died, and who had returned during each thaw ever since.

Since the day of her first flow, Ana had hoped to see a handsome boy from another clan stride through one of the village gates like a gander in search of a goose. She was old enough to be partnered now. Grandmother had instructed Ana and Kore on ways to give and receive pleasure, so they would perform the act of love in the way that would most please the Goddess. Grandmother also showed the girls how to stretch themselves inside with lengths of carved antler, polished smooth and coated with beeswax, so their first sowing ritual would be painless.

Arina's steady breathing told Ana that her sister was asleep. Ana closed her eyes and tried to stop thinking about the ritual to come. It was nearly dawn before she finally fell asleep, too.

Like Ana, Kore had been too excited to sleep well. At breakfast, the two drowsy girls chattered about which boy in their clan was the most handsome, and which they would choose that night.

"Girls, enough," Grandmother Mari said. "We are all sons and daughters of the Goddess. Tonight, *Who* is not important. *What* is all that matters: Will you honor the Goddess the way I have taught you? If anything else is on your minds today, then I worry for our crops."

The girls bent their heads, avoiding one another's eyes, until Mari was out of earshot—not out of remorse, but to keep from giggling.

"You'd think she'd remember what it was like the first time," Kore said.

"Grandmother is very old," Ana said. "After all, she has seen more than fifty winters and summers."

After breakfast, Ana and Kore bathed and washed their hair, helping each other tease out the tangles with bone combs. They painted one another with red ocher, drawing three parallel lines on their cheeks, spirals around each breast, and straight lines on their bellies and thighs. Each girl put on her new string skirt and a necklace of bone beads before joining the rest of the clan in the public space outside the temple.

At midday, Mari stood in front of the assembly, holding the tether of the first bull calf of the season. She looked every inch the village leader in a narrow skirt sewn from deerskin strips and a sleeveless deerskin jacket decorated with egg-shaped beads and fringe. She wore a necklace and bracelets of shell and copper beads; her long hair was clean, twisted into coils and kept in place with combs carved from horn.

Ana and Kore walked up to her, Ana on her right side, Kore on her left, and the three of them entered the temple, leading the lowing calf. Mari put on the mask that looked like the wide-mouthed face of a frog. Kore, in the temple for the first time, gasped and shivered to see her great-aunt's familiar face hidden, transforming her into their Priestess. Ana squeezed her cousin's hand. Even though Ana had been assisting her grandmother with temple rites since she was a little girl, she, too, felt the awe of seeing Goddess Power inhabit her grandmother. The Priestess lifted the polished copper knife from the bench and led the girls and calf into the sanctuary.

They bowed to the statue of the Giver-of-Life, who sat on a painted pottery throne. The Goddess wore a carved bird mask with owl and hawk feathers arrayed in a fan around the top. Her hands cupped her large breasts, and between her legs, spread for birthing, the head of her newborn was crowning. The Priestess handed Kore the calf's tether before lighting the sacred fire and leading them in the prayer of offering. After the prayer, the Priestess handed Ana the bowl of regeneration. It was a fine clay piece, made by another Priestess long ago. The bowl was wide and deep, with phallus-shaped handles. Ana held it under the calf's throat as the Priestess lifted the knife, and with another prayer of offering, slit the calf's throat. The temple filled with the sharp odor of spilled blood.

Ana had to kneel to keep the bowl under the pulsing flow as the calf's knees buckled. The Priestess held one hand on the animal's head, praying, until it bled out.

When the calf was dead, they pulled the body into the antechamber and the Priestess removed her mask. The dead calf would be retrieved by the oldest women of the clan after they left. They would skin it and roast it whole for the next day's feast; afterwards, its bones would be buried at the edges of the fields.

When they emerged from the temple, Grandmother took the bowl, dipped her fingers into the blood and painted three vertical lines on the foreheads of Ana and Kore, who then led the procession out to the fields.

The blood on Ana's face felt warm and sticky. She couldn't remember ever being so excited. She had done the work of the Goddess all her life, but always as an apprentice, a child. Today the men of the clan were seeing her as a woman for the first time. Ana knew that in her ocher body paint, she looked beautiful and desirable. She was conscious of her body, and walked with graceful steps to show off her slender waist and round hips.

Behind them, the rest of the women, also wearing string skirts, lined up two by two. Each carried a small clay temple, with a tiny clay Goddess inside. Each temple contained one handful of grain. The men, naked except for beaded belts woven in bright colors, followed at the back of the procession, carrying sacks of barley, millet, lentils, and flax.

When they arrived at the fields, the women walked along the prepared ground, reaching into their clay temples to sprinkle the blessed seeds a few at a time. The men walking behind them did the actual sowing, tamping the earth over the seeds with their feet. When they finished sowing, they rested, men in one group, women in the other. They fasted except to drink beer, wishing the blessings of the Goddess on their fields with every cup they drank. At sunset, Ana's grandmother led them in prayer:

"We hail the sun that gives us light and warmth. We hail the rain that waters our crops. We hail the earth that shelters our seed. We hail the grain that feeds us. Blessed be She who gives us light, warmth, rain, earth. May she give us fine crops and a good harvest. We honor her tonight and for all time."

With the end of the prayer came the moment Ana and Kore had been waiting for all day. The men stood in the center of the group. Some of them—those who hadn't drunk too much beer—already had erections. By tradition, Ana and Kore were granted first pick. Ana walked up to Onno, a boy with fine-looking eyes who matched her in height, and took his hand. Her cousin chose a boy she used to climb trees with when they were children, and their Grandmother picked the handsomest of the grown men. Some women chose their current partner; others chose someone new. There were a few more women than men—there always seemed to be a shortage of men—so the last man was shared by two women. The two remaining women took each other's hands. There were many ways of honoring the Goddess this sacred night.

The couples spaced themselves out around the fields, and waited for the rising moon. When Ana's grandmother saw the first arc of the moon rise above the trees, she chanted a final blessing, and the ancient ritual commenced.

The morning after the sowing ritual, Ana woke at sunrise feeling languid and content. Onno lay on his back, snoring. In the daylight, with a line of drool on his cheek and smudges of red ocher on his chest, he seemed much less handsome than he had the night before.

Ana looked down at herself. The pigment that had so beautifully decorated her breasts and belly was almost rubbed off, and her torso was caked with dried sweat and dirt. Her thighs felt sticky, and they itched. She stretched a kink out of her back and strolled down to the river. The water was chilly, so she quickly rinsed herself clean and ran back to her home, where she hoped Shela would have the fire going.

Ana was grinning with happiness. She was fully a woman now, and she was sure she had done honor to the Goddess the night before. All her life she'd seen the whole village return smiling the morning after the sowing ritual. Now she finally understood why.

15

As she reached the wattle-and-daub village wall, she could smell the roasting calf, and her mouth watered. By the time she crossed the threshold of her own home, she was ready for breakfast. Happily, Shela was already up, and stirring a pot of porridge on the open hearth.

"Ana," Shela whispered, because Arina was still asleep. "What was it like?"

Ana slipped a tunic over her shoulders and tied a skirt around her waist before sitting down next to her sister.

"Is the porridge ready?" she asked. "I'm so hungry this morning!"

Shela filled a clay bowl and handed Ana an antler spoon. "So, tell me."

Ana blew on the hot porridge to cool it. "You know I can't tell you about that part. You're too young. Only grown women can talk about it."

"I know, but I'll be old enough next year, most likely. Can't you tell me anything? Did it hurt?"

"Of course, it didn't, silly. That's what the Temple training is for. You'll find out soon enough."

"So, did you like it?"

Ana couldn't help but smile. "Yes, I liked it. A lot." She reached over to give Shela a hug and a kiss. "Thank you for making this. It tastes so good."

As more people returned from the fields, Ana and her sisters looked forward to the festival day, a welcome respite from daily chores. As granddaughters of a Priestess, they had been apprenticed since childhood to the sacred work of the Goddess: baking bread, weaving, and working in clay. The Temple annex housed a beehive-shaped oven, querns for grinding flour, a storehouse of grain in large clay pots, smaller pots of honey, salt, dried fruits, and nuts. This was where Arina learned from patient teachers how to bake the offering loaves.

The central feature of the weaving room was the warp-weighted loom leaning against one wall. The loom was an ancient gift from the Goddess, and with it a skilled weaver like Shela could make beautifully patterned cloth. Stringing the warp threads onto the horizontal beam was tedious work, in Ana's opinion, but Shela said the repetitive task was relaxing. During fine weather, she would move the loom outdoors. She dyed their yarns outdoors, too, using a variety of barks and roots to color wool and flaxen fibers.

Ana was the potter. Her first job as an apprentice had been to make the loom weights to which the warp threads were tied. The weights were small, simple cylinders of clay, easy for young fingers to mold. If they cracked when they were fired, it was no matter. Ana would merely try again, and her mistakes would be crushed into powder for tempering new clay.

As the oldest she was also a priestess-in-training, and her other primary duty was to become a healer like her grandmother. It had been many, many cycles of the moon since Ana's clan had faced a winter so harsh that the herds wasted away, or a growing season so dry that all the crops failed. But sickness was common. Infants often died before they experienced one full cycle of seasons. The elderly sometimes developed a cough that Ana's grandmother could not cure. The unlucky clan member would grow thin and weak, and finally cough blood, and then a grave would have to be dug. So, Ana also learned the rituals for dying: how to place a man on his left side and a woman on her right, which artifacts to bury with them, which prayers to say to guide them through the passage to whatever the next life might bring. A healer was needed for the beginning of the cycle, too. Ana had assisted Grandmother at several births already; she knew how to cut the cord and which prayer to recite when she buried the afterbirth.

Ana was also learning all she could about decoctions, such as how to cause a needed flux and how to stop a harmful one, and poultices to ease the pain of a bee sting or draw out a swelling. There was so much to remember about the healing arts that Ana liked to scribe her grandmother's instructions in clay so she would not forget them. Grandmother had been teaching her the secret runes ever since Ana was a little girl. She made notes like "tea of willow bark for pain" or "chickweed poultice for itching" on bowls and cups before she fired them in the kiln.

Once a moon, Ana would check how much clay she had on hand. If her stock was getting low, she would take an empty pallet over to the clay pit, and dig a new supply. It was hard work with a digging stick, especially during a drought, so she tried to do this chore soon after a soaking rain. The wet clay would be much easier to dig, and when left to dry for a day or two, not so heavy to haul back. Whenever Ana was out walking, she kept part of her attention on the ground itself, hoping to spot a good vein of clay in a color she did not have.

This was Ana's task on a fine warm day one moon after the sacred rite. The sun was already climbing when she set out with her digging stick, a bag of reed netting over her shoulder for collecting greens, and a small jug of water tied around her waist with a leather thong. She wore a sleeveless linen tunic and short linen skirt dyed bright yellow. Around her neck she tied a strip of leather hung with obsidian beads and purple shells. An armlet of deer bones circled her left arm above the elbow.

Ana strolled upriver, where she saw families of ducks and geese, schools of minnows, clusters of tadpoles, water beetles, all the creatures that made the river their home, while keeping an eye out for emerging edible plants. After a winter of eating dried meat, dried fruit and stored roots, it was always a joy to seek out dandelions and cress, wild onions, and sorrel. It was a bonus to come upon a patch of plantain leaves, so useful for healing wounds. She picked the leaves and stuffed them in the net bag.

After a while she turned north toward the forested hills. Far beyond these familiar hills, people said, stood mountains so high their tops were capped with snow. Ana had never seen the mountains, but her Grandmother assured her they existed. Old legends said that long, long ago, some of the mountains breathed fire and smoke, and her ancestors had sacrificed young boys and girls to the mountain, but that sounded like nonsense to Ana, the kind of scary stories told to youngsters to make them behave. The north wind came from those mountains after the harvest time, when the nights were long and the land itself froze hard as rock. How could such a place be hot enough for a mountain to breathe fire?

In the dappled shade Ana saw tardy violets blooming, and ground ivy. She rested alongside a rocky creek, replenishing her water jug and then leaning against an oak tree to enjoy the trickling sounds of the water and the green fragrance of the ferns. She lay amid the old tree's roots in that dozy, dreamy state of relaxation that always made her feel both protected by and closer to the Goddess. Eyes half closed, she watched a yellow butterfly land on a rock to sip the water puddled on its surface. She heard a faint, rhythmic sound that at first she couldn't place, then she recognized it as hoof beats. But the forest edge was a very odd place to hear wild ponies. They were creatures of the plains, where they could see far and run fast when danger threatened. She thought she must have fallen asleep and dreamed them, but the hoof beats grew louder. Then they were so close she felt the ground shudder. The butterfly fluttered up and out of sight. Alarmed, Ana stood up.

Just as she did, a pony burst out from the underbrush almost on top of her. Ana shouted and ducked away from the pony's flailing legs. The pony, which had no desire to injure its hooves, whinnied and shied at the motion. But the most amazing thing, from Ana's point of view, a thing so odd she thought she really must be dreaming, was to see a young man sitting on the pony's back.

It was no dream. The pony reared, front hooves slicing the air, rear hooves stumbling against tree roots. Its body twisted away from Ana as it lifted up, and the young man, caught off guard, was unbalanced. He was flung off the pony and landed hard on his back, with an ugly thud as his head snapped back against a rock. The pony screamed, planting a hoof on the man's chest as it galloped through the creek and crashed off into the woods.

The young man lay still. Ana, who could feel her heart thudding in her chest, called to him, "Are you hurt?" Of course he was hurt. She felt foolish for asking.

She grabbed the net bag and knelt to examine him. His eyes were closed, but he was breathing, thank the Goddess. She squeezed his hand, but he didn't respond. She looked at his head, lying against the rock, and ran her fingers gently through his black hair. Her hand came away sticky with blood. This was not good.

Ana took plantain leaves out of her bag. They should be washed and warmed before use, so she quickly rinsed them in the creek and rubbed them between her palms. She placed them between his head and the rock. She lifted aside the leather vest that was his only upper garment to check the damage to his body. The imprint of the pony's hoof was clearly visible, an angry looking red welt at the base of his rib cage. Ana could feel at least one broken rib, but when she touched it, the young man did not stir or cry out in pain, a very bad sign. She felt his arms and legs—nothing broken there, thank the Goddess. Ana shook her head. She would have to get help, but she was not sure he would even be alive by the time she returned with her grandmother. Still, she had to try, so she ran back toward the village.

Ana had covered a lot of ground this morning, but she took a more direct route home. At least half of the journey was downhill, and she was surefooted, so she sped as fast as she could. Still, it seemed like a long time before she saw her kinsmen working in the fields. She waved at them because she had no breath for shouting. She ran up to the nearest cousin, Boros, and gulped for air, her hand to her side. Everyone in the field dropped their tools and ran over to her.

When she could, she gasped out, "Man...hurt...get... Mari." They understood her enough to send someone to fetch her grandmother. Cousin Tiso gave her a drink of water. By the time her grandmother strode up to them with her medicine bag slung over her shoulder, Ana was able to speak more coherently.

"Grandmother, there is a man hurt, very bad. He hit his head on a rock, and he has a broken rib. I used plantain for the bleeding, but I am afraid he will die. You must come."

"I'll go with you, Ana, but if he lives, we will need to bring him here," Mari said. She looked at the others. "Boros, Tiso, come with us.

Bring an axe." She turned back toward Ana. "Tell me what happened as we walk."

"I was resting near a brook. I heard a pony. It came out from the trees very fast. The man was on its back."

"A man on the back of a wild pony?" said Boros. "You must have been dreaming."

"That's what I thought at first, but I was awake and I saw what I saw."

"How is that possible?" asked Tiso. "No one can get close enough to a pony to even touch it."

Ponies were indeed very fleet-footed, and easily startled. While it was entirely possible for a hunting party to sneak up on a herd and fling spears into one of them, it was foolhardy to even think about approaching close enough for contact. A pony's hooves were deadly.

Ana thought back to what she had seen.

"He had a thong around the pony's head. He was holding that with both hands. But the pony lifted its front hooves. The man fell off and hit his head. The pony stepped on him and then ran off."

"Was he awake when you left?" asked Mari.

"No. That's why I ran back."

"You did the right thing," Mari said. "But it is surely a strange tale that you tell."

Ana knew her tale was odd indeed, but not impossible. Perhaps the man had found an orphaned pony, and raised it as one would a goat or sheep. If it was very young, it might well have been docile enough for him to feed and care for it. A grown pony would also be strong enough to carry a man, though how he could stay on its back without falling off she couldn't imagine. Still, the Goddess allowed strange things to happen sometimes.

"What if we can't find him?" she asked. "What if he awoke after I left, and crawled away? He must be dazed. He might be deep in the woods. What happens if he runs into a wolf, or a boar, or a bear?"

"From what you told us, Ana, it is far more likely that he has already died," Mari said. "There's no point in wondering. We'll find what we find when we get there."

The sun was lower in the sky before they reached the creek. Ana didn't know whether to be relieved or fearful when she saw that the man had not moved.

Mari knelt to see if he was even alive. His color was very pale, but he was still breathing. As Mari examined him, Ana had time to wonder what clan he might be from, because he didn't resemble any of the people from any village she knew of. His hair was dark, almost black, and his skin would be tanned if he weren't so pale. He was very hairy, with the dark shadow of a beard on his cheeks, a thick mustache, and dark curly hair on his chest through which the ugly, hoof-shaped welt showed clearly. Like Ana, Mari felt the wound there, and agreed with the diagnosis of a broken rib. She gave Ana a brief smile of approval before lifting the man's head carefully to see where Ana had applied the plantain. Mari nodded with satisfaction that the blood had stopped flowing.

"This head wound is bad," she said. "I can feel broken bone. We must get him back to the village right away."

She asked Ana for more plantain, and applied some to his chest. She bound the leaves to his body with vines, and instructed Boros and Tiso to cut saplings to make a pallet. They worked as quickly as they could, and laid him on the pallet, tying him down with vines to keep him from sliding off. Then each of the men took one side of the pallet to drag it along the forest floor.

It was a little easier going once they left the forest, but dragging the pallet through tall grasses was still hard work, and they all took turns, even Mari. It was nightfall by the time they reached home.

There was not much they could do before daylight. Ana and Shela took turns sitting up with the man, but he never stirred. At sunup, Mari rose, went into the Temple to pray for him, and then gave him a more thorough examination. The girls helped her remove his strange clothes. Besides the vest, he wore leather breeches and boots. He wasn't very

22

tall, about Ana's height, but his body was well formed and muscular. The bruise on his side was no larger than it had been the night before, a good sign that he was not bleeding inside. There was nothing to be done about the broken rib; it was not possible to set it as one could a leg or an arm. It would heal or it would not; that much was solely in the hands of the Goddess.

The head injury was another matter.

"It is not good that he has not woken," Mari said. "I have seen this before. It happens when blood pools up under the skull. If it doesn't come out, he will surely die."

"How can we get it out?" asked Ana.

"We have to open his skull."

Ana had heard of this procedure, but she had never seen it performed. Grandmother would have to use a special tool, a thin cylinder of stone with a very sharp point. They would take a small bow, like the kind that could be used to start a fire if one had no flint, and use the two implements to drill into the skull so they could remove the blood. If they were successful, the man might live.

A procedure so dangerous was not undertaken lightly. Both women prayed to the Goddess to guide Grandmother's hands. They placed figurines of the Goddess all around the injured man, and rubbed him with tansy and chickweed. Mari used a sharpened clamshell to shave away the hair around the injury, and to cut his scalp through the swelling and down to the bone. Ana took the ceremonial copper knife, which had been laid in the fire, and applied the hot tip to the wound to stop further bleeding. She cradled the man's head in her lap, holding it steady, as her grandmother began the most dangerous work.

Ana disliked the scraping sound the tool made as it slowly widened the existing crack in the man's skull. She was glad he was not awake. This would be a terrible thing to go through with full awareness. After what seemed like a whole morning of bowing, her grandmother stopped and carefully chiseled out the remaining bone. She showed Ana the dark stain on the sheath that covered the brain. She used a small scraper of bone to carefully scoop out the clotted blood.

When the wound was as clean as she could get it, she daubed it with plantain and covered it with a wrap of linen. There was no more she could do. Given time, the bone might re-grow and close the wound. Whether the stranger had that time, only the Goddess knew. It would be one of Her great miracles if he survived.

To no one's surprise, the injured man developed a fever. Once again Ana and Shela took turns watching him through the rest of the day and into the night. They washed his face and arms with water infused with feverfew and meadowsweet; once, his eyelids fluttered, and once, he moaned. Grandmother got up twice during the night to see how he was doing.

"He is very strong," she whispered to Ana toward dawn. "Perhaps the Goddess will favor him."

Ana dozed, waking when the rooster crowed. When the light reached into the room, she saw that the man's eyes were open. He was staring at her.

He licked his lips and tried to speak.

"Hush," whispered Ana. "We are taking care of you. The Goddess protects you." She poured a cup of water, put a hollow reed into it, and held it for the man to drink. He winced when he turned his head, taking only a few sips before falling back to sleep.

Ana felt his forehead. It was cooler than before. She was glad the Goddess would be merciful today.

When the man woke again that afternoon, Ana's grandmother was there.

He mumbled something neither of them could understand.

"Be at peace," she said to him. She patted his hand. "Rest now."

He tried to speak again. She shook her head. "Rest."

Whether he understood or not Ana could not tell, but he closed his eyes. His attempt to speak had taken all his strength.

Ana's grandmother motioned her outside.

Shela was waiting to take her turn at watching the man. Arina gave Ana a slice of barley bread. Ana was stiff from sitting up much of the night, and tired from having had little sleep in two nights, especially after running so hard and so far to get help.

"How is he?" Shela asked.

"It is as I feared," said Grandmother. "I think his body will survive, praise the Goddess, but I don't think he will be right in the head. It happens sometimes with these kinds of wounds. Some people cannot walk or sit up after they heal; sometimes they cannot speak. He makes sounds, but they mean nothing. It is very sad."

"Where did he come from?" Arina asked.

"I have no idea."

"Ana, did he really fall from the back of a pony?" Shela asked.

"No one but Ana saw that," Grandmother said before Ana could reply. "But your sister doesn't tell lies or embellish stories to make herself seem important. If she says a thing happened, then I believe her." She smiled at Ana and told her to get some rest.

Ana felt better after she had slept for several hours. Feeling very dirty after all she had experienced over the past three days, she walked down to the river to bathe as soon as she woke up. The afternoon was hot and the cool water refreshed her. She immersed herself, then floated, wondering about the young man and where he could be from. He was very nice looking, in a different sort of way. Ana hoped he would truly get well. She immersed herself once more, grabbing a handful of fine grit from the river bottom to scrub her skin clean. She soaked and scrubbed her tunic and skirt as well. She laid them flat on a rock to dry off in the sunshine while she combed her hair. She rubbed her skin with crushed burnet leaves before putting her clothes on. She felt—and smelled—much better after that.

Ana went back to check on the young man.

"I think there is something wrong with his mind," Shela said. She was standing in the doorway. "He just makes funny grunts and gargling noises, and he doesn't seem to understand anything I say. He just made water where he lay, but he pushed me away when I tried to clean him up."

"Let me try," said Ana. She went inside. The stranger was trying to raise himself up to a seated position. His face was gray with pain and beaded with sweat. Ana gently pushed him back down. He was so weak he was as easy to shift as a child. She went into the next room, where her herbs were stored, and came back with a handful of juniper berries.

She held out her hand. "For the pain."

He looked at her hand warily, and then at her face.

Ana pointed to her side and grimaced, then she pointed to her head and did the same. She put a berry in her mouth and chewed. She made an exaggerated sigh, and smiled. Then she held the berries out to him again.

He understood. He took three of the berries and chewed them slowly, looking at her the whole time.

Ana nodded. "Good. They will help."

She reached for the cloth he was lying under, but he grabbed it and would not let go. He made a growling sound, guttural and harsh.

Ana pointed to the wet stain on the cloth. "It is all right," she said. "I just want to clean that." She nodded again and tugged firmly on the cloth. He was too weak to hold onto it, and he moaned with what Ana interpreted as frustration as she uncovered him. She rolled up the cloth and set it aside. The bruise on his side looked terrible, a large patch of purplish-blue, almost black. She knelt next to him, dipped a cloth in tansy-infused water, wrung it out and lay it on top of the bruise. Even the weight of that small scrap of linen pained him. He closed his eyes, but he did not cry out. When he opened his eyes again, she gave him more juniper berries. Then she took a wet cloth and spread it across his lap.

He muttered something, trying to shake his head and reach for her hand, but he could do neither. He tried to take a deep breath and groaned. She waited until he was able to open his eyes again.

"It is all right," she said again, using the tone of voice she would use with a child. "I must clean you off."

He closed his eyes again as she gently wiped his penis, his scrotum, his thighs, moving his legs very carefully not to cause him pain as she reached under him with the cloth. She took away the washing things and returned with a small woolen cloak that she shook out and used to cover his midsection. He opened his eyes only when she was done. His face was red and he would not look at her.

Maybe Shela was right to think his mind was damaged. Ana could think of no other reason why anyone who endured such pain so bravely could feel shame at needing basic care. His reaction was so different from that of her clansmen that she wondered again where this stranger could possibly have come from. How could anyone grow to adulthood and be so ignorant? Were there no healers among his people?

His eyes were closed again, his breathing even. He had fallen asleep. That was good. A wounded person healed more quickly when he slept.

The next time he woke up, Ana was there with a bowl full of fermented ewe's milk and honey. She fed him a spoonful at a time. He was a little more relaxed with her, and more alert. But when her grandmother walked in, he tensed up.

"How is our injured stranger?"

"Getting stronger," Ana said, "but he doesn't seem able to talk. He is very—unusual. He must be from far away, maybe from beyond the mountains, don't you think?"

"I don't know. I have never met anyone from so far away. But it is possible, I suppose." She reached for his head to unwrap the bandage and remove the packing. Her patient looked at her warily, but did not protest. She sniffed the wound, and satisfied there was no pus, closed the gap by stitching the skin together, using sinew and a bone needle. She covered the seam with fresh plantain leaves and a clean linen wrap. Throughout the whole procedure, the man bit his lip to keep from crying out. He did not even moan. Grandmother admired his courage. She patted his hand to signal she was done.

"Well, the wound is clean, the fever is gone, and he is eating. These are all good signs." She pinched his left foot, which he pulled back, and then the right, and he did the same. He glared at her.

Mari nodded. "He has the use of his limbs, praise the Goddess. I think he will be all right, at least in body. He seems to trust you, Ana. Do you mind taking care of him from now on? The calmer he is, the faster he will heal."

Ana smiled. "I'm happy to, Grandmother." Mari touched her granddaughter's cheek and smiled back. She was not so old that she couldn't recognize what a handsome young man he was, and how intriguing his strangeness was to her granddaughter. She hoped Ana understood that he would probably be simple for the rest of his life. If so, then perhaps he would make a pleasant companion for Arina. There were worse fates.

She looked at the stranger and said, loud and slowly, "You are in good hands. I will stop by in the morning to see how you are."

He doesn't understand a word. A pity.

How long would it be, Ana wondered as she watched him fall asleep, before someone missed him, and came looking for him?

But no one looked for him as the days went by.

The stranger healed surprisingly well. He ate, and got stronger, and his bruise began to fade. He breathed easier each day, which both Ana and her grandmother noted with approval. His head wound healed cleanly. Grandmother was a great healer, Ana thought, as she carefully cut and pulled out the stitches. *I hope someday to be half as good.*

One day not long after, when Ana had taken away the man's night soil and returned with a jug of fresh water to bathe him, he showed how much better he was. As soon as Ana knelt and placed a wet cloth over his penis, it stirred with life. She smiled, more because it meant he was truly improving than out of any response to him, but then he placed one finger on the curve of her breast. She looked at his face then. His expression was easy to read.

She had not been with anyone since the sacred rite. Although she and Onno had enjoyed each other that night, neither of them would consider someone from within their immediate clan as a possible long-term partner. Someone from another village would be much more suitable.

Ana liked this dark-haired stranger with the long straight nose and dark brown eyes. Her body responded easily to his look and his touch.

She bent to kiss him, taking care not to put any weight on his injured side. His mustache tickled her face, but his mouth was soft, tasting of juniper berries. He cupped both of her breasts as they kissed, and she felt his hips stir in response. She didn't want him to hurt himself, so she quickly knelt astride him, and guided him into her. He looked surprised at first; then he lay still, his eyes half closed, watching her move her hips. He climaxed much too soon, but instead of continuing for her own satisfaction, Ana lifted herself off him, knowing what little strength he had. Indeed, his face showed pain mixed with pleasure as he breathed too hard for his still-mending ribs. She kissed him again, very lightly, finished washing him, and covered him again as he fell back to sleep.

Ana went back to him with the noon meal, a roasted chicken leg and some greens. He grinned as soon as he saw her, and she smiled back. She knelt to feed him, although he could feed himself perfectly well by now. She pulled the chicken meat off the bone and put bite-sized pieces into his mouth. He licked her fingers every time she gave him a morsel. When he finished the meal he pulled her closer and kissed her. She kissed him back, but when his kisses got too hungry she sat up, and shook her head. She mimicked sleep, and pointed at him. A well-trained healer, Ana knew when he needed rest, and when he needed something else. He rolled his eyes, but lay back obediently. And then he asked her something. The sounds he made still had no sense in them, but from the tone she could tell he had asked her a question.

She shrugged and shook her head. "I don't know what you are trying to say."

He pointed at her and asked again. Her face lit with understanding. She pointed to herself. "Ana."

"Ana," he repeated, still pointing at her. She nodded and pointed at him.

He mimicked the gesture, saying, "Dumuz."

"Dumuz," she said, trying to match his pronunciation. She pointed to him. "Dumuz." To herself: "Ana."

"Ana." Suddenly his voice was no longer strange or crazy, but deep and melodic. "Ana," he repeated, infusing her name with the rough sweetness of honey fresh from the comb.

Dumuz regained his strength through the rest of growing season. After the ugly bruise faded, he was able to breathe easier and to move around more. One day he stood up with Ana's help, and soon he could walk across the room. If he tried to do too much his head hurt, though, so they expanded his activity in short, careful stages. When he was well enough, Ana took him to the pottery shed and showed him the large cistern, stepped down into three levels for washing out roots and rocks. She explained how the first level produced a coarse-grained clay good for patching walls and mending fences. The second level resulted in a medium grain suitable for everyday cups and bowls. And the third level gave Ana a very fine-grained clay used for all the most important ceremonial pieces.

She looked at Dumuz and realized that he couldn't understand a word she had just said. But he smiled, touched her cheek with his hand, and said something in the throaty language that was his own way of speaking. She tried to repeat his words. Although the sounds were very strange to her, unlike any dialect she'd heard from people who lived up and down the river valley, she could see that it gave him much pleasure to hear her try.

She had more success teaching him her own language. He quickly learned the words for foods, for bowl and cup, spoon and knife. When he was able to walk outside, Ana taught him house, fence, river, sun, moon, sheep, goat, dog, cat. It was easy and fun to teach him the words for activities like walking, speaking, eating; for different kinds of birds, for clothing, colors. They laughed at his mispronunciation of body parts and body functions, but had no trouble understanding and responding to each other's body language.

Abstract ideas were much harder to convey. It was many days before he was able to make Ana understand that he wanted to meet their clan leader. She had as hard a time making him understand that Grandmother was, in fact, their clan leader. He seemed amazed that the men of the clan accepted Mari's leadership. Ana was puzzled by his surprise. How could any clan lack a Priestess? Why would he think a clan would be led by a man? The Giver-of-Life was female. It was natural that Her Priestess should lead Her people.

Dumuz seemed unaware that the Goddess who controlled the seasons was the reason for the fertility of their crops and livestock, that She was an intimate part of everyone's life from birth through adulthood and into the afterlife. Her clansmen treated one another with respect because to do otherwise was unthinkable: every man was the son of the Goddess and every woman Her daughter. Every home had figurines of the Goddess under its foundation posts. Every home had a shrine to Her. Ana wanted Dumuz to know that every activity they did, no matter how small, was dedicated to the Goddess. Sometimes his ignorance of such basic concepts made her wonder if he did not have something wrong in his head after all.

She was frustrated that they couldn't communicate better. Their bodies understood one another, but she wanted to know who her lover was—what kind of man he had been, and who he might yet become. Eventually, he was able to explain that he came from the east and north, far from this river valley, on the far side of the mountains, as Ana had thought. But why he was so far from home and all alone was still too complicated a tale for his limited vocabulary.

Despite the obvious differences, the entire clan accepted Dumuz with the graciousness Ana's people had always accorded a stranger, although privately most of them thought his head injury had rendered him even more simple than Arina. Still, Ana had obviously taken him as her partner, and she was a Priestess-in-training, so she must know what she was doing. Ana's grandmother had even sacrificed a hen, that most domestic of creatures, to the Goddess to bless their joining.

When Ana missed her monthly flow, and felt her breasts begin to swell, she gave thanks to the Goddess for the gift of new life, but it took a lot of pantomime before she could explain her condition to Dumuz. She was relieved when he reacted with joy, as any man in her clan would do. His ways were so different that she hadn't known what to expect.

By that time, Dumuz was feeling well enough to contribute to village life, but this, too, was something of a puzzle. He couldn't make beads or farm tools, he didn't know how to catch fish or dig for clams, he didn't even know the difference between barley and millet. He did not have the stamina yet to help in fields, or haul firewood. He could make a good bow and spear, though, and when his strength returned, he used his hunting skills to contribute hares and quail to the evening meal.

Occasionally, he had bad days when his head hurt too much for him to do more than lie down with a cool, wet cloth on his forehead. Ana worried about this, but Grandmother said it was to be expected when someone was healing from such a drastic injury. After the worst of the pain passed, when Dumuz was able to sit up, he liked to watch Ana work. She showed him how she made a simple bowl by molding a lump of clay with her fist, punching the hard clay until she made a depression, and using her thumbs to deepen it. As the bowl took shape, she pulled and turned the clay, drawing the sides of the bowl thinner and making the opening wider. When it was the size she wanted, she smoothed the outside with a sharp piece of bone. Then she used the bone to incise the bowl with curving lines that looked like fast-flowing water.

She gave Dumuz a handful of clay and watched as he tried to imitate her. She laughed to see the thick, lumpy, uneven form that he made, as bad as her first attempts when she was just a child. After a while, he gave up, laughing as well.

"I see why you are so strong," he said, giving her arm a squeeze to be sure she understood. Somehow, he made the simple words carry much meaning, acknowledging her skill as well as her strength. He had graceful hands, and communicated much with gestures. Ana got in the habit of watching him closely. Most days she could tell his mood simply by the way he stood.

One cool evening, not long after their meal of grilled pike and wheat porridge, Ana watched as Dumuz sat on the river bluff, gazing into the northeastern distance. She could only imagine how homesick he must be. She had never been away from this village for more than a night or two. Before she began doing the work of the Temple, Ana's grandmother had wanted her to know about every aspect of village life, so she spent a few summer nights under the stars with the goatherds and shepherds, and once she traveled with a group of her clan folk when they went downriver to trade. She had never been alone in her life.

She was, in fact, surprised that Dumuz was still here. Ana had expected him to leave as soon as he was well enough; she would not have thought it unusual to wake some morning and find him gone, even though they honored the Goddess with their bodies almost every night, and often when they woke, and sometimes after the midday meal. She wondered whether Dumuz would stay with them when the harvest was over, or whether he would leave before the north winds brought snow. It made her very sad to think of this, but lately she often felt sad for no reason, or utterly happy for no reason. She thought the coming baby might be influencing her moods, but she wondered what could possibly make an unborn baby sad or happy.

Ana walked over to Dumuz with one hand on her belly, which was getting rounder and larger every day. The weight of it made her a little clumsy and she grunted when she sat down. Dumuz put his arm around her as she leaned into him comfortably. She had hoped simply to soothe his troubled heart, but as so often happened when they were alone, he began to kiss her. Ana was glad he still desired her. She remembered how, at the start of the sowing season, she had been so proud of her firm breasts and narrow waist. Now she had no waist at all and had to tie her skirt lower and lower. She liked how quickly Dumuz untied it, and the extraordinary pleasure he seemed to take in all of her new curves.

He preferred to be on top when they made love, another sign that he came from a different and strange people. In that position he almost always climaxed before she did, but he was learning to wait for her, or to change position to give her more control. Her growing belly would soon make his favorite position impossible, though. Ana would have to consult with her grandmother on the best way to love without hurting the baby-to-come. She needed to know, because she was like tinder to his flint.

Afterwards, they lay in the dusk, watching the eastern sky as it darkened.

"You always look to the east," Ana said.

"I am looking for Luguk." By now Ana knew this was his name for the pony that had run away.

"You still miss him, even though he hurt you?" She touched his side and his head to make sure he understood.

He nodded.

"Do you think he will ever come back?"

Dumuz sighed. "No, I think he found a wild mare to stay with, just like I did." He smiled so she would understand he was joking.

She got the joke, and smiled back. It was one of the things she loved about him, his humor, his not wanted to offend, an odd tenderness in so strong a hunter.

"Ponies belong with ponies," she said. "People with people."

"Yes, but Luguk was my"—he used his own word to finish—"friend."

"What is 'friend'?"

"Friend is..." he waved toward the village.

"Clan?" she guessed.

"Not clan." He brought his hands together and intertwined the fingers. "More."

"Kin."

"Not kin." He frowned, trying to find a way to make himself understood. "Do you like all your kin?"

"Yes."

"All the same?"

She thought about that. "I weep when any of my clan are hurt."

"Same tears for all? For Shela? Arina? Mari? Tiso?"

"Yes."

"Same tears for me?"

"No." She thought of his terrible injuries, how he almost died. Then, he had been a stranger in need. Now, the thought of his being injured hurt her, too. She put her arms around him. "You are more than kin, more than clan."

He kissed her cheek.

"That is friend."

She looked at him, still puzzled. "That can't be right. You make it sound as if you and Luguk—" words failed her, so she thrust her hips forward and back.

He shook his head, and his face turned so red that Ana burst out laughing.

"I don't have the words. Luguk—no." He shook his head again. "No."

He cradled her face in his hands. "You, Ana, are more than friend." He pulled her face closer and kissed her. "You are sun. Moon. Stars."

She responded to his kiss, but she was uncomfortable to hear herself compared to such powerful and mysterious aspects of the Goddess.

"Not sun, not moon, not stars." She put his hand on her belly. "I am a field ripe with grain. I am the earth, and you are my farmer. Plow me, Dumuz. Plow me."

It was Tiso who brought the news of the windfall one cool morning not long afterwards. He had walked some distance downriver to try a new spot for fishing. When he saw them, he ran back to the village.

"Wild ponies!" he called out. "Wild ponies stuck in the marsh, one full grown, one much younger."

Pony was a rare but welcome source of meat to be dried for the dark season between harvest and sowing, when bitter cold storms could last for days.

A handful of men were spared from the day's harvesting to get the ponies. Dumuz was as excited as any of them until he saw them take up their hunting spears.

"Ana, no, ponies are to ride, not to eat!" He tried to explain that only a desperate, starving man would kill a horse, and then only the oldest of the herd, not prime breeding stock, and never a foal. But such ideas were beyond his skills with their language, and totally foreign to their way of life. Instead of a weapon, he grabbed a long leather strap.

Dumuz and the hunting party began walking downriver. Ana went, too. From Tiso's description, it wouldn't be more than an hour's walk, and her back was beginning to ache from working with clay, so the exercise would do her good. She understood more than any of them how much the ponies could mean to Dumuz, but she also knew how much more they would mean to her clan.

They approached the bend in the river beyond which lay the marsh, a treacherous area where seemingly solid ground could suddenly give way to muck. Tiso motioned for them to be quiet from this point on. They stooped low, using reeds for cover, and soon had the ponies in sight. They stopped to consult on how best to handle the situation.

The mare was half on her side, exhausted and sweating. She had tried to heave herself out of the mud, but she was stuck deeply, up to her chest. That she'd been struggling for a long time was obvious, and even Dumuz realized the kindest outcome for her now would be a quick death. Once she was dispatched, they could use Tiso's fishnet to snare her head and, with effort, pull her body to more solid ground.

She'd be much too heavy to move any farther. They would have to butcher her on site.

The foal, though, was another story. It stood on a hummock of solid ground, wide-eyed and nickering. It was half-grown and scrawny, too thin to be worth killing for food. Dumuz made his plea as well as he could, offering to kill the mare for them in exchange for the foal. No one could deny he was the best spearman among them, so they readily agreed to his offer to spear the mare, but they didn't understand when he asked them to spare the foal's life.

"Ana, you understand me? Tell them. Tell them for me."

Ana explained that Dumuz thought the foal would not give enough meat to make it worth carrying back to the village. That seemed a fairly reasonable statement, but when she added that Dumuz wanted to bring it back to take care of it, their skeptical expressions were clear enough for Dumuz to understand.

Ana asked them to agree with him for her sake. "The Goddess spared Dumuz for a reason. Maybe he can teach us something about these animals."

The men looked at one another and shrugged.

"Well, of course, if it would please the Goddess," Tiso said. Ana gave thanks for her training, and for the authority it was beginning to give her.

Tiso handed Dumuz his spear. Dumuz nodded, putting his hand on Tiso's shoulder. He motioned for everyone to stay down.

"Watch where you step," Ana whispered, but Dumuz was already moving into position. He walked carefully in a hunter's crouch to a place where he could stand up and aim for the mare's throat. A spear through the eye would be quickest, and most merciful, but she was still struggling, so the big blood vessel in her neck was the next best target. He waited for her to stop thrashing. He was concerned about being upwind of them, but the animals were panicky, with no energy to spare for noticing him.

The mare tired again and lay against the mud with her neck in a graceful arch. She must have been a beautiful animal before she was covered in filth and sweat. Dumuz stood, took aim and hurled the spear, almost before she could react to his sudden appearance. She screamed when the spear hit true, a high and horrible cry that made the foal back up, snorting. It ran from the smell of the blood that gushed out around the spear. For a moment, it looked as though Dumuz would be able to catch the foal with his bare hands, but at the last second it swerved away from him. More surefooted than its mother, it galloped into the river, through the shallows and up the opposite bank.

Dumuz ran after it, calling to Ana and the others not to follow him.

Following Dumuz was exactly what Ana wanted to do. She was worried he would disappear along with the young pony, never to return. But she could only hinder his quest to catch it, so she turned back to the gory sight of the dying mare. It took only a few minutes for the animal to lie totally still with dull eyes. Ana gave thanks to the Goddess for this gift of so much food; duty done, she left the men to figure out how best to retrieve it without getting stuck themselves. She faced the river and sat down to wait.

Tiso had dispatched a runner to go back to the village with the news of their success. The rest of the hunting party struggled to move the heavy mare onto more solid ground. Once that task was accomplished, with much good-natured cursing and sliding, and more than one of the men getting covered head to toe in the muck, they rinsed themselves off in the river. By that time, more clan folk had arrived. They congratulated the hunting party, but Ana was pleased to hear the men give full credit to the absent Dumuz.

One of the men cut the mare's belly open. No part of the animal would go to waste. The vast entrails were scooped up into baskets and taken to the river to be washed. Brain, liver, heart and lungs were choice meats to be roasted fresh; legs, tail, eyes, and tripe were ingredients for soup; skin, sinew, bone and the stiff hairs of the tail were raw materials for garments, tools, thread. All the remaining flesh would be smoked or dried, the fat rendered, and everyone in the village would benefit. Even the hooves would be hollowed out into drinking vessels.

Only the blood would be left in the swamp—an unfortunate loss, but nothing they could have prevented.

The sun was low on the horizon when the butchering was done and everyone was ready to carry home some part of the mare. Dumuz had not returned. Ana wanted to wait for him, but clouds of mosquitoes were already rising from the swamp. It was neither practical nor safe for her to stay out here by herself, so she went back with her clan, carrying only a light load of horsemeat in a basket balanced on her head.

The sun went down, the cooking began, but Ana had no appetite for horseflesh. She waited up as long as she could, and slept badly, feeling in the dark for a comfort that wasn't there. She had always expected this day would come, but she was unprepared for how long and chilly the night felt without her beloved. As long as he was next to her, Ana could pretend that her feelings for him were only physical, that he hadn't filled her heart when he filled her body. But on this first night without him, she felt a longing that made her whole being ache. Worse than the loss of her mother or father, worse than any physical pain she'd known. No one expected any woman to stay with one man all her life, although some chose to do so, but Ana and Dumuz were still new to one another, still learning, and could have had much happiness together.

She felt the baby move for the first time, a sudden tiny pressure and release. All the women of the village would rejoice with her at this sign of the baby's growth and health. She wished she could share the moment with Dumuz.

"Sleep, little one," Ana whispered, rubbing her stomach gently. "Be glad you can."

Morning dawned foggy and cool, and if anything, lonelier than the night before. Ana ate only a few spoonfuls of porridge before going to the clay shed. Here she took out her frustration on the damp red clay, pounding and punching it, but the resulting shapes were so far from the refined vessels she usually made that she gave up. She wrapped herself in a woolen cloak and walked down to the river, to the bluff that gave her a good view downstream.

Little Arina wanted to bring her some lunch, but Grandmother suggested she leave her sister alone for the day. Ana did not know or care that she was the subject of village gossip for the entire afternoon. It was nearly sunset before she saw an oddly shaped creature walking on their side of the river bank. It seemed to have the head of a man and the body of a horse. At first Ana thought she was going insane, but that seemed ungrateful if the Goddess was granting her a vision. Then, when the figure came a little closer, it resolved into Dumuz, holding the young horse around the neck with the leather strap. Only then did Ana finally weep. She broke down and sobbed into her hands, getting control of herself briefly, only to lose herself in emotion again, whether anger or relief or joy or a mix of all three, she couldn't tell. She ran down the bluff and along the bank to meet him. He was tired and filthy but smiling until he saw her tears.

"What's this?" he asked as she put her arms around him and pressed her face into the curve of his neck. When she lifted her head, her tears had made a clean spot on his skin and a smudge on her cheek.

"I thought...I was afraid...." She couldn't speak. She wouldn't let go of him. He put his free hand against her cheek and kissed her.

"You thought I would leave you for a scrawny little pony?" he asked, but the joke in his voice and his grin faltered when he saw the hurt on her face. He pulled her close, and whispered in a voice at once harsh and tender, "Beloved, I am here, and I am staying here." He held her tight until she yelped and pulled back, startling the little pony that had nibbled her hand.

"Easy, easy, easy," Dumuz said to the horse in his own language, soothing it, hoping Ana's abrupt motion hadn't undone the hard work of catching and calming the foal over two days and a night.

For her part, Ana tried not to feel put out as he crooned to this trembling animal in almost exactly the same tone of voice he had just used toward her.

Dumuz put the pony in the goat pen, which would serve as its paddock until the goats returned from grazing in the hill pastures. He filled the wooden water trough with buckets of river water, and took a scythe to cut down some grasses for the pony to eat, before he finally came inside to have food and water himself.

Ana had built a comfortable fire while he was caring for the pony, and was heating water so she could wipe off the worst of the mud. She noticed him wince as he sat before the hearth.

"Your head hurts?" she asked. She wasn't surprised, not after all his exertion over the past two days. She got up to fetch tansy, adding it to the water.

While he ate two bowls of mutton stew, she dipped a cloth in the warm water and wiped him clean, much as she had done when he was only her patient. In the firelight she couldn't see his head well enough to see how the site of the old injury looked; his hair had regrown and the stitched wound had healed over. But Ana knew he still had a soft spot in his skull where the bone had been removed. She was concerned that if he fell again or was struck there, he'd be re-injured too badly to heal. She felt his head carefully, but could detect no swelling or excess heat, and the area smelled only of sweat.

After Dumuz finished eating, Ana made him lie down with a wet cloth over his forehead. He was so tired he fell asleep within moments. Ana-the-healer was glad he did; Ana-the-lover a bit less so. She lay down next to him. He made a small, contented grunt, put his arm around her, and that was all she knew until morning.

The next day, the pony was the center of village attention. Everyone had to see this creature Dumuz went to so much trouble to save. The foal was leggy and thin, with a dun-colored coat and a dark brown mane that stood straight up from its neck. Its ears were pointed back, giving it a wary expression, and it shivered a little as it walked in circles, shying at all the people who stared and pointed, but who backed up hastily any time the pony came near the fence, flicking its dark tail. It whinnied when it saw Dumuz, who climbed the fence instead of opening the gate.

41

He had a handful of barley, which made the foal come close. It snorted and blew air from its nostrils before eating from his hand.

"You're not going to feed that thing all our barley, are you?" Boros asked. "We need that for making beer."

"No. I will lead her out to graze, like the other animals. I'll cut extra grass for her before the snow falls."

"What will you do with it?" asked a little boy named Gat.

"When she grows up, I'll ride her." He had to pantomime what he meant.

The villagers laughed. Riding a pony was a silly idea, and no one had really believed Ana's story that he had been riding a pony the day she found him. After a little more watching and joking, the adults left to take care of their daily chores. Only Ana, her sisters, and a few small children stayed to watch Dumuz. Arina was afraid of the pony and huddled against Ana with her face in Ana's tunic. Ana thought it was a good thing for Arina to be afraid of it. She wanted her little sister to stay away from this wild creature. She had seen what damage pony hooves could do.

"Why don't you go back to the temple and make us some millet cakes," Ana suggested to her. "You don't have to go near the pony." Arina, looking relieved, skipped away.

"May I touch it?" Shela asked.

Dumuz shook his head, but he smiled at her eagerness. "Not today. She's afraid. She needs to know us better."

He ran his hands over every inch of the pony, which stood calmly now that the crowd had gone. Ana and Shela marveled that the pony let Dumuz lift each hoof to inspect it, that he could touch the pony anywhere on its body without it kicking him. When he stroked its neck and rubbed its ears, the pony made a soft nickering sound. Dumuz patted the horse on its rump and climbed back out of the pen.

"She has good bones. She will grow strong and run fast," he said to them. "She will need a place of her own before the snows come."

"We need a place of our own, too," said Ana, glad to hear him talking like this. She took his hand and placed it on her belly. "I can feel the child moving now, can you feel that?"

He shook his head.

"You will, soon. We have time, before the baby comes, to build a home. There is room for a small house on the west side of the temple."

"I don't know how to build a house."

"My kin will help us build it."

Dumuz nodded. "Is there room to have a shed for the pony?" He moved his hands together. "Next to the house. Yes?" The pony nickered as though she knew he was talking about her. He smiled. "I need to give her a name."

"A name?" Shela asked. "What for?"

"Don't your village dogs have names?

"Yes, but that beast is not a dog. We don't name goats or sheep."

"The pony will be more like dogs than like goats or sheep. When we know her better, we can give her the right name."

The time between leaf fall and the beginning of the snow was a busy one for Dumuz. Boros and Tiso helped him cut tall, straight oaks to use as corner posts, and haul them back to the village. Grandmother made sure they cut holes for the posts in exactly the right spots, and Ana made the proper figurines to bury beneath each post to ensure the blessings of the Goddess on their new home. As she had promised, Ana's kinfolk showed Dumuz how to construct a solid floor out of planks covered with a thick layer of clay, and walls out of wattle-and-daub.

"What did you live in before?" Tiso asked him as they thatched the roof.

"In summer, just the earth and sky. In winter, frame like this," he picked up four saplings and pantomimed tying them at the top with strips of leather. "Covered with hides. Easy to put up, easy to take down. We moved from place to place."

"Why didn't you stay in one place?"

43

"Hunters need to move with animals, Tiso. We go where they go."

The idea of moving one's home to follow animals was very odd. The village livestock were never pastured more than a day's walk from the village during the warm season, and the animals were kept inside the village walls during the cold one. Ana wondered what it was like to live without a permanent village, for a whole clan to pack up and move to go hunting instead of raising grain. To rely solely on hunting for sustenance seemed so risky, she couldn't understand why anyone would choose such a life. Nor could she understand the amount of time and energy Dumuz spent, in addition to building their house, to care for an animal that was not providing food or milk. Every morning he fetched water and grass for the pony, and every evening he used bundles of dried reeds to burnish the pony's coat. He untangled its tail with his fingers, all the while talking to it, until, just as he had said, it became as tame as the village dogs, following him around the pen like a pup. At night, he sat in front of the fire with strips of leather, making what he called a harness to fit around the pony's head. To Ana's surprise, the pony soon accepted wearing the harness all the time. Ana had to admit it made sense, because now Dumuz could lead her simply by looping another strip of leather through the harness.

In the meantime, Ana prepared the interior of their home, first building the shrine, a three-legged altar made of clay and decorated with water symbols. When it was finished, Ana took it from the kiln and placed it in the northeast corner of the house. She made a statue of the Goddess, masked and seated, and to please Dumuz, gave the Goddess a male consort, also masked and seated, holding a sickle in his right hand. She placed them on top of the shrine, along with two small offering bowls, one for water and one for grain.

After the shrine was in place, Ana decorated the interior walls with meanders, spirals, and patterns of dots. She arranged stones for a hearth, made a small clay oven, and set a quern next to it. She stood storage jars in one corner, and hung dried herbs from the rafters. It was small but cozy, with thick walls that would keep the house cool in hot weather and warm in cold weather.

The house and its adjoining lean-to shed were finished in time to move the pony out of the goat pen when the animals came back from their warm-weather pasture. Dumuz made bedding for the pony from stalks of grain after they were threshed, and he had a stockpile of field grasses drying for fodder. The coming season would be a harsh one for the whole village, herd animals and people alike. The ground, when not covered with snow, would be frozen hard. Through long nights that would be even colder than the freezing days, they would have to be on guard all the time against hungry wolves that howled and sometimes paced close to the village fence, which would always be gated shut by sundown. No one would go outside the fence alone, not even in the daytime.

Thank the Goddess, they'd had an excellent harvest, and good fishing and hunting. They had enough grains, lentils, dried fish, and smoked meat to make it through the dark, cold season. On good days when the sun shone and the snow thawed a little, Dumuz and the other young men would go out to hunt hares and partridge, out of boredom as much as the desire for fresh meat.

Dumuz was not used to such plenty. His people had often been close to starvation by the time the snow melted for good, and more than one man had lost toes or fingers to frostbite from the need to hunt no matter how cold it became. Even so, their grain stores were precious. He could feed the growing foal only a handful of grain every few days, and even that was too much for some villagers, who could see no use in the pony except for food.

"Once she is big enough to ride, you will see," Dumuz had assured Ana so that she could explain it to the rest of her clan. "I will be able to travel farther to hunt. She will carry many goods to trade. She will serve us well. She will earn her grain."

One cold night Ana looked over at the pony, who dozed in a corner of the room with one leg partially lifted. At first, she had objected to bringing the animal inside on the coldest nights, not wanting her home defiled by its urine and feces. Even though the pony's droppings were less fetid than those of an ox, she insisted that Dumuz remove them immediately and replace the thick layer of straw that she hoped would keep the floor clean. Despite her distaste, she had to admit the pony's increasing bulk helped keep the interior of their house warmer. But Ana was glad to know that once the pony was full grown she would be able to withstand the cold weather in her own shed.

Ana shifted a little closer to the hearth with a grunt. It had been nine moons since she'd last had her flow, so the birthing would be coming soon, likely before the sheep and goats were dropping their lambs and kids. And about time, too. Her breasts were hard, tight, and getting painful; her belly was enormous. Sometimes she could see it ripple as the baby shifted position. Sometimes she could see and feel the outline of a hand or foot against the taut skin. Every night she rendered a bit of animal fat with dried burnet and rubbed the warm compound on her belly to keep the skin supple. Even better were the evenings when Dumuz applied it for her, as he was doing this night.

Dumuz was almost fluent in their language now. He was finally able to tell her how he came to be riding in the woods on the day she first saw him.

"We suffered through a time so cold that many of our elders froze to death. That's when my father died. When the thaw came, my tribe packed up. We traveled west and south. We entered the territory of another tribe. Our head man met with their head man. We thought we had permission to camp and hunt. They must have changed their minds. Maybe their hunts had gone badly, too. Maybe they were starving, like us. I don't know. When the sun set, they attacked us."

"Attacked you? Like a bear or wolf? Why would they do that?" asked Ana.

He shrugged. "Why does any tribe attack another?"

"I don't know. That's why I asked."

Dumuz stopped rubbing her belly and stared at her.

"Are you making a joke?"

She shook her head. "I have never heard of such a thing."

46

Dumuz was nonplussed. "Can it be that in your whole lifetime, no village has fought with another village?"

"In my lifetime, and that of my ancestors, as far back as stories go. Why should any village fight another? What purpose could there be in that?"

Dumuz laughed harshly. "Because one village has what another wants, of course."

She looked blank.

"Grain? Goats? Copper beads?" he suggested.

"Each village grows the grain it needs and tends its own herds," she explained, patiently, as though she were talking to Arina. "If we want more copper beads, we travel up or downriver to trade our bone combs and antler knives for them."

"Land, then. Surely your people have fought someone for this land."

"This land has belonged to our village since far beyond anyone's memory. There is plenty of land along the riverbank for many villages. You can walk three days along either bank before you come to another settlement. You could start your own village anywhere you want. There are fish enough for everyone."

Dumuz shook his head. "It is different where I come from. There is never enough food. Everyone wants the best hunting grounds."

"How sad." The baby pressed against Ana's ribs. She pulled her tunic back down and shifted position, trying to get more comfortable. "Go on, Beloved. Tell me what happened to your clan."

"As I said, they came at night. Our watchman blew a horn to warn us. Still, I barely had time to mount Luguk before the horsemen were among us. In the battle, I killed one man right away. Then another knocked my bow out of my hand. All I had then was my knife, no match for a bow, but one of our attackers had lost his bow, too. He was fleeing, and I chased him. Luguk was fast as the wind. We outran the other man, and I knocked him off his horse. I dismounted and killed him with my knife."

Ana drew breath sharply.

"Ana, if I had not killed him, he would have killed me."

"I don't understand all this killing." She reached for him. How could this hand, so soft with oil and burnet, kill another person?

"Killing happens when people have little but need much."

She shook her head. It was hard for her to imagine a clan, no matter how poor, not sharing what they had. "How sad. What happened next?"

"I was many miles from my people. I had ridden Luguk hard, and he needed rest, so the sun was coming up by the time I got back to our camp. It was on the other side of a small rise. I dismounted, let Luguk graze. When I got to the top of the rise. I could see my tribe below me, all dead, every one. Nothing was left but their bodies. Hides, bows, knives, water skins—all gone. I didn't see any of the men who killed my people. Their tracks led east. Maybe they thought there were more of us that way. Alone, I couldn't go after so many. I went back to Luguk and rode west."

Her eyes filled with tears. "Did you bury your dead first?"

"It is not our way to bury anyone. We have no digging tools, and what is a body when the life is gone? Just flesh and bone. We let the animals take it."

Ana shivered to hear of this harsh treatment of the dead. "And then?"

"I rode all day, and then I needed to eat. I made a snare and caught a hare for my dinner. I made a new bow, a crude thing, and a few arrows. With those, and more snares, I caught enough small game. I kept riding west. I crossed the mountains, and that took a long time. There was snow, and not much to eat. After I got through, I headed south. I kept to the forest because I didn't know who lived along the river, or what they might do if they saw me. All was well until we came upon a beautiful forest spirit, who stood up right in front of Luguk." He kissed Ana. "Apparently, the spirit spooked him so badly that he threw me off his back. But I can't remember that part."

She pulled him to her and held him close. "It makes my heart ache to think of all you went through. I'm glad that you ended up here, but how sad what came before."

To make her feel better, he talked instead about how happy he was going to be to finally see their baby. Ana was glad to hear him speak of tomorrow, not yesterday. She hated the wistfulness in his voice whenever he described racing across the steppes atop the galloping Luguk, the feel of the wind on his face and in his hair, the dusty look and smell of wild northern plains so different from this fertile river valley. He couldn't wait until the days grew longer and warmer and he could ride again.

The pony was thriving and putting on muscle. He named her Marsh Hawk, because of where they found her, and the spirit she had shown him that day. Ana liked the name, although she feared that one day, Dumuz and Marsh Hawk would fly away together.

But not tonight. She felt Dumuz grow heavy with sleep. She shifted away from him, unable to breathe, and pushed herself upright. As she did, she felt warm liquid gush between her legs. Now she understood why she had been so uncomfortable all evening.

She nudged Dumuz awake. "Dumuz, get Mari. Our baby is coming!"

The arrival of the baby was cause for celebration throughout the village. Although Mari told her it had been an easy birth, Ana had felt as though she were being turned inside out. Then she heard the baby cry and felt her tired body flush with love. She named her Dana, bringing together Dumuz' name and her own.

The baby's arrival also meant that Marsh Hawk went back to her shed. As the days grew longer and warmer, Shela seemed more interested in the pony than her new niece. She watched every day as Dumuz led the pony outside the village fence, where he made her walk, then trot, then canter in a circle around him, using only a long leather thong and a series of clucking noises to cue the pony to start, stop, change gait. One day, Dumuz tied a blanket on the pony's back while he exercised her. When she was tired, he draped himself over the blanket. Marsh Hawk tossed her head at first, but then she continued to walk forward.

The next day, Dumuz mounted the pony. After a few moments of head-tossing and kicking, Marsh Hawk calmed down and they walked through the village gate.

Everyone stopped their work and stared as pony and rider walked by. Mari, who had been rocking great-granddaughter Dana in her arms, nearly dropped the baby in amazement.

Ana put down the figurine she was decorating, wiped her hands and walked over to the gathering crowd. She took Dana from Mari and put the baby in a sling she wore around her shoulders. She didn't need to say "I told you so." She felt deeply satisfied to see the expression of wonder and awe on her Grandmother's face, and on the faces of her kinfolk.

"Dumuz looks tall and handsome atop that beast, doesn't he?" she asked, opening her tunic so the baby could suckle.

"How does he keep his balance?" Grandmother asked.

"His skill is a gift from the Goddess, I expect. What else could it be?"

"Long hours of hard work, perhaps?" Shela said. "Like learning to weave or work clay."

Grandmother laughed and put her arm around Shela. "All aspects of life are Her gifts, child, even long hours of hard work. I am very thankful the Goddess has let me live long enough to see such a wondrous thing."

The three women walked with the rest of the villagers as they followed Dumuz back outside the fence. Even Arina came alongside Ana to watch as, after walking the pony across the ditch, Dumuz kicked her into a trot. After a few steps Marsh Hawk, feeling new grass under her feet and soft air on her face, leaped into a canter. Ana gasped, expecting to see Dumuz thrown off again, but he gripped with his knees and held on to her stubby mane. True to her name, the pony seemed to fly across the meadow, getting smaller and smaller, like a hawk in the sky.

A few moments later, they turned and galloped back. The villagers began to run out of the way, but Dumuz slowed Marsh Hawk to a trot and then a walk. He slid off the pony and led her by the harness to the waiting crowd. The pony held her head high. Her nostrils were wide and her eyes seemed lit from within. Dumuz' face also looked lit from within. Until now, Ana had seen that look only when they made love. She knew she should be pleased to see her lover so happy, but she was not sure how she felt if riding a pony gave him as much pleasure as loving her. She held the baby even closer.

Marsh Hawk puffed and snorted and stamped her feet at the crowd, who moved quickly to stay away from the sharp hooves. Only Shela walked forward. She placed her hand on Marsh Hawk's muzzle, calming the pony, and looked over at Dumuz.

"Teach me to ride, Brother." The villagers laughed.

Dumuz laughed, too. "Ride? Girls don't ride."

Shela scowled at him. "Why not? Did the women of your clan walk when you broke camp?"

"Of course not," Dumuz answered. "But they sat behind their men. They held on to the men while the men controlled the ponies."

"Didn't your women have two arms and two legs, like you?"

"Of course, but a riding a pony takes strength and skill."

"So, were you born with strength and skill? Did you ride that well the first time you tried?"

Dumuz rubbed Marsh Hawk's flanks thoughtfully. "No, Shela. I fell off the first time I rode. I had to learn how to balance. My father taught me."

"Then you can teach me," Shela said.

Dumuz raised his eyebrows and looked over at Ana, who shrugged and said, "We women have less between our legs to injure from bouncing on a pony than men have, Dumuz. Why not do as she asks?"

The villagers laughed at her good joke, and Dumuz laughed with them. "But women have more to injure above the waist," he countered. "Horses bounce a lot." That, too, drew a laugh.

"I will wrap my breasts, then," Shela said. "And you can start teaching me tomorrow after Marsh Hawk has had a good rest."

Dumuz and Ana had a long talk that night, after Marsh Hawk was in her shed and the day's work was done. They lay together next to the hearth, with the baby between them.

"Your clan is very different from my tribe," he said, stroking Dana's tiny hand.

"In more ways than how you speak, and where you live, and how you get food, and who gets to ride horses?"

Dumuz smiled. "In all ways, it seems." He looked up at her. "Did you know I was hoping for a boy?"

Ana was dumbfounded. "You didn't want our daughter when she was born?"

He caressed the baby's head. She had straight black hair like his. "I love our baby, and her mother, surely you know that by now."

"Then why would you hope for a boy?"

"Men are supposed to beget boys. Boys learn to hunt and provide food. Women merely cook it."

Dumuz was full of surprising statements today. This one made Ana laugh heartily. "Women don't 'merely' do anything, or haven't you noticed?"

"I have noticed. In your village, women are special. Especially you and Mari. I suppose Dana will be a priestess someday, too?"

Ana leaned up on one elbow.

"Probably. But there's nothing special about us. Every village lives as we do."

"All of them? Up and down the river, all the people you trade with?"

"Certainly. All people are the same. A baby girl, a baby boy, each is a precious gift from the Goddess. How could one wish for one kind over the other?"

"Where I came from, it wasn't like that."

"Tell me. It's a strange way to serve Her."

"Ana, my people did not serve your Goddess. We worshipped Gods. Powerful male Gods, and many of them."

"The Goddess has many consorts."

"That's not what I mean. I had never heard of your Great Goddess before coming here."

Ana sat up at that. Dana fussed at the sudden motion, so Ana picked her up and rocked her.

"How that can be? Why would She allow that?"

Dumuz sat up, too, and stirred the fading coals. "Because different people have different Gods. I met other tribes whose Gods were not ours. Sometimes our Gods were more powerful than theirs. The tribe who killed my people must have had more powerful Gods than we did."

"More powerful? Sometimes the Goddess takes life, but She gives it back again, too. Babies are born. Sheep have lambs. Eggs hatch into chicks. People, animals—she renews us all. Plants, too. Trees shed their leaves and die when it gets cold, but they are born again when the sun's warmth returns. Crops grow, are harvested and their stems die, but they give us seeds to nourish us through the cold season, and seeds to sow. The cycle repeats, over and over and over. The new cycle is beginning even now. The sun will soon rise in the east, and the moon will be full."

"So? The sun rises every day. The moon waxes and wanes. That is nothing new."

Ana wondered yet again about the strange tribe of Dumuz, who knew so much about riding a pony, but knew nothing of the cycle of seasons. She explained how important it was to plant crops at the right time, and how the sun and moon worked together to help them know that. She showed him her Grandmother's counting sticks, and told him how they helped Grandmother determine the moon's cycle, and how the sun's rising in the East gate told when the cycle was new, and when it was half over, and how each season had its own ceremony to mark it.

"I like your ceremonies," he said softly, watching the baby fall asleep in Ana's arms. "I liked the harvest ceremony, when the whole village got together to make beer from barley. I didn't know you could do that. All we ever drank was fermented mare's milk."

"Exactly. The Goddess showed us how to change grain into drink. She transforms everything. Even Marsh Hawk's droppings will help change seeds into grain. But we must sow crops at the right time. Too soon, and they may rot in the ground. Too late, they may shrivel and dry up. The moon tells us the right time."

"I see. My people had no crops, so we didn't pay attention to the sun and moon. Either it was cold or it was not. Those were the only two things that mattered. Whether hunting would be easy or hard."

"For us, what matters most of all is making sure the Goddess blesses our fields to make them fertile. That's why the Sowing Festival is the most important of all the ceremonies. Now that you are with us, you will be part of it, too, on the night of the second full moon after the Sun rises in the East."

"Tell me about it" he said, yawning. He lay down again. Ana placed the baby by his side, and explained the ceremony in detail.

He sat up again. "Maybe I didn't hear this right. All the men and all the women at the same time?"

Ana laughed. "Not all of us in a big pile. By two, or sometimes three. On that night, the Goddess is in all of us. I am not Ana, Boros is not Boros, Shela is not Shela. We are all Goddess. We are all Earth. We mate as all the creatures of the Earth are mating then, to honor the One who gives all life."

"And the *women* pick the men?"

"Of course."

"What if someone else picks me?"

Now Ana yawned. They had been up a long time. "We do as the Goddess wishes. It would dishonor her to refuse." She yawned again, and reached for his hand. "Don't worry, my love. The Goddess brought you to me. I won't choose anyone but you."

This time, it was Shela's turn to lead the sacred procession to the fields. She had woven for herself a string skirt of exceptional beauty, with a pattern of red and yellow chevrons on the belt. Ana carefully painted the ritual marks on her sister's body, taking care to avoid the tri-line tattoo on Shela's shoulder, marking her as a woman of childbearing age. The tattoo was still tender. Shela had begun her monthly flow later than Ana had done, on the day the moon rose in the east; she'd scarcely had time to complete the preparations for the Ritual.

Ana was proud of her younger sister, and proud of herself, too. She was still nursing Dana, so she felt particularly close to the Great Mother this time. And for all the time that Dumuz had been with them, each full moon had risen brightly, remaining bright and uncloaked until She set. All was well.

At their Grandmother's signal, Shela took the tether of the first bull calf and they walked into the Temple. Ana watched Shela's face as Grandmother put on the Frog mask and became the Priestess. Shela's eyes widened but she remained composed. Ana nodded her approval.

They entered the sanctuary for the fire-lighting and prayers. This time, Shela held the bowl of regeneration. Ana reached for the calf's tether but to her surprise, the Priestess handed her the sacred knife. Ana had never killed an animal before, except to swat a mosquito or green-headed fly. She had always known this ritual sacrifice would be hers to perform one day, but she had thought that day was far away. Her hand trembled. She prayed to the Goddess to guide her so the creature would not suffer much. The Priestess took her hand and showed her where to cut. Ana took a deep breath, and jabbed the knife into the calf's throat, slicing quickly across.

She didn't move back fast enough to avoid being splashed by the blood that arced from the calf's neck. She cleansed the knife with water from a decorated jug and wiped the blood off her arm. The Priestess prayed while Shela captured the rest of the calf's life offering.

When they came out of the temple, Ana was surprised once more. Grandmother took the bowl from Shela, but then she gave it to Ana, signaling to the whole village that Ana was no longer merely an apprentice. Ana held the heavy bowl in her left hand, dipped three fingers of her right hand into it, and painted the blood lines on her sister's forehead. During the procession, she walked next to Mari. When they reached the fields, Mari gestured to Ana to sprinkle the blood on the ground.

Ana didn't get the chance to see how Dumuz was coping with his first ceremony until after the sowing was finished. Tiso had helped Dumuz prepare by bathing in the river and showing him how to wear the beaded belt.

Ana knew that Dumuz was strangely reluctant to be naked in front of the whole clan. Every man and woman from the village was not only comfortable with the idea, but looking forward to it. She didn't understand why Dumuz could feel any shame about it. She tried to imagine herself in his place, encountering this custom for the first time, but she could not. The Ritual was too much a part of her life, too holy and important, so she gave up.

"You know how my body reacts when we are naked," he had told her the day before when she showed him the belt he was to wear. "Everyone will see!"

"That's the whole point of the ceremony," she explained, yet again. "We are supposed to become aroused. It is the Goddess working in us, helping us celebrate the new life we see everywhere around us by making new life ourselves. Our mating is important. The ceremony depends on it."

In the end, Ana had suggested that he might want to drink some beer before the procession began, to stay relaxed. Obviously, he had taken her advice. He was already drunk when the others were taking their first cup.

She found him near a willow grove, where he had gone to relieve himself. She shifted Dana from one breast to the other. Unlike other children, suckling infants were not only welcome at the Ritual, they held a place of honor along with their mothers, who in feeding their babies so clearly embodied the very essence of the Mystery of life.

"Well, it's certainly easier to make water wearing only this thing than breeches," he said.

"See, there are advantages to everything. What do you think of the ceremony so far?"

"Tiso said you became a full Priestess today. He was impressed. Me, too. You look different somehow—more beautiful, maybe. Must we wait for the moon to rise before we mate?"

"Yes, we must wait, but it won't be long. Come back to the others with me."

"Ana, I can't—seeing you like that with the baby, look what it's done to me!"

Ana laughed. "Well, take care of it yourself, if you must. It may help you wait until moonrise!" She walked back to the rest of her clan, knowing that she, too, would have a hard time waiting for the moon. She had felt the Goddess power in her body this whole day, stronger than she had ever felt it before. She knew that her clan members felt it, too. She could tell by the deference they had shown her ever since she had bloodied her sister's forehead. She had always been respected, as one who did the holy work of the Goddess, but her new status, granted at a time when she had a baby at her breast, nurturing new life as the Great Mother nurtured all, made them regard her with a kind of awe. Even Dumuz, unaccustomed to their ways, had seen the power in her and been affected by it.

If only the sun would set!

Finally, after the infants were nestled together beneath the hedgerow, each sleeping soundly thanks to a few sips of beer, the adults gathered together for the prayer. When Ana finished chanting the ancient, holy words for the first time, she motioned to Shela. Shela looked around the crowd of grinning men, old, young and in between. She walked straight up to Dumuz and took his hand.

Ana inhaled sharply. Mari touched her hand, as lightly as a moth's wing, but it was reprimand enough. Ana willed herself to smile and stand still as Dumuz was led away, looking over his shoulder at her with a what-now expression on his face. In answer, she walked up to her cousin Boros and led him in the opposite direction. They were all Goddess tonight, she reminded herself. It was the act itself that

57

mattered; who was paired with whom made no difference whatsoever. As a new Priestess, she should know that better than anyone.

As a woman of only fifteen summers, still feeling the mood swings of recent birthing, she wanted to slap her sister's face.

Ana's aching, milk-filled breasts woke her before anyone else was stirring. She stood up without giving Boros another glance, picked up her daughter, and walked back to the village. She went into the temple, where she knelt before the Great Mother and prayed. She had done her duty during the Ritual, but her body had no longer hummed with the Power that had been upon her all day. She'd had to use all her skill to ensure that she would climax, because not to do so would have been sacrilege. But Ana feared that by not performing the Ritual with a full heart, she had failed to honor the Goddess. So she prayed, but she felt no better after praying. She would have to ask Grandmother for her advice. Mari would know what Ana should do. Ana felt like a very poor kind of Priestess to have so many doubts.

By the time Dumuz came home, she had bathed herself and the baby, fed Marsh Hawk, and was sitting outside in the morning light, playing with Dana by patting her tiny hands together. The baby smiled and cooed at her, which did more than any prayers to make Ana feel better.

Dumuz stopped when he saw her. He was blushing so hard his whole face and neck were red. He had a hard time meeting her eyes.

"Ana."

She looked up, making sure her face and voice were as normal as possible. She knew how much he needed that. She even smiled at him, a true smile he could see in her eyes.

"Good morning, Beloved. There are millet cakes and a jug of fresh water inside. I took care of Marsh Hawk's breakfast, too."

"Ana, we must talk."

"No need."

"Last night—"

"Dumuz, last night belonged to the Goddess. The rest of the nights belong to us. Why don't you bathe and dress and bring the millet cakes out here? It's a beautiful, blessed morning."

Dumuz blushed again as he realized he was standing naked in front of returning, sober villagers. He went inside the house and came out a few minutes later in breeches. He sat down next to her and sipped from a cup of water.

"My head aches this morning."

Ana's reaction was immediate. "I'll get the tansy."

"Don't get up. Not that kind of ache. Just the kind you get from drinking too much beer."

"Ah. Only time can cure that, but drinking water will help." Dana yawned. Ana laid the baby in her shoulder sling, pulling the cloth up to shade her from the increasingly warm sun.

She smiled at Dumuz.

"How can you act like nothing happened last night?" he asked more sharply than he intended.

"All that happened was that my sister chose you, as was her right. It hadn't occurred to me that she might do so, but it should have."

"So now what do we do?" Dumuz was clearly worried.

"About what?"

"Is there some arrangement to be made? Will she live in our home? Is there some kind of bride price to pay?"

"What on earth are you talking about?" asked Ana. "What is a bride price?"

"It's what's paid to a woman's father when a man takes a wife."

"Take a wife? I don't understand. And what do you mean 'paid'?"

"In trade. You know. A man gives a father something of value, like so many deer skins, or a copper knife."

Ana gasped. "Are you telling me that your tribe traded goods for women as though they were livestock?"

"No, not exactly. It's not that simple. But I don't know what to do here. Shela has no father. Is there another male relative I should talk

59

to? I should have done so with you, too, but I didn't know how to speak your language well enough to ask."

Ana stared at him. She had almost stopped thinking of him as a foreigner, but this conversation was so absurd she didn't know how to reply.

He tried again. "Ana, don't you understand what I am trying to say? I took your sister last night."

"I would say instead that she took you," Ana said drily. She took a deep breath, not wanting to feel again the sharp flash of anger she had felt last night. "Did the two of you fully honor the Goddess?"

Dumuz looked away from her. "Yes."

Of course they had. It was right that they should. "Then you fulfilled your duty. You have no further obligation to Shela." Ana knew this, and believed it, but she also knew that the hurt she felt was wrong.

He looked at her again. "None?"

Ana didn't meet his eyes. "None at all, Dumuz. Last night was a Ritual. We bond that way for that night and that night only. It has nothing to do with choosing a mate. Look at everyone returning to their own homes, their own mates. Most of them were with someone else last night." Ana shifted the baby slightly. Dumuz didn't react to what she said. She had thought her explanation would make him relax, but he still sat tense and troubled. She had to ask. She forced herself to look at him.

"Of course, if you and she desire each other today, that's different."

"I don't desire her—not now. But Ana, you must know, I desired her last night. I didn't mean to, but I was drunk and..." He blushed again. "She was surprisingly ... skillful."

Ana kept her voice neutral. "Of course she was. We are all trained in the art of giving and receiving pleasure, because some things come naturally to a couple, but some things do not."

Dumuz ran his hands through his hair and lowered his voice. "What if she has a child?"

"All children born from the Ritual belong to the Goddess. If Shela is given that gift, she will care for her child as any other woman does."

"Does the father have no duty to the child?"

Ana marveled again at how much basic common sense needed to be explained to her otherwise intelligent lover. "Look, suppose that tonight she beds with Tiso, and the next with Boros, and in nine moons she has a baby. Which of you would be the father?"

Dumuz' face took on such a bemused expression she had to laugh. "Well, I suppose if the babe were yours, the hair would make it obvious. But for most clans, it would be hard to tell. We know that a baby belongs to a particular woman because we see it come from her body. That is all we can know, and all we need to know. Once a baby is grown past suckling, everyone helps care for it. That's what makes us kin and clan. It's the only arrangement that makes any sense."

Dumuz rubbed his aching forehead. "Ana, it is so different among my people. A woman belongs to one man. Some men have more than one woman, but a woman would never have more than one man."

"That's not fair."

Dumuz thought about that. "No," he finally admitted. "I suppose not."

By this time more and more members of the village were returning, all looking tired and pleased. The quiet peace of dawn was being transformed by the everyday sounds of morning: conversation, the baaing of sheep and goats eager to be milked, floors being swept. The scent of the roasting calf masked the odor of animal dung, making Dumuz' stomach rumble with hunger. He stood up and went inside for a millet cake.

When he came out, holding a cake out to Ana, Shela walked by, dressed in her everyday tunic and skirt.

"Good morning, Brother," she said. "Will you give me another riding lesson this afternoon?" Her tone was innocent enough, but Dumuz wondered if by "riding" she meant Marsh Hawk or himself.

"Um, why don't you take her for a walk instead?" he said. "You are doing well enough to ride quietly on your own now. Just don't go too far or too fast with her."

"Thank you. Right now I'm going to check on that delicious-smelling calf."

Ana realized she had been holding her breath. She released it slowly, but the motion disturbed Dana, who stretched and yawned and fell back to sleep. A bee droned past them.

"I am not sure I will ever understand your people," Dumuz said. "But I will try." He took Ana's hand and held it to his chest.

"I swear by my own Gods and by your Goddess that you are the only woman I want. I wanted you since the day I woke from darkness to see your face bending over me. Is it possible for someone not of your clan to be blessed by your Goddess? Because if it is, then I am certainly blessed by Her."

Ana leaned into his chest with relief. "She has blessed us all, my Beloved. Let's go inside."

In the afternoon, most of the villagers, Dumuz among them, napped away the effects of the night's revelry. But Ana was too restless to sleep, even after she and Dumuz made love. He had been especially tender and attentive. She was happy that he had tried to make amends for the previous night by delighting her in ways that she thought she fully deserved. But when the pleasant afterglow of lovemaking faded, the fear returned that her jealousy had put her clan's welfare in jeopardy.

Unable to sleep, she got up and walked around the village. She passed the women who tended the sacrificial calf, nearly done roasting and smelling even more mouthwatering than before. She passed Arina, who was engrossed in forming millet cakes under the guidance of Daria, a woman who had lost a child during the winter, and who more than anyone else in the clan needed her little sister's joyful company. She was glad she did not see Shela, who was probably still out riding Marsh Hawk. She circled the whole village, ending up at the temple, where her grandmother was sitting in the shade with a bag slung across her shoulders. She rose stiffly.

"I've been waiting for you, Ana," Mari said. "Come, let us look for fresh mint."

Ana was glad for this excuse to have a private talk. She both desired and dreaded receiving the wise old woman's guidance. What if, after all the years of training, she was now unfit to be a Priestess? How could she bear the shame?

Mari said nothing until they were through the fence and walking toward the hills. The grass was soft and fragrant, and the sun was warm, but a cluster of mare's tails was gathering in the northwest sky.

"I think we will have rain soon," Mari said. "The tears of the Goddess, my mother used to call it, blessing the earth for us."

"Why would the Goddess be crying?" asked Ana.

"I think they were meant to be tears of joy, in thanks for the Ritual."

Ana fell silent. She didn't know how to begin telling her grandmother how she had wronged the Goddess last night.

"How is Dumuz?"

"Sleeping off too much beer."

Mari chuckled. "Dumuz and the rest of the village, I think." She paused. "And how are you?"

"Oh, Grandmother—" was all Ana managed to say. The suddenness and vehemence of her tears took her by surprise. Mari put her arms around her granddaughter and held her without saying a word until she stopped sobbing. She patted Ana's back and led her to a large, flat stone. A small green snake, which had been sunning itself there, uncoiled and fled into the tall grass as they approached. Ana wiped her eyes on the hem of her tunic.

"Ah, that feels good," Mari said as she sat down. She massaged Ana's back. "I worry that I have gone too fast with your training, child. You are still young to be a Priestess. It should have been your mother to whom I gave such a heavy load."

"Grandmother," Ana whispered. "I hated Shela last night!"

"I know. How could you feel otherwise? You are a young woman in love, who recently gave birth, and your sister chose your man."

"But a Priestess should feel only joy at the consummation of the Ritual. I felt much anger. At both of them."

63

"Ana, a woman feels what she feels. A Priestess is still a woman, after all. You cannot deny what you feel, but you can choose not to show it."

"You stopped me."

"You stopped yourself. The Goddess may have guided my hand to yours, but you understood and regained your composure quickly. Your face did not betray your feelings."

Ana took a deep breath. "I'm glad of that. But Grandmother, I'm worried that I may have dishonored our Great Mother, because I performed the Ritual, but with no joy in my heart."

"I would expect nothing more, even from a woman of greater years. Do you think you are the first Priestess to feel this way?"

Something in the way her grandmother asked brought Ana out of her own misery. "*You*, Grandmother?"

"All of us, at one time or another, I am sure. I think that is why the Ritual is about the physical act itself: only about the body, because in the right circumstances—say, when one is a bit dizzy from fasting and drinking beer—the body can do what is needed no matter what the heart says. The important thing for a Priestess is to make sure the Ritual is completed. The woman inside must cope with her feelings as well as she can, but the outward Priestess must not deviate from her duty."

"Then, do you think the crops are safe? I've been so worried about that—I wonder if I'm really worthy to be a Priestess?"

Mari kissed Ana on the cheek before pushing herself upright.

"My child, we have followed our sacred custom, and now the crops are in the hands of the Goddess, as always. But I think I really have pushed you too far too soon, and I am sorry for that. For now, you must trust me. If you were able to honor Her last night, you are indeed worthy, and all is well. Now let's go back. I need some rest before tonight's feast."

"We haven't picked any mint."

Mari waved her hand. "That's all right. Now that I think about it, I still have some hanging from the ridgepole."

They walked back to the village, arm in arm. Ana realized for the first time that she was taller than her grandmother. When did that happen?

When they got back, Dumuz was still asleep. Ana checked that Dana was sleeping, too, and then she lay down next to her beloved. She was asleep almost before she closed her eyes.

To Ana's great relief, all the grains and legumes grew strong and full that summer. Lambs and kids thrived, fish all but jumped into the fishermen's weir nets. It was a summer of plenty like no other she could recall. Shela made only one reference to the Ritual, informing Ana that Dumuz was too hairy for her taste. Except for that one remark, it might never have happened at all. Shela even had the good sense to stop riding Marsh Hawk, although the reason might have had more to do with her growing interest in Tiso than in trying to avoid awkward interactions with Dumuz.

Dana was growing into a plump and vivacious baby who could get away from Ana in a twinkling with her fast, purposeful crawl. Ana could get no real work done while Dana was awake, but she took great joy in playing with her daughter, in kissing her fingers and toes, in feeding her and holding her close afterwards until she slept. Ana was very glad that Dana had a happy disposition. Some babies woke up cranky, but Dana always smiled in the morning. Other babies cried most of the time; sadly, babies like that seldom thrived. Ana thanked the Goddess that so far, her baby was healthy and happy. Only recently did she start to fuss, now that her front teeth were pushing through the gums. Arina baked hard little cakes for Dana to suck on while she teethed.

In the brief hours when Dana napped or contentedly teethed on a millet cake, Ana took advantage of the opportunity to work on new vessels for the trading fair that would take place at the end of the harvest season. Her village was going to host the event; traders from upriver and downriver would be arriving to set out their wares on the floodplain across from the village. There would be no chance of flooding at that time of year—even the beaver pond was shallow—so it was the perfect time and place for a fair.

Normally Ana would be disappointed not to be traveling outside the village for the fair, but with Dana it was going to be much easier to have the fair come to her. It would be much easier for Grandmother, as well, who became more tired as the days grew shorter. She woke up with a coughing fit more days than not, and Ana thought she was losing weight. On the day the sun returned to the east gate, when day and night were the same length, the Head Priestess performed the solemn ritual, but Ana noticed how she swayed a little when she raised her arms in prayer, and coughed when she finished the chant.

As they went back to the antechamber, the Head Priestess removed the owl mask, replaced it on the clay bench, and pointed along the row of masks. "They will be yours to wear before the first snowfall," she said.

Ana had denied it vigorously at the time, but Mari was a great healer, and she knew what she knew. Every night since then, Ana prayed that the Goddess would give Grandmother the strength to keep on. She placed the masked face of the Great Mother on her bowls and jugs, decorating them with her most skillful incised designs and scribing a dedication to her Grandmother on her best work.

Dumuz, too, was working hard to prepare for the fair by making bows, arrows and spears. Old Danu, Tiso's mother's uncle, showed Dumuz how to chip obsidian into sharp arrowheads and spear points following the ancient technique. Dumuz, who had only used bone and antler weapons, admired the ultra-sharp edge and thin profile of the obsidian, which would penetrate the hide of a wild boar much better than the arrows and spears he had previously used. Like Danu, he looked forward to trading with people from the more northern clans to replenish their dwindling stock of the glossy black stone.

The whole village was busy with harvest activities. Those who were young and fit spent long hours cutting grain. Those whose bones ached too much for such strenuous work tended the herds, milked the animals and made cheese, smoked meat and fish. Children gathered acorns and nuts. The harvest would culminate in the making of barley beer. The beer making was preceded by the blessing of the grain that would be converted into malt, with additional blessings at each stage of the process. First the barley was soaked in water for two days. Then it was spread out to germinate. After that, children and adults took turns dancing on the sprouted barley, rubbing it with their feet to break the sprouted grains off the shoots. The malted grains were then heaped up and covered with straw until fermentation began. Once the characteristic odor seeped up through the straw, the grains were uncovered, spread out, and danced on one more time. Then the malt was dried and ground.

Some of the ground malt would be stored, and the rest would be covered with boiling water to start the first beer of the new season. After a few hours, the liquid would be strained, cooled, and set aside in clay jugs to bubble and froth into beer.

The trading fair would take place during this last stage in the process, which required at least half a lunar cycle to complete. When the new beer was ready, the first tasting would be accompanied, as always, by solemn blessings. But once the brewing was deemed a success, the full harvest celebration would begin and last for three days. It was a happy time of music, dancing, and practical jokes; a man who drank so much he lost consciousness might wake up buried to his neck in the trash midden.

Everyone deserved such merriment after the hard work of the growing season. It was a last chance for the clan to gather outdoors before the cold, dark days began. When the snows started in earnest, families mostly stayed inside, close to the hearth, telling ancient tales of days when there was no growing season, when all was ice and snow and cold, and the Mother Earth herself was fast asleep. The only break in the long, gloomy season was the day when the sun made her passage farthest to the south and the light began its slow return, but even then, it would be many days before the sun was high enough to give not just light, but also warmth.

Ana thought about all these things when it was time for the hard work of firing the pottery, and prayed for her Grandmother with each hunk of wood she added to the fire in the kiln. She could no longer deny the fact that Grandmother was coming to the end of her days. Ana had trained intensely, all her life, to take over from her. She knew every prayer, every ceremony, every ritual; she was developing into a healer nearly as skilled as Grandmother; she worked clay as well as anyone; she was using the counting sticks to track the moon's cycles. She was ready to serve the Goddess and her village.

But what if she herself were to grow ill? It would be years before Dana could begin the sacred work. Ana would need an apprentice. She would have to talk to Shela. But Shela had a wildness in her, like Marsh Hawk before she was tamed. Shela's hands had the patience to weave beautiful cloth from flax and wool, but her spirit lacked the patience to memorize complex prayers and rituals. Still, Ana felt obligated to approach her; as sisters it was only right to do so. But what if Shela refused? Sweet, simple Arina would never be able to learn even the simplest of prayers. Who among her young cousins might be right for the task?

She stoked the fire, and sighed. It wasn't so many moons ago that she was a carefree apprentice herself, learning to shape loom weights and spindle whorls, secure in knowing that Grandmother could answer any question that came to her.

How much longer would she have her Grandmother's wise counsel? What would happen when Ana, who felt she had much knowledge, but little wisdom, was the one to whom expectant mothers came for help with birthing?

She prayed the Goddess would spare Grandmother for just a while longer.

When preparations for the trading fair were almost complete, Dumuz went into the hills with many of the other men to help bring the goats and sheep down from their growing season pastures, assisted by barking dogs that nipped at the animals' feet to keep them orderly. When they returned, it was time for the solemn part of the Harvest Ritual: the blessing of the grain. For the first time, Ana went into the temple by herself to get ready. Her long hair was tied back by a leather thong strung with beads. She wore the leather skirt and sleeveless tunic of the Priestess, a bracelet carved from a single large shell, a necklace of bone and unpolished copper beads. In the antechamber, she stood facing the six masks that she had seen Grandmother wear, ever since she could remember, to mark the cycle of the seasons. Bear, who came down from the hills with her cubs to mark the sun's appearance in the east. Frog, the layer of many eggs, for the Sacred Rite. Crane, the bird of life, for the longest day. Owl, the bird of death who mourned the sun when she passed the east gate on her southward journey. Fish, who disappeared when the north winds froze the river, to mark the end of Harvest. Hedgehog, who rolled into a ball to die and then sprang from the ball into new life, to mark the sun's return after the shortest day.

Ana hesitated. To put on any of these masks was to acknowledge how weak her grandmother had become. The old woman needed to sit or lie near a fire, even on warm days; many days she did not leave the hearthside. On rare days when she felt well enough, she left her home, leaning on Ana or Shela, moving slowly with the help of a walking stick. She would sit in the sunshine, the former Priestess full of power and wisdom, now a crone who dozed at midday.

It was as it should be, Ana knew that. Grandmother had been more blessed than most, to live so long and so well, when many who had died much younger rested in the burial ground on the south side of the village. And wasn't it fitting that Grandmother's health should be leaving her at Harvest's end, when so many birds flew south, and bees slept, and the bear would soon retreat to her den?

Ana took a deep breath, picked up the Fish mask, and placed it over her head. It was made of woven reeds covered inside and out with a slip of clay, with a gaping mouth through which she could see straight ahead, but not to the side. She stood still for a moment, waiting to feel the transformation that she always saw when Grandmother put on the mask and took on the Goddess power.

But she felt no different. With sorrow, she forced herself to enter the sanctuary, fumbling a little as she lit the sacred fire. She prayed as hard as she could, but still, she felt no different. She heard the music starting outside, and knew she had to face them.

Ana bowed to the seated, birthing Goddess and left the temple. Because of the mask she had to duck through the entrance; when she emerged, she stood as tall as she could, and raised her arms to begin the chant. She heard her clan gasp, almost in unison, as she stretched her hands to the sky. She looked through Fish's mouth, and saw on their faces the same expression of awe they had always shown to the Priestess.

So, they saw the Power in her after all. But if they could all see it, why couldn't she herself feel it?

The first traders began to arrive. Across the river, people were erecting reed shelters and laying out their goods. Most of the traders were young men, but there were women, too, some with suckling babes, some with small children who ran excitedly, exploring the riverbank for snails and crayfish.

Ana's clan were beginning to move their goods, carrying them upriver to a meander where deposits of silt made an easy place to ford across. Despite the festive atmosphere, day-to-day chores had to be completed, but instead of the relaxed rhythms of everyday, people were bustling about, eager to finish their work and walk over to the fair. Ana's main concern was that someone should always be with Grandmother.

Grandmother had other ideas. She walked out of her house, leaning heavily on her stick. "Take me out to the river bluff so I can sit there and watch the activity," she told Ana. "I may not be able to walk any farther, but my eyes still see well enough. Leave me food and drink and I will be fine until someone comes back."

Ana caught the eye of Kore, who said, "Mari, may I sit with you? I am too heavy with child to walk all that way." It was only a small untruth. Six moons along, Kore was not so big that she couldn't walk to the fair. But she was having a difficult pregnancy. She still vomited almost every day, and was unable to eat much more than thin porridge. Lately, she'd felt some cramping. Ana had been giving her angelica tea, which soothed her stomach, but Ana did not think Kore's child would wait a full nine moons, and children born more than one moon early never lived long. Ana was glad Kore could watch over Mari, but after she got them settled on the bluff, with Dana snuggled in between, she still fretted about leaving them alone over here.

"Nonsense," said Grandmother. "Go have a good time. There are enough people going back and forth to help us if we need it. We'll take good care of this little one. And you can see us from the meadow. Wave at us, and we'll wave back to show we're fine."

The long speech made Grandmother breathe heavily. Ana waited until her breaths came easier, using the time to feel Kore's belly. It was soft, and she felt a small flutter under her palm. All was well, then.

Dumuz was waiting for her with Marsh Hawk. He had brushed the pony until her coat gleamed. Over her back, he had fastened two large woven baskets with leather strips. Most of Ana's pots were packed inside, wrapped in woolen cloths. Dumuz' arrows were tucked beneath the crisscrossed leathers.

"Sorry, they didn't all fit," he said. "But if you lead Marsh Hawk, I can carry this basket and the spears."

Ana took the pony's lead. Marsh Hawk nuzzled her hand, and she gave the pony's soft muzzle a pat. She had come to like the beast, although she had no desire to ever climb upon its back.

The walk upriver eased her worries. The morning air smelled clean and crisp, now that they were upwind of middens and manure piles. High in the sky, a skein of white swans flew south, their trumpeting calls sounding clear but faint on the light northwest breeze. A flat, easy path led along the bluff, sloping gently down to the ford. Purple and white asters dotted the fields, and cattails had split open, revealing their fluffy interiors. Ana made a mental note to come back and collect the fluff, a warm, soft stuffing for boots and mitts.

Marsh Hawk forded the river easily. At this time of year, it was perfectly safe; only after the snows melted did the river run too deep and fast to cross. Like most people who lived alongside a river, Ana had learned to swim when she was a child. It surprised her that Dumuz didn't know how. He never went into the river just for fun, only to bathe after working hard on a hot day. Even then he rarely went in deeper than his waist. She would have to teach him, so when Dana was old enough, they could all have the fun of swimming with her in the cool water.

After they forded the river, they stopped to dry their feet. Ana put her leather sandals back on, Dumuz his boots. Then they proceeded around the meander to the meadow where the fair was in progress. Like any fair, this one offered a variety of useful goods. Clans from the north brought the flint and raw obsidian Dumuz and Danu wanted; those from the south brought shells and raw copper. There were everyday tools and household implements, woven materials dyed many colors, even a few livestock. Those who knew metalwork brought worked copper implements like knives and ax heads, or round pendants of copper beaten flat. Most popular was the trader who brought the most valuable thing of all: salt, brought up from the far south, where people lived at the edge of the great sea that Ana hoped someday to travel to, as Grandmother had once done.

Ana's eye always went to the pottery first. Right away she spotted two new styles of decoration: pots with raised bumps of clay, like the Hedgehog mask, and pots with incised dots. Some pots were raised up on pedestals. These looked so elegant, she was already thinking about how to accomplish it without having them crack apart in the kiln. Then she noticed how silent the fair had become.

She looked up from the pottery display. All eyes were fixed on Ana and Dumuz. No—on Dumuz and Marsh Hawk.

The two had become such a part of village life, she had all but forgotten how different Dumuz looked, and that no one else had ever seen a tamed pony. Although most people just stared at them with open mouths, a few people actually ran away, which made Marsh Hawk shy.

"My pots!" shouted the trader whose wares Ana had been admiring. "That beast will smash my pots." Others began to scream, "Get it out of here!"

Dumuz concentrated on calming the pony, who became more frightened as the clamor grew. He backed her up slowly, past all the goods. When cups and beads and bone combs were safely out of range of her hooves, he untied the baskets and set them on the ground.

"I'll take her home," Dumuz said to Ana. "I'm sorry. I forgot what a strange-looking pair we make."

"No, I'm sorry, Beloved. I should have realized—Dumuz, it's just they've never seen a pony that wasn't wild."

"They've never seen a wild man like me, either. See how they stare? I can feel their eyes on me. I will stay in the village, with the old women and the babes."

"Dumuz, no," Ana said. "Come back and show them the fine arrows and spears you made."

"Maybe tomorrow," he said, leading the pony away.

Ana watched until he was out of sight beyond the curve in the river, then she turned to face the traders. "I thought we were hospitable to strangers." No one met her eyes.

Boros came over and lifted one of the baskets. He motioned with his head. "We're set up over there."

Ana followed him, too angry to look at any more pots. She set up her wares in silence while the rest of the traders began to talk among themselves, gossiping about Dumuz, no doubt. Their voices sounded like the buzzing of botflies.

In a little while, a woman from the northernmost village stopped by.

"Your pottery is very skillfully made," she said, picking up one of Ana's inscribed bowls.

"Thank you."

The woman nodded, running her hands along the inscription. "Very skillful indeed." She looked at Ana curiously. "Who was that dark-haired stranger?"

"He is my mate."

The woman made no attempt to hide her shock. She put down the bowl and looked at Ana with a frown. "You chose to mate with him willingly? Your people accept him?"

"He is a good, kind, and generous man," Ana answered, trying to control her anger. "He's learning our ways gladly, and he contributes much to our village. He teaches us many things, as well."

"We have seen his sort near our village," the woman said, with scorn plain in her voice.

Now it was Ana's turn to register shock. "Tell me about them."

"They are neither good nor kind, and far from generous. There were three of them. We call them *Takers*. They come on the backs of ponies like that one," she inclined her head toward where Marsh Hawk had stood. "They have taken many of our lambs and kids. Beware of them. You may see them coming south before the snows fall."

She walked away, leaving Ana with much to think about, and more to fear.

Ana looked across the river at the top of the bluff where Grandmother and Kore were seated. She raised her arm, and both women waved back.

A shadow flickered across the sun. She shaded her eyes to see what caused it: a bird, a large one, a bird of prey. Then she gasped. It was an owl, in broad daylight, an owl flying straight across the river toward the bluff where the women sat waving.

"Do you see that?" she asked Boros, who was walking toward her with the last of the baskets.

"See what?"

She pointed. "That bird—do you see that bird flying across the river?"

"No, I don't see anything." He shrugged. "You are more far-sighted than I am, anyway."

Ana looked at the rest of the traders. If anyone else had seen the owl, they would have been staring as well, but all were intently examining one another's goods, haggling over their trades. She looked again at the bluff, but she couldn't see the bird anymore. Grandmother raised her arm, but she didn't beckon Ana, she merely waved again. She must not have seen it, either.

Only Ana had seen the great night hunter flying during the day, flying straight at Grandmother and Kore. The Goddess could not have sent a surer sign of coming death.

By the time the fair was over and the traders had begun their journeys north and south, everyone in the village knew about the three *Takers.* It was hard for Ana's people to imagine anyone like Dumuz stealing livestock. Animals were as necessary to the success of a village as their crops, even more so in bad times. As long as there was even dry grass for grazing, there would be milk and meat.

To take animals—or anything—from a village was unheard of. Hospitality to strangers was immediate and generous. Travelers brought with them news and stories. Young men often traveled to another village in search of a mate. If chosen by a young woman, the stranger would settle in her village and become part of her clan.

Even if a stranger were ignorant of their customs, as Dumuz had been, all he had to do was ask, and food would be given, and drink, and shelter. To treat such a person with anything but kindness would be a sacrilege against the Goddess, who gave all the bounty of the earth to her people. In a time of plenty, with game and fish easy to come by, travelers often brought food with them to share with their hosts. Generosity was matched with generosity, as it had been since this area was settled in ages past.

Dumuz tried, unsuccessfully, to explain to the village why any stranger would behave with such disregard for civilized behavior.

"Outside this valley, beyond the mountains, the world is harsh," he said. "There are no crops, and there may not be enough game for everyone. People travel to survive. If I had come across your herd of sheep when I first arrived here, I would have taken a lamb or two, not knowing they belonged to anyone, and to be honest, not caring if they did. I would be hungry and would need to eat."

"But you would only have to ask," said young Gat. "Whatever we have, we would share. And if you were truly starving, we would slaughter a lamb ourselves to feed you."

"But for people like these *Takers*, asking would not enter their minds. And hospitality to strangers—that's a dangerous thing where I came from. Men like that killed everyone in my tribe. We were just looking for a place to set up our shelters and hunt for a few days." He could see how puzzled they were about the strange customs he was describing. On some faces, he saw frank disbelief.

He asked the question that had been troubling him. "What will we do if they come this far south?"

"Do you think they will?" asked Gat. His question seemed almost eager.

Dumuz shrugged. "I did."

Gat smiled. "So? Now you're one of us. Besides, the beer is almost ready. Nothing bad ever happens during the Harvest Festival!"

Dumuz had as little success making Ana understand the danger. "What if they come this far south?" he asked again.

"We will have to meet as a village to discuss it."

"What good will that do? You will need action, not talk."

"Well, what good is action without talking about it first? It's what we do when any big decision must be made."

"You talk and talk until everyone agrees?"

"Most of the time it works that way. But sometimes a clan cannot come to agreement. When that happens, one of the parties will move away and start a new village. That way harmony is maintained for everyone."

"Talk will do no good if these men come here. They will come with great speed, too swift for talk. Could you persuade your clan to do something, please? Maybe fortify the outer wall, or make it higher? You are their Priestess. They listen to you."

"In matters pertaining to the Goddess, I serve Her with my prayers and my work. I serve my people by healing them and by guiding them in the necessary rituals—I have no influence beyond that."

Dumuz sighed in frustration. There were times when a group needed a leader. This was one of them. He could not understand why they had no head man to take charge at times like these, and he told Ana so.

She just laughed. "Imagine trying to get everyone in the village to do something just because one man or woman told them to! You might as well try to keep the goats in one spot without fencing them in."

Ana had more immediate worries in the here and now than three strangers far to the north. Kore had not felt her child move since the first day of the fair. Ana feared the owl had done its work. If the child was dead, and rotted inside Kore, then Kore would die, too. To prevent that, Ana would have to break Kore's water—a very dangerous procedure—to make her go into labor and expel the dead child. If the baby was still alive, however, and Ana forced Kore to deliver almost three moons early, then the baby would not survive. She wished Grandmother could advise her on which course to take, but Grandmother could not help her. After her day of watching the fair, she was too tired to do anything except sleep by the hearth. Each day her sleep became longer and deeper. Now she did not wake, even when Ana squeezed her hand, and shook her shoulder. Finally, Ana pinched her arm, but Grandmother merely frowned; otherwise she did not react. She had eaten no food, and drunk nothing, since the sun had risen, set and risen again. She had not made water all day.

At the fair, Ana had traded four of her finest ceremonial bowls, and two of Dumuz' spears, for a shiny round pendant of worked copper hung from a leather thong. She had given it to Grandmother that first day, before leading her home from the bluff. Grandmother said she had never seen anything so beautiful, and had put it on right away. It looked like a small sun gleaming in the afternoon light. She still wore it. Ana hoped it might have some positive effect on her Grandmother, since it was made of the precious metal, and lay right where her heart was beating, but she didn't think Grandmother even knew it was there now.

Ana took a damp cloth and wiped the old woman's wrinkled face. She could see that Mari's lips had taken on a blue cast. It wouldn't be long now.

Ana went into the temple, and returned with a basketful of Goddess figurines, some only a few inches high. Each figurine was inscribed with one of Her symbols: water, snakes, eggs, birds, fish. Ana arranged them around her Grandmother's prone body so she would be surrounded by Goddess Power during her passage. The largest, carved from the thighbone of a doe, was unpainted, a narrow figure wearing a blank, triangular mask. This one she lay atop her grandmother's chest, right below the copper medallion.

When she had finished, a shadow in the doorway made her look up. Kore stood there, holding her stomach. "My water broke," she said. Ana got up and led her to the other side of the fire. Kore lay down heavily. Ana lifted her skirt and gently examined her. Kore's birth canal was moist with the fluid leaving her womb. It was easy for Ana to feel the opening her body was making for the baby's passage. It would be some hours away, Ana thought, relieved that she did not have to perform the delicate procedure of inserting a sharpened reed in there to break the water sac.

She removed her hand and smiled to reassure Kore, though she knew this birthing would not have a happy outcome.

"I need another pair of hands, Cousin. I will get Shela and be right back."

"Don't be long, Ana," Kore said. "I'm afraid."

"The Goddess will protect you." Ana lowered Kore's skirt. "We have plenty of time."

Once outside, Ana paused to take a deep breath and say a quick prayer. "I need much help tonight, Great Mother," she prayed. "Guide my hands to help Kore, and bless Grandmother on her passage to you."

She found Shela first, behind the house, kissing a boy she had met at the fair. He must be a good kisser, Ana thought, since he made Shela forget Tiso ever existed.

"Sister." Her voice was sharp with authority. "I need you. Find Arina right away. Grandmother nears her passing, and Kore's child is coming."

Shela, for once, let her mind rule her heart. She ran to get her sister. Ana turned to Shela's young man, who clearly had been ready for much more than kissing.

"You won't get any more kisses for a while, Owin. Shela and I have a long night ahead of us."

Soon the house was filled with women. Shela sat dry-eyed by her grandmother's head, wiping her brow with a cool cloth. Arina leaned into Daria's arms and wept.

Ana had her hands full with Kore, but between contractions, she looked across the hearth at Grandmother. It took the work of her whole body for the old woman to take in enough air. Her chest and shoulders rose and fell in short, jerky spasms, and her mouth worked like a netted fish gasping on the riverbank.

Kore's labor proceeded much faster than normal for a woman's first birthing. Not long after sunset, she pushed out a tiny, downy boy, living, though no baby that small could live for long. Ana rubbed his little body with a bit of rough cloth until he opened his mouth and let out a faint wail. She laid the child in Kore's arms, the cord still attached, and looked over at her Grandmother. Grandmother had opened her eyes for the first time in days and turned her head toward the baby. A smile barely creased the corners of her mouth. She sighed. Then she was still.

The baby lay silent. It had taken all his strength to utter that single weak cry. Even in the golden glow of the firelight Ana could see how blue he looked.

"I'm sorry, Kore," she said. "He won't be with us for much longer. But Grandmother heard him, did you see? She will take him with her, and make sure he is safely in the arms of the Goddess. Your baby was in such a hurry tonight, I think he knew that she was waiting for him."

It was a comfort to Kore that her newborn would not leave the world by himself. Still, they all wept as Ana began to massage Kore's belly, to encourage the passing of the afterbirth.

Afterwards, Daria sat with Kore while the three granddaughters took turns washing their grandmother's body. They used Shela's softest linen, dipping it in warm water, fragrant with tansy and burnet. Ana polished the copper pendant until it seemed to be made of firelight itself. She replaced it around her grandmother's neck, put bracelets on her arms and ankles, plaited her thick gray hair and coiled it on top of her head, decorating the braid with bone hairpins.

They wrapped the dead baby in linen, and laid it next to the old woman's body. Kore had asked that the baby be buried with Mari to make sure that what Ana had told her would be true.

By morning the single grave was dug, by clansmen who took turns using stone-headed pickaxes to break up the soil. After everyone in the village had paid their respects to the former Priestess who had lived so long, and to the baby who had not lived nearly long enough, they wrapped Mari in a linen shroud and walked in procession to the cemetery. Ana and Arina led the way, followed by Dumuz, then Boros, who tapped a goatskin drum, and Tiso, who played a slow song on a bone flute. Kore, who had insisted on walking with them, was supported by Shela and Daria. Like the three sisters, Kore wore a shawl over her head. Ana carried the white figurine, the Goddess in her most frightening aspect. Death, although commonplace, was something to be feared. What followed it, no one knew, but since the Goddess who took life also gave life back, cycle after cycle, then perhaps people returned to walk the earth again. It was a great Mystery.

They laid Mari on her right side, the baby boy on his left, facing one another. They placed Goddess figurines between the bodies, and placed two cups and a water jug at their feet. Daria helped Arina add two honey cakes. Ana held the figurine aloft and prayed for their safe journey, as one by one, each member of the village used the wooden scoop to pour the earth on top of them.

Part II

Snow fell not long after the Harvest Festival, and once it fell, it stayed. Sometimes a thaw would occur only a moon or so after the shortest day, but not this season. Once the Earth Mother was frozen, she remained so, just as she did in the stories of days when men hunted improbable shaggy monsters as big as houses, with long, curving teeth. Normally Ana enjoyed hearing these old tales as much as anyone, but after hearing about the *Takers*, she was uneasy. She could hear wolves howling with hunger on the coldest days. She dreamt of owls night after night; sometimes, she woke screaming, ducking from the bird's talons.

Dumuz would have to hold her tightly, rocking her and talking to her as he did to Dana, soothing nonsense syllables until she calmed down and told him what she had dreamt. Then he would wrap her in sheepskins, walk with her to the doorway, and lift the hide to show her the snow shining blue and serene in the moonlight.

"See? Nothing stirs. All is well."

He would lay her back down, place Dana next to her, and Ana would finally fall back to sleep under his protective arm.

She didn't tell him about the other dreams, the ones where he mounted Marsh Hawk and galloped away toward the rising sun.

Each time the full moon rose, Ana waited to see if She was going to remain bright, or cloak herself again. It seemed She must, because what else could cause so much heartache this season? There was the day Tiso fell into the frozen river. He was tired of dried meat, and wanted to try spearing a fish near the eddy where the water still ran no matter how cold the day. But he lost his footing, and slipped beneath the ice before anyone could pull him out. The last thing they saw of him were his hands frantically grasping for purchase on the edge. They weren't even sure where his body lay, frozen somewhere below the hard crust of ice. They would have to wait until the river thawed to see where the waters would release him.

They would have to wait until the ground thawed, too, to dig graves for those who had contracted the sickness that made them cough up blood. Gat and his brother had both succumbed.

It was so cold for so long they had brought all the livestock indoors to keep the animals from freezing to death. Every household lived with a couple of sheep or goats and a cow or two. Ana was sick of the stench of manure. During the shortest, coldest days, she woke up queasy from it several mornings in a row, but it wasn't until her flow stopped that she realized why the familiar smell was affecting her so strongly.

It was Ana's one sign of hope, and she clung to it throughout the long nights, the way Shela and her mate, Owin, clung together whether it was night or day. They were now living in the house that Dumuz had built for Ana. Ana and Dumuz had moved into the larger home next to the temple, the Priestess' home, where Ana had grown up. The house was crowded now, with Dumuz and Ana, Arina and Dana, Marsh Hawk and the other animals.

Ana was touched by how solicitous Arina became once she knew Ana was expecting again. Though Arina would never be more than a child no matter what her age, she was a very responsible child, who was proud of her job of baking bread for temple offerings, and eager to imitate the way Ana cared for Dana. Arina helped feed the baby now that she was weaned, first with the liquid that remained after soaking wheat or barley meal, then with loose porridge, often with a bit of honey mixed in. In fact, if Ana didn't stop her, Arina would often slip the baby a fingertip of honey as a treat. It was hard to scold her when she made angelica tea for Ana's morning sickness, or let Dana play with the beloved straw doll that Shela had crafted for Arina during the Harvest Festival.

The only time Arina was not close at hand were the ritual days, when Ana put on one of the Goddess masks. Then Arina cowered behind Daria in fear. Ana had tried to explain to Arina that the mask did not change her into a frog or hedgehog, but that was too hard for

Arina to understand. Or maybe even Arina sensed the Power in Ana on the holy days.

Of all of them, Arina seemed the least touched by the hardships of the season. She loved to see how snow sparkled when the weak sun shone its light on the crusty surface. She danced when fine, powdery flakes fell on her tongue. She marveled after an ice storm left icicles dangling from every tree and roof. She made Ana and Dumuz taste a broken icicle to see for themselves how delightfully hard and cold it was. When Dumuz went outside to chip ice off the woodpile, he had to keep an eye out for Arina lobbing a snowball at him. Her aim was so poor he sometimes stepped into the path of the snowball so it would splash against his sheepskin jacket. His feigned astonishment made her laugh every time. Sometimes—only when Ana was not looking—Dumuz would make designs in the snow when he made water, trying to draw a duck or bunny for Arina. His silly, lopsided efforts always made her clap her hands and giggle.

When the river ice finally broke up with loud cracking noises, and the village was filled with the sound of running water as melting snow dripped from rooftops, Arina's monthly flow started, too. The timing was so coincidental that Ana could only conclude the Great Mother was blessing her sister. Ana had been wondering what to do about that when the time came. If she put the tri-line on her sister's shoulder, she would be announcing her womanhood to the clan, her eligibility to participate in the Sacred Ritual. She asked Arina if she wanted to undergo the ordeal. For her part, Arina was eager for the tattoo, but when Ana explained to her what the Ritual involved, and how she was to prepare for it, Arina cringed.

"Must I?" she whispered.

Ana thought about that. No one had ever told her that a woman had to participate in the Ritual; on the other hand, she had never heard of anyone refusing. In fact, it was an event most women looked forward to with eagerness. It marked her passage into adulthood, made her a full participant in the sacred cycle, and initiated her into the physical pleasures that any woman desired once her flow began. But although

Arina now had a woman's body, she was, and always would be, a child in her mind and heart. The Ritual was most definitely not for children.

"No, sweet, you do not have to join the Ritual if you don't want to. You can Honor the Goddess just as well by staying in the village to help take care of children and prepare our feast."

Arina's relieved face told Ana that she had given the right answer.

As the thaw deepened, the sun rose in the east gate, and on the night of the full moon after that, Ana put on the mask that made her Priestess of the Goddess Bear, She who brought forth her offspring from the Earth. The moon rose bright and remained uncloaked, but Ana still worried that, thaw or no, the fields would not be ready for the sowing after the next full moon. What kind of Ritual could they hold if the ground was too hard or too wet? She did not relax until she saw catkins thick on the willow branches.

Then, for the first time in many moons, Ana stopped dreaming about owls. Dumuz, in her dreams, remained at her side, as he did while she was awake. Shela was expecting now, too, and their fertility was mirrored by that of the animals. As though to reward them for enduring so many long, cold days and nights, the Giver-of-Life had touched all their livestock with abundance. They had more lambs, kids and calves than at any time anyone could remember, with many twins and even one set of triplet kids. Hens' eggs hatched out fluffy little chicks who peeped and scooted in front of every threshold. Even Marsh Hawk felt renewed life flowing in her veins. She snorted and kicked up her heels whenever Dumuz walked over with the lead in his hand to take her on a gallop.

It was everyone's favorite time in the cycle, except maybe for the men who specialized in brewing beer for the Harvest Festival, but it was Arina's favorite time most of all. No one could help but smile to see how delighted she was to cuddle every chick, every pup, every cavorting kid and bleating lamb. The babies she loved best were the soft little ducklings that bobbed up and down among the reeds. She liked nothing better than to creep through the marshy shore—mud and mosquitoes notwithstanding—and push the reeds aside to glimpse the brown and yellow ducklings, or the black-and-white striped grebe chicks riding on their mother's back. She could lie there for hours, watching them.

It was nearing mid-afternoon on a fine day when Shela asked "Where's Arina?" as she stooped to give Dana a hug. "Daria is making bread, but Arina isn't with her. I looked all over the village, but I can't find her."

Ana rinsed clay off her hands and sighed. "Yesterday she was telling me all about the new ducklings, so I guess that's where she is. She probably has her head stuck in the reeds, or is sitting with a lap full of peeping fluff."

She stood up and stretched, rubbing the small of her back. "I'll get her. I could use a walk. Want to come?"

"Sure," Shela said. She stood up with grace; her pregnancy was not so advanced as Ana's. She was having an easier time all around, with no sickness, clear skin, and seemingly boundless energy. She held out her hand to Dana. "Come, little one, take Auntie's hand."

"You will have to carry her before we get even halfway there," Ana said, taking Dana's other hand. "Shall we swing?"

"One, two, three," they counted, lifting Dana up on *three*. She giggled with pure joy as they walked along, swinging the toddler up and down between them.

They were halfway down the path along the bluff when Ana said, "Oh, that's enough swinging. My arms are tired." Dana began to fuss, so Shela picked her up and blew raspberries onto her cheeks to bring the giggles back.

"Shh," Ana said.

"What?"

"I thought I heard something."

"What? I don't hear a thing."

"I don't either, now. But I thought I did. And now there's nothing at all. We should hear something—frogs, at least, or birds."

The marsh was strangely silent, even for midday. No wrens chattered, no blackbirds sang. They listened for a moment more.

"Are you sure you heard something besides our own footsteps?" asked Shela.

"No, I'm not," Ana said. "It was very far away, almost like the sound of a drum. . .or hoof beats."

Shela shook her head. "Couldn't be hooves. Marsh Hawk is in the shed."

Fear flooded over Ana's body like scalding water poured from a stewpot. She began to run.

They found Arina where they expected she would be, lying among the reeds, not far from a mallard's empty nest. Her tunic and skirt had been cut off. Her eyes and mouth were wide open, expressionless. Dark smudges on either side of her mouth and on her neck showed why no one had heard her cry out. Her forearms were bruised, too, as were her small breasts, and her thighs, spread wide, with a pool of blood between them. There was so much blood. . . .

Ana stood, frozen, staring down at Arina's slender body. She didn't need to feel for a pulse at her sister's throat to know she was dead. Shela, covering Dana's eyes with her hand, flushed red with rage.

"Who? Who among us would do this? Who *could*?"

Ana didn't answer. She didn't have to. Shela knew as well as Ana did that no one, *no one* in their village could ever commit such a horror.

She dropped to her knees, raising her eyes to the sky to appeal to the Goddess, but all she could do was howl.

Dumuz reached them first, running with a spear in his hand when he heard Ana's screams. It was he who saw Arina before the others, and covered her with his vest, and carried her home. It was he who went back to the river to track them, first on the near side and then across the swollen ford without once thinking about his fear of the water. He picked up their tracks downstream, heading east.

It was he who spoke shortly afterwards when the village had gathered in a stunned group in front of the temple. The clan was divided between those who cried with grief and those who flamed with anger.

"There were three of them, on horseback," Dumuz said. "I found their tracks."

"*Takers?*" Daria asked, in a voice hoarse from crying.

Dumuz knew as well as anyone that no one in this river valley would assume a young girl was his to use for his own cruel pleasure. Let alone three of them—he could imagine them taking turns, and laughing. It made him want to vomit.

He shrugged. "No way to tell for sure without seeing them."

"But why?" Daria wailed. "Why, why, why?"

"Some people are no better than animals," Dumuz answered.

"They're worse—no animal would hurt its own kind, not that way," said Boros. He looked at the group. "We cannot let this act go unpunished."

"Punish them how?" someone asked.

"Kill them, like they killed her!" another shouted.

"Then we'd be no better than they are," an old woman said, shaking her head. "How could we honor the Goddess by doing that?"

"You can't," said Dumuz. "None of you can. I will do it."

That silenced them.

"I am the only one among you not born of the Goddess," he said. "Besides, I am the only one who can ride after them. They will not expect to be pursued by a horseman. They don't have much of a head start, and they won't be riding hard. I will."

"But what will you do when you catch up with them?" Boros asked. "One man against three?"

"My straight arrows will kill them all. I will then cut off their manhood, as they deserve."

He walked away from them to collect his bow and quiver and the lead for Marsh Hawk. *Cutting off their manhood was the least they deserved.* He hoped they would still be alive when he did it. They were indeed were far lower than animals. Killing them would be no worse than squashing a bloodsucking tick.

He had not felt such red-hot wrath since the night his tribe had been attacked. His desire for revenge was righteous and fitting, according to the code he had grown up with. He did not want to admit, though, that this vengeful impulse caused him some disquiet now. He had seen the looks on everyone's faces when he described the punishment he was about to mete out.

He told Ana he was going after them, but he wasn't sure she heard him. She'd had to be led away from the marsh, wailing, half carried by her kinsmen. Dumuz had laid Arina next to their hearth, but when Ana saw her there, she began to howl again, so they brought Ana to Shela's house instead. Now Ana was seated before her sister's hearth, calm once more, but it was not a natural calm. She would not look up, would not answer Dumuz. He touched her cheek with his fingertips. She stared at the fire, unmoving.

Shela followed him outside. "Take me with you," she said.

"I can't." Dumuz' face was like the Goddess' death mask as he mounted Marsh Hawk.

"I can ride behind you. I can throw a spear."

"Yes, you can do that, but two riders would slow Marsh Hawk too much. I need speed to surprise them."

"Only you against three of them? How can you possibly succeed?"

"Because my will is strong and I must. And I need you to take care of her."

Then he was gone.

Take care of her—did he mean Arina? Or Ana?

Shela watched him gallop hard in the direction of the rising sun.

Shela had to take care of both her sisters. Ana could not bear to look at Arina, and Shela would let no other hands touch her. So Shela prepared her little sister for burial by herself. She washed her sister's broken body with tenderness, alternately aching and raging to see how her womanhood had been literally torn apart. There was nothing in

Shela's experience to prepare her for that. To take any woman against her will was an abomination, a sacrilege against all they held sacred. To do so to a woman-child like Arina was so evil, she could not begin to comprehend it.

Giving and receiving sexual pleasure was the central truth of her people's existence. All life came from the act, and life itself was sacred, imbued with the Power of the Goddess. That it be done with ease in the body's joy was unquestioned. That's why young women were prepared in the Temple after their first flow, and why the Goddess visited boys while they slept, so each would be able to participate in the holy ceremony with full understanding of Her greatest gift.

Though day-to-day lovemaking might have had less to do with holiness and more to do with lust, each joining was still an expression of Her power, the most fundamental way for anyone to honor Her. To make love was to respect the Goddess and all her creation, it was as simple as that. What kind of subhuman monsters must walk the earth not to know such a basic truth?

Shela wrung out the washcloth as she wished she could wring the necks of the filth who had made this washing necessary.

When she finished, Shela laid Arina on a clean linen shroud. She had woven it with care, and dyed it yellow using the skins of dried wild onions that Arina herself had gathered. She placed Arina's hands on her chest, with a duck figurine above them, and a hedgehog, the little life-giver, below.

Shela went next door where Ana still sat unmoving and silent. She knelt in front her older sister with a cup of water.

"Here, Ana, drink some water." When Ana made no response, Shela brought the cup to her sister's lips and tilted it. Most of the water ran down Ana's chin, but some of it got in, because she coughed.

"Ana, it is time for the burial." Ana began a keening cry. Shela held and rocked her until she stopped. "Sister, you must perform the ritual. The grave has been dug. We have no one but you to send our little one on her journey. She feels no more pain, but she needs you to help her on her way. We all need you. You are our Priestess. You must be strong."

Shela made Ana stand up, and removed her tunic and skirt. She washed Ana as though she were a child, dressed her in fresh clothes, and put the shawl on her head.

"Now, let's go to the temple and get the White Goddess."

Shela led Ana outside. The clan had gathered, waiting. Daria held Dana, hushing her when she called, "Mama!"

Inside the sanctuary, Ana stood, trembling. Shela led her to the wooden chest where the figurines were stored.

Ana took a long, shuddering breath, then picked up the white figurine and went outside. Arina's shrouded body lay in the strong arms of Boros. Shela kept pressure on Ana's arm to make her start walking. Ana was dry-eyed now, but the rest of the people wept.

It took all of Ana's will to complete the ritual, but she held up the figurine and recited the prayers her sister so deserved. Afterwards, she went back to her own home, enervated. She lay down before the fire, unable to sleep, unable to move, except to hold Dana close in her arms.

To no one's surprise, the sun rose and set three times with no sign of Dumuz. Few expected him to return. It was all but certain that he would be killed. He was probably dead already. He was a good hunter, more skilled with a bow than any of them, but it was one thing to surprise a buck, and another to sneak up on three armed men. The boys of the village admired him for his courage in taking on such a hopeless task. He would be the topic of stories and songs for many moons to come.

Only Shela kept vigil for him, sitting on the river bluff, facing east, every morning and every evening. At night she took comfort in Owin's arms, while Daria watched over both Ana and Dana. On the third night Ana stirred for the first time. She took up a cooking pot and began making porridge, almost as though nothing had happened. But her eyes were as empty as an owl's.

On the fourth morning after the burial, Shela saw a single horse and rider walk slowly out of the fine mist. She crouched low, prepared to raise the alarm, until they were close enough to recognize. She ran to them, thanking the Goddess for protecting them both.

Dumuz slipped off Marsh Hawk's back and leaned against the pony. They looked exhausted. Dumuz had wrapped a cloth around his left bicep; he was wounded on his side as well. Fresh blood seeped from both wounds.

He nodded in answer to her unasked question.

"It is done."

Shela took Marsh Hawk's lead as they began to walk toward the village. She was not sure why she felt so little reaction to his news. She should feel—not happiness—that would not be right, but surely at least satisfaction? Yet his words only covered her with sorrow, like the mist.

"How badly injured are you?" she asked him.

"It will heal. Marsh Hawk is tired. She stumbled a few times. It made me bleed again. You can believe me when I tell you they bled much, much more."

Shela had never known anyone who had deliberately killed another man. She knew Dumuz had fought once before, and killed some of the men who attacked his kin, but that was long ago, and in his own homeland. And anyone would defend herself if, say, a wolf attacked. Murder for revenge, though, was completely out of her experience. She glanced over at Dumuz. His eyes looked straight ahead. She couldn't read anything on his face except weariness. He held a filthy parcel in his left hand.

"What are you carrying?" she asked.

"A present for Arina."

She shivered. He had threatened to take their manhood, and Dumuz was a man of his word.

"Take care of Marsh Hawk for me?"

"Of course."

He walked toward the burial ground. Arina's fresh grave was easy to find. He bowed his head and then knelt.

"I'm sorry I was not here to help send you on your way, Little One. I don't know where you have gone, but I am sure those men will not be anywhere near you. They will not be sent to the other side with prayers, as you were. I left their meat for the vultures. May wild dogs eat their bones. But first, I took these for you."

He unwrapped the grisly package: three sets of severed hands, penises, testicles. "I will burn the weapons they used against you. No part of them will defile any part of your Mother Earth. Be at peace, Sweet One. I will miss you even more when the snows come."

He wept for her, not knowing or caring that the village was abuzz from the moment Shela walked through the east gate leading Marsh Hawk. She would answer no questions while she rubbed the horse down. She set out dried grasses and filled the water trough, then went into the stores for a handful of grain.

"Good girl, Marsh Hawk," she said as the pony nuzzled the grain with her soft lips. "You did well."

The gathering crowd stepped back in awe when Dumuz walked up to them, bloodied and carrying his parcel. He walked into the middle of them, placed the parcel on the ground, and unwrapped it.

There was a collective gasp.

"It is as I promised you. They will harm no one again, not in this life or the next. I have removed what they used for weapons and left their bodies to rot and be consumed by animals. Their spirits will never know peace. Bring me dry wood so I can burn this offal."

At first no one moved, but then Boros fetched the wood, as well as tinder and flint. Dumuz made the fire out in the open, outside the village wall and downwind, so their village would not be defiled by the vile smoke. The clan watched in silence. The expression on Dumuz' face would not let them ask questions. Not until the fire had consumed flesh and blackened bone did he meet their eyes.

"*Takers?*" asked Daria.

Dumuz swallowed hard before answering. Shela could see the tracks of tears on his face.

"*Takers.* Yes. As you were told, they looked just like me."

He looked around the crowd. No one met his eyes except Shela.

"Where is Ana?" he asked, as he stood up.

"Inside. She won't come out. She won't eat or sleep or do anything, Dumuz. Maybe now that you're back..." She turned from him. "I will leave you to your reunion."

Ana was watching Dana eat cold leftover porridge when Dumuz walked in the door. She looked up. Her face drained of color. She moaned and collapsed.

When she woke in his arms, she touched his face to prove to herself he was real.

"You are hurt! Your head?" she asked.

Dumuz helped her sit up. "Always the healer," he said, with a wry smile.

She took a closer look at him. "You've been crying. Oh, my love." Tears filled her eyes, and spilled over, and would not stop. It was the first time she had cried—not howled, not wailed, not keened, but truly cried—since the unspeakable day. They held each other and wept; Dana wept, too, not knowing why, weeping only because her parents were weeping. Dumuz scooped her up and held them both until it seemed they had no tears left, and Dana had cried herself to sleep.

Ana made him lie down then, stripped off his filthy clothes, and examined him from head to toe. She wouldn't let him get up until she saw for herself the extent of his wounds, smelled them to make sure no pus was forming, cleaned and dressed them. She washed his whole body, as she had done when he first came to her, and just as it happened then, she saw his desire form at the touch of the warm, wet cloth in her hands.

He sat up. She saw his face shift with the emotions—hunger, sorrow, fear—and thought her own face must mirror his. Would she be able to love him without thinking of how monsters had perverted the act? Would either of them be able to wholly lose themselves in the other, ever again? How could they make loving one another natural and sacred once more?

She put the washcloth down, and took her tunic off. Her eyes teared up again.

"It wasn't you. I know that in here." She placed his hand on her head. "But help me know it here." She placed his hand on her breast. "And here." She moved his hand down and slipped it under her skirt. But despite her plea, she flinched from his touch.

He kissed her other hand, each finger, one by one, then the palm, the base of her thumb, her wrist. He kissed her forehead, each eyelid, her nose. He kissed the renewed tears falling down her cheeks. Finally, he kissed her mouth, lightly as the wings of a butterfly on a wild rose, letting her open up to him again, slowly, one petal at a time.

Preparations for the Sacred Ritual restored the clan to a much-needed sense of routine. Everyone anticipated the cleansing grace the Ritual would provide, especially after so much violence and sorrow. The climax of the act would give them not only the renewed blessings of the Goddess, but also a physical release from a growing tension among the community.

No one was openly hostile to Dumuz after he had admitted that he was from the same stock as the *Takers*, protected as he was by being mated to one of their clan, especially the woman who was also their Priestess. Nothing in Dumuz' past behavior suggested he was in any way like the *Takers*. Yet even though many admired his decisiveness and his bravery, the savage way he had avenged Arina's rape and murder was beyond their understanding. Some even feared him now.

He was not asked to participate in any of the tasks to make the clan ready for the Ritual, nor was he asked to help with any of the ordinary work of the village. No one asked him to go hunting or fishing; no one brought worn-out spearheads for him to sharpen; no one invited him to sit by their fire and chat at the end of the day. To his face, everyone was as polite as they had been when he first arrived, but that meant they were treating him like a stranger again. He missed the easy joking, the approving hand on his shoulder. Children who used ask him for lessons in bow craft now ran away from him.

He spent all the days before the Ritual taking care of Marsh Hawk and riding her on the plain.

For this season's Ritual, as sometimes happened, there were no young women attending for the first time, but Ana, her sister, and at least three other women were with child, and there were two young mothers with suckling babes, so all was still to the good. Now that Dana had outgrown Ana's breast, she would stay behind with the rest of the children and elders. Ana would be able to carry the bowl of the bull calf's blood unencumbered.

Wearing the Frog mask, Ana performed the ritual slaughter as she had been taught, and then led the procession to the fields. A light rain the night before had left the fields muddy but not too wet for planting, so she could relax that the sowing would proceed and the Ritual properly consummated. She blessed the seeds and the sowing, blessed the beer, and as the afternoon waned, shared the anticipation of her people who so desired to feel the Goddess's approval of their fertility, and to put aside the dark reality of vengeance.

When it was time, she gathered them together. Unlike the year before, Ana hoped, and even prayed, that one of her kinswomen would choose Dumuz to show that he was still a member of their clan. With no first-timers to start things off, she motioned to Shela, as the youngest, to begin. Not surprisingly, Shela took Owin's hand. One by one, women and men paired, and this year their numbers worked out evenly. Finally, only Dumuz stood before Ana, unwanted, unclaimed. She could see his face in the growing dusk. She knew he understood how much his status had changed.

She took his hand without a word, and held it tightly. They stood side by side until the moon rose.

The next morning, Ana busied herself cleaning up the temple, even though the village elders had done a fine job of that the day before.

While she paused in her sweeping, she overheard raised voices, and the name of her beloved. She stood near the door, out of sight, listening, hearing how deeply divided her people had become. Many in the village thought that Dumuz should be asked to leave. A few, mostly the oldest who had lived with their traditions the longest, thought that asking anyone to leave would affront their code of hospitality and possibly affront the Goddess herself. It might be different if he were not mated to the Priestess, she heard someone point out.

Ana was appalled. Until last night she had assumed it would be just a matter of time before Dumuz was accepted again. She thought it might take a full cycle, or more, but surely her kinfolk understood that he was not to blame for what happened. Did one judge an entire people based on the actions of a few? Weren't his own kinfolk victims of *Takers* as well?

"First him, then three—who knows how many more of them might be out there?" she heard Daria say. "Maybe they came looking for him. Many others may now come looking for all of them."

That possibility had not occurred to Ana. She felt the blood drain from her face at the idea. It would be worse than any of her nightmares.

She held her rounded belly with one hand. If the debate was not resolved, the village would split in two. She had to do something, but what? If she left with Dumuz and Dana, the village would be without a Priestess. She had not had time to choose or train an apprentice. For Dumuz to leave by himself—in that case, Ana herself would feel split in two. She bowed her head, imploring the Goddess for guidance, asking her to find a way out of this dilemma.

After the group passed by, she put down the broom and walked to the weaving room where Shela had set up the loom and was tying threads to the warp beam. A small pile of warp weights lay in a basket near her feet. Normally Shela hummed to herself as she did this task. Today she was frowning.

"I may need a few more weights," Shela said. "I want to make a tighter weave with this batch of wool. It is very fine."

Ana picked up one of the weights. She recognized the design on it. She had made it a long time ago. "Did you hear them talking?" she asked.

"I've heard plenty. Some are actually blaming him for all the snow we had, and saying that even the coughing sickness was his fault. What nonsense." She looked up from her threads. "If he leaves, and you go with him, Owin and I will go, too. We can start a village of our own, and leave the rest of these fools to their ignorant gossip."

Ana was surprised her sister had thought it through so much, and grateful for her support. She clenched and unclenched her fists.

"I suppose if we have a bad growing season, they will run him out of the village," Ana said bitterly. "What else do they think he will do—keep the sheep's wool from growing? Turn milk sour? He's just a man, a good, good man."

"Yes, he's a very good man. But he's also a hunter, who tracked and killed three other men. He lives among us, but he's not of us, and now, he never will be."

She made a noise of frustration because she had tangled the threads. She let go of the wool and looked at Ana.

"May the Goddess forgive me, but I'm glad he killed them, and glad he cut off their hands and their manhood. Mostly, I am glad they will never do to another girl what they did our sister."

"I am glad for that, too, but—"

"There is no *but*. If you saw a viper crawling toward Dana, would you not pick up a rock and beat it to death?"

"No, I would pick Dana up and run away."

As the growing season went on, it became worse than Ana feared. Everything from a splinter to spilled stew was being attributed to "a bad force" in the village. Dumuz started taking overnight hunting trips every few days.

"It's easier for you when I am away," he said, one morning while he picked up his quiver and bow. "Ana, we both know I should leave this village and never come back."

She reached for him, pressing her cheek to his. "Promise me you'll come back. Swear it, by your Gods or mine. Swear it!" She kissed him before he could say a word, her mouth open, her tongue reaching for his. He responded as fully as she hoped he would. She untied his breeches, so he could lift her onto him. She wrapped her legs around his waist as he pushed her against the wall. "Plow me," she whispered. They lost all sense of self, letting their passion dissolve into a desperate frenzy, bodies fused together by a Power as strong as they had felt during the Sacred Ritual.

Dumuz was smiling when he guided Marsh Hawk out of village and kicked her into an easy canter northward. As long as Ana could make him feel like that, he would indeed come back to her, as he had finally sworn once they were lying in a tangle on the floor, panting and sweating like Marsh Hawk after a hard gallop. He would just have to win the villagers over as he had done before, by making himself an integral part of their lives again. Hunting was the best way, he decided. It was easier for Ana during his absences, and if he continued to bring back game to share, no one would deny his value to the village. They just needed more time to get over their grief, that was all. Eventually they would forget, or at least forgive.

He let Marsh Hawk choose her own way along the gently rolling hills. Her hooves stirred up the fragrance of mint and other plants he couldn't identify, but he was sure Ana could. When they came back, he would stop and pick some herbs for her. He hoped she would be able to use at least some of what he brought home, even though in his ignorance he would probably gather mostly weeds. He didn't want her walking this far while carrying their next child.

Marsh Hawk slowed to a walk as they passed into the forest. She continued on as though she had a destination in mind. It was the sound of water that drew her. He could hear the creek now. They reached it, and he dismounted to let her drink.

He looked around and laughed out loud. Marsh Hawk had brought him to the very spot where he had first seen Ana. She herself had brought him back to see the place after he had healed. He had been hoping to find Luguk that time, or at least a trail to follow, but rain had erased the pony's tracks. Ana had leaned against this very oak, to show him where she had been napping when he and Luguk had parted ways. They had made love that day, too. Ana considered this place blessed by the Goddess. It was the place that brought them together, a place where a man should have died from his injuries, but did not.

He heard a rustling in the bushes. Marsh Hawk lifted her head and snorted. Wild boar, maybe? Dumuz reached for his bow as a small dark shape poked through the undergrowth. It was only a bear cub, but Marsh Hawk reared up, whinnying. Dumuz grabbed her lead to regain control. He heard a loud growl behind them, and turned to face it.

Ana had gone to the river—staying well away from the marshy, reedy spot where the ducklings were growing up—to wash all the clay off her hands and arms. She had made the warp weights for Shela, and even some spindle whorls. It had been a long time since she felt this serene. Perhaps the Goddess had heard her prayers and would soon give Ana the wisdom to hold the village together.

She was shaking her arms dry when she saw Marsh Hawk racing toward the village, froth flying from her mouth, streaks of blood on her side.

"Oh, Great Mother, have mercy!" The mare would not have come back alone and terrified unless Dumuz were badly hurt—or worse. She ran up the bluff to get her bag of healing herbs. Marsh Hawk's galloping tracks would be easy to follow. Ana took no time to tell anyone where she was going, to ask for help, or to worry about Marsh Hawk's condition.

She held her belly as she ran. She could not afford to stumble, but the sense of urgency made her want to fly. It was as easy as she had thought to see Marsh Hawk's trail. Her hooves had uprooted grasses, trampled herbs, even broken the branches of shrubs. It wasn't long before Ana recognized the patch of woods where Marsh Hawk had come from.

Of course he would come back to this spot. "Great Mother, let it be only a broken arm. Let him be lying against the oak tree, waiting for me to come to him."

He was indeed lying against the oak tree. It took no healer's knowledge to understand what must have happened. Ana saw the big, flatfooted, claw-tipped tracks and the same shaped tracks in miniature. She saw the red stripes across her lover's chest where the mother bear had slashed him, and the same red marks along the arm he would have raised to protect his face. With a single powerful swipe, she had knocked him backwards against the great tree's roots, the roots Ana had once nestled against to take a nap.

She lifted his head tenderly, feeling for the vulnerable spot. As had happened so many moons ago, her hand came away sticky with blood. This time, the blood was already congealing. This time, he was beyond her skill. Her experienced fingers could feel how the skull had fractured in two places on either side of the old injury. When he was thrown against the tree, his head had cracked open, like a flawed clay pot fresh from the kiln.

She laid his head back down and kissed him for the last time. All she could do was wait and weep. They would come soon, looking for her if not for him. When she told them what must have happened, they would all understand. The Goddess Bear had answered Ana's prayers.

She would bury him next to Arina. He was, in the end, part of their clan.

The harvest was a fine one the season after Dumuz died, and the season after that. The trading fair that followed took place about four days' journey downriver. Ana stayed home with her children, working her clay, and using a model of the temple to teach Dana the first of many lessons she would learn as her apprentice. Dana would make a good priestess one day. She had a quick mind, like her father.

The clansmen had left the village with their wares on foot. It would have been an easier trip if Marsh Hawk had still been there to carry the heaviest items. But Marsh Hawk had arrived back at the village that day not only terrified, but badly mauled. When she burst through the village fence, she collapsed, screaming and bleeding from her gut. Shela had held the poor beast's head while Boros stuck a knife in her throat. They had cut out her heart and buried it as a gift to the Goddess, and butchered her flesh while a search party went looking for Ana and Dumuz.

Neither Shela nor Ana would even taste the meat.

These cooler days, with a breeze carrying the sweet smell of hearth fires, were happier times. When Ana's clansmen returned, they came back with the beads and shells and salt she expected. They also brought the news she had been hoping for. Although clans who lived in the north near the mountains were building additional walls and ditches just in case, no *Takers* had been seen anywhere along the river.

So, they were safe again.

But for how long? Ana wondered, as she walked along the river bluff, holding little Dumuz on one hip.

Were the *Takers* just an isolated few, cut off from their tribe by violence, wandering through strange lands, like Dumuz had been? Or were they the first of many to come? Would there be more of them in her lifetime, or her children's? Would they all be men of pure violence, or would they be more like Dumuz—violent men who could learn to live in peace?

And if, by some awful fate, they were indeed men of pure violence, how would her people fare? Would all their food and livestock be taken from them, or would they meet violence with violence, taking with taking? Who would be more powerful then, the *Takers'* strange Gods who rewarded killing, or the Giver of Life who had existed since before the first seed had been sown?

Ana sighed. She seemed to have nothing but questions in her heart these days. Until Dumuz, there had been nothing to ask questions about: Everything was as it had always been. Did Grandmother ever have need for questions like these? She didn't think so. Ana was glad that Grandmother had died when she did and never saw the evil that came upon their village. Yet how Ana missed the old woman's wisdom.

She kissed her young son, who yawned and tucked his small thumb into his mouth. The Goddess takes from us, but she always gives back, Ana thought. Life for life. As it had always been, it would still be—whatever changes the future might bring.

She lowered herself carefully to the ground, leaning against the trunk of an old crabapple tree, and shifted little Dumuz so he rested more evenly on her chest. She watched her baby fall asleep to the river's liquid lullaby. She hoped her son was having happy dreams. She wished he could dream about his father. She would have such stories to tell him when he grew older—how his father had come to their village, how he had tamed a wild pony, and how much he had loved his son even before he was born. She rubbed his little back lightly, tracing a circle over and over. But something pressing against the small of her own back was making this position uncomfortable. She laid her son gently on the grass and reached behind her, expecting to feel a rock. Instead, she put her fingers around an apple.

The apple Ana held in her hand looked unlike the fruit of any crabapple tree she had ever seen. This one was huge, the size of a man's fist, with bright red skin. When she tasted the apple, the flavor was not puckering tart, but sweet as honey, different from the dried apples sometimes brought for trade by people from the north. The flesh was white and crisp and so full of juice it dripped down her chin. She wiped it off with her fingers and licked the juices from them. She ate the whole apple down to the core, pricking out the big black seeds with her thumbnail. She wrapped the seeds in a leaf to save them for planting.

She stood up and saw that the tree's branches were full of ripe apples. She picked as many as she could reach. When she stepped out from under the crooked branches, she saw another apple tree, and another. She realized she was standing in a forest of apple trees. But what kind of forest was this? The trees stood in straight rows as far as she could see. She turned a full circle, but no matter where she looked, she saw row upon row of apple trees. Had some giant come down from the far mountains to plant trees the way her people planted barley?

She wondered how far this strange forest extended. Where was the familiar river? In which direction was her home? She turned a full circle a second time. She looked up, but the sky was overcast, with no sun to guide her. A cool wind blew, making her shiver. She rubbed her arms for warmth. She wasn't afraid, not yet, just puzzled by the strangeness of the place. She looked down at her sleeping son. Then she laughed, knowing what to do. She walked a short distance to a tree with a good thick trunk and low branches, and began to climb. All she had to do was get as high in the tree as she could, part the leaves, and look out over the treetops to see where she was. Any child would have known that, and she climbed as easily as a child, enjoying the feel of the bark beneath her bare feet. When the branches became thinner, she moved more carefully, testing each limb to make sure it would bear her weight. When she had gone as high as she could go, she bent the supple twigs to either side, and peered out. She had chosen her lookout well, for she had a clear view, but all she could see in this direction were more apple trees. She turned carefully on her perch, all the way around, but no matter where she looked, she saw nothing but apple trees, row upon row upon row.

Disappointed, she started to climb down, but she couldn't move. Her foot must have become wedged in a crook of the tree. She reached down to pull it free, but her hand felt nothing but bark. She looked down at her feet. They weren't there, or rather, they were there, but they were covered in bark. Bark was growing up her legs, and twigs were sprouting from them, leafing out, flowering, and bearing fruit all at once.

She had no time to feel anything more than wonder. She stood up straight and stretched out her arms as the bark embraced her. The last thing she saw was the round, red globe of a ripe apple.

BOOK TWO: DÉJÀ VU
USA, Central Wisconsin, 1960

Part 1

Lucy upended the bucket of apple peels onto the compost pile, reaching into the bucket with one gloved hand to scrape it clean. She tossed the bucket aside and picked up the pitchfork, lifting clods of compost and flipping them over the fresh peels. She watched the worms writhe across the steaming pile, nosing themselves back into the safety of its decomposing depths.

Peeling apples was a chore Lucy had performed so many times she was sure she could have done it in her sleep. Some days she felt as though she had been paring and coring apples all her life. All she knew anymore was the sight, smell, and taste of apples. At one time she had loved everything about them, but even the minimal perfume of their pale pink blossoms in springtime choked her now. In fall, the overpowering scent of full bushel baskets in the warehouse made her dizzy. She didn't want to think of how the apples squished when they were pressed for cider.

Even worse, Lucy had begun to hate the impatient customers who lined up to buy cider by the gallon, and their whining children, who begged for one of the thousands of apple cider donuts she had to bake each fall. She hated the unending cycle of grafting, pruning, spraying, harvesting; the worry of cold winters that damaged buds and the worry of winters that were not cold enough to set fruit. She wanted to go on vacation, to see the Southwestern desert and Caribbean rainforests and the Arctic tundra, all places where apples cannot grow.

Mostly she wanted to feel like someone who truly mattered, not simply Goddard's pie baker and donut saleswoman and keeper of stinky compost.

Goddard was a good man, she knew; he was wholesome and kind, a good provider, and even a decent lover. There was nothing wrong with Goddard, not really, except his almost conjugal love for the orchard: he fingered the young leaves, he caressed the baby apples when they were still hard and green and sour on the branch, he inhaled their scent during cidering time. And the way Goddard handed a customer change, holding their outstretched hand in both of his for just a few seconds too long. Maybe especially the way Goddard spread his arms when he preached on Sunday mornings when he stood in front of the altar in the Church of the Orchard. She wanted to lie in bed until after dawn and never again play the same songs on the wheezy organ at these church services, held for the Mexican workers Goddard hired every harvest season. She had begun to wince every time he used an apple variety as a metaphor.

"Behold the Macintosh," he might say on a September Sunday. "Crisp and tart enough to pucker the mouth, yet when baked into a pie does it not become sweet as honey on your tongue? So you, too, blessed by the warmth of love, can shed your tartness for human sweetness and a kind heart."

As he spoke, Lucy would rest her fingers on the organ keys and ever so softly begin playing, slowly increasing volume just the way Goddard wanted as he reached the climax of his sermon, adding a foundation of rich bass notes that were entirely too beatific for the banal hymn. After Sunday dinner and its invariable apple cobbler, Goddard would put on a sweater with frayed elbows and wander the orchard, speaking to each tree he passed, almost blessing the heart-shaped Red and Golden Delicious, the plump globes of Staymans.

Lucy used to walk with him when he made Sunday rounds, strolling up and down the rows, inspecting every tree they passed for any of the multitude of ills that could wither a twig or rot a fruit. But she disliked the lump of plant material that formed like a tumor where the scions were grafted onto hardier rootstocks. She felt increasingly hemmed in by the endless, neat corridors of pruned branches, every tree lined up in a straight row. Row after row after row after row.

She wished she could break free and run down a curving path, or through a field of prairie grass open to the sky, or through the canyons of skyscrapers she saw only in magazines. Just once, Lucy wanted to hear the blare of taxi horns and the scream of sirens instead of the endless soughing of wind in apple limbs. Instead, she was trapped in this orchard where Goddard made all the decisions and Goddard gave all the orders and everything, absolutely everything, had to be done the way Goddard directed.

The predictability of her days stretched before her to infinity, unwinding like the spring of the kitchen timer that would tell her when the latest pie was done.

She was beginning to think that Goddard loved the trees more than he loved her, or anything else. One day, Goddard had chanced upon a black rat snake looped over the branches of an old, half-bare tree. He'd attacked the snake with his walking stick, beating it bloody despite her protests that it was a harmless creature. But Goddard tolerated no intruders in his orchard.

After that incident, Lucy began to stay indoors on Sunday afternoons, her restlessness translated into unsatisfactory fits of closet cleaning or window washing.

The machinery started up in the cidering shed. The thump and bump of apples as they fell from the conveyor belt into the press sounded to her like the beat of Goddard's walking stick, and the cloudy amber juice that flowed from the first pressing was too much, in her mind's eye at least, like that snake's blood seeping into the brown grass at the base of the twisted old trunk.

Lucy dropped the compost bucket and walked back into the house. The timer buzzed. Yes, she thought, as she turned off the timer and removed the golden pie, whose fragrance made her stomach hurt, it's time, all right. *Time to get out of here.*

She told Goddard her plans that night, fidgeting with her apron as Goddard knelt before the fireplace, stoking the applewood fire.

"That isn't reason enough to leave me," he said. "It was just a snake. How can you let a snake be more important to you than I am?"

"It's not just the snake."

How could Lucy explain that she was afraid the next time she put the blade of a paring knife to the skin of a Granny Smith she would hear the apple wail in pain? That she was sick of apple pie and apple pandowdy and apple dumplings and apple brown betty and applesauce?

And she wasn't just sick at heart. The orchard was making her physically ill, to the point where she would vomit at the smell of a cored Jonathan.

"You can't leave in the middle of cidering time. It's our busiest time of year. I forbid it."

Although Goddard clearly thought he had settled the matter, Lucy packed her bags and left on the morning of the first frost, taking only her makeup case and one small bag of city clothes. She left behind her dungarees and her clodhoppers, her field coat and tattered corduroys. Lucy wasn't quite sure where she was going, but she had a vague desire to head east, maybe as far as the ocean. She imagined that the sound of waves crashing onto the shoreline must be more soothing than that of wind making dried leaves crackle. Maybe the salt air would blow away the last vestige of apple from her body.

Lucy walked into town, and bought a bus ticket for New York. She knew from the look in the station manager's eyes that she would be the topic of gossip by the time the noon whistle rang, but she didn't care anymore. She sat outside despite the chill, warmed by her own racing pulse. She was leaving. It had been 100% her own decision, the first decision she had made since forever.

It was more delicious than any apple could be.

The Greyhound bus rolled in on schedule, halting with a screech of brakes and a cloud of diesel fumes—not quite the exotic chariot her imagination had led her to expect. Grimacing at the noise and smoke, Lucy handed the driver her ticket and sat down near a grimy window up front. Her suitcase fit on the upper rack but she held onto her makeup case, running a finger along the multicolored stripes on the curved edge while she waited for the driver to close the doors. She was the only passenger getting on at this station, and only one or two passengers were on the bus already.

Lucy avoided their eyes, savoring her anonymity and solitude. She wiped the window with a tissue and stared outside as the bus pulled onto the two-lane road. With each monotonous field of feed corn they passed, she felt lighter. This was right, the tires said as they rumbled over joints in the road. This was right, the brakes screeched as they pulled into each stop.

Once the bus turned onto the highway, Lucy felt as though the cars, hordes of them, it seemed, were escorts carrying her along to a tomorrow that would be nothing like today. She peered around at the other passengers in the now-crowded bus. Most lay back against the seat, dozing, but Lucy was too excited to nap. The landscape was changing, becoming crowded with small houses and then the factories, rail yards, and stockyards of Milwaukee. She was eager to see each new scene, especially when pavement overlay dirt and they drove through treeless city streets.

In Chicago, the bus stopped in front of a rest stop under an overcast sky. Lucy followed the other passengers into a snack bar that seemed to cringe under the weight of a huge sign reading "The Frying Pan." The letters flickered on and off in buzzy red neon light, the only bright spot in an otherwise gloomy afternoon. Inside, rancid smoke from the deep-fryer lay in plumes beneath the ceiling.

"Sorry, fan ain't workin'," said the hostess.

Lucy followed the other passengers into the waiting line where she encountered a less-than-perfect aspect of travel, limp hot dogs and tough hamburgers resting under a warming light. She didn't care, as long as no one offered her apple pie for dessert. She paid for a hot dog and medium coffee and carried her tray toward the orange melamine tables that were crowded with travelers. Not ready to be sociable, she found a small unoccupied table in the back.

Lucy looked down at the food, and sighed. The thrill of being on her own faded with the reality of the journey. She wasn't very hungry, but dinner was a long time away, and she hadn't thought to bring any food of her own. She bit into the cold hot dog and was immediately sorry. She put it down and sipped the coffee. It tasted like the paper cup and was barely lukewarm, but it was sweet and smelled like coffee beans, sort of.

The boarding call sounded over the loudspeaker. Lucy re-boarded and dozed off until a bump in the road jolted her awake. She turned toward the window and frowned. They were rolling past something she'd never seen before: a vast framework of steel girders and pipes. Fires shot out of some of the pipes and black smoke billowed from others. The air outside the bus seemed filled with black grit. Then Lucy realized it was rain, a dark cold rain that fell onto the highway to be splashed into a greasy slurry by the bus's large wheels. For the first time on the trip, Lucy wondered whether she was heading in the right direction.

Eventually, lulled by the rhythm of the road, Lucy relaxed and closed her eyes. Dusk seemed to fast-forward toward midnight. She heard moans and cries of pleasure—it seemed as though everyone on the bus was hot with sex, and the smell of it was overpowering. She opened her eyes and glanced across the aisle where an old man leered at her and reached into his pants.

The bus jolted to a stop, waking Lucy, who was curled up on her side, her head on the empty seat next to her. She sat up, confused by what must have been a bizarre dream, and looked around.

Everyone else was preoccupied with getting their belongings and lining up in the narrow aisle, eyes front. No one leered at anyone. No one glanced at Lucy at all. She felt as anonymous and invisible as she had felt in the orchard. She followed the others off the bus.

"Where are we?" she said out loud.

"Nowheresville, lady," said a young man in a leather jacket.

Lucy looked around. It was pitch dark, and outside of the yellow glow of a streetlight she couldn't see anything. As she moved away from the exhaust fumes she smelled the familiar odors of cow manure and fertilizer, and knew she was back in the country again.

She went straight to the rest room, where a young woman was kneeling on the grimy floor, repacking a duffle bag. She had a weapon in her hand, and Lucy stepped back.

"Don't be scared," said the girl on the floor. "It's just my Ruger. I never travel without it. See? It's a P-series, 9 millimeter. Aluminium alloy, stainless steel slides, resin grip panels. The frame is new technology: plastic polymer with a fiberglass filler that acts like a natural shock absorber. And it's a decocker. Isn't that sweet?"

Lucy shook her head. "I don't know anything about guns."

"It's not a gun, it's a pistol. I can get one for you, if you like."

"No, thank you."

"Suit yourself." The girl put the pistol in her bag and left the rest room. Lucy hoped she wasn't getting on the same bus.

Lucy left the rest room, bought a cheese sandwich from a vending machine, and boarded for the next leg to Cleveland.

The sun was rising when they got there, which Lucy took as a hopeful sign.

After a quick breakfast of coffee and a buttered roll, she got back on the bus to start the second day of her journey. She was looking for a seat when a lilting voice said, "There's room here, honey." A dark-skinned woman with long, blood-red nails patted the seat next to her. She had gold rings on every finger, several gold necklaces, and huge hoop earrings that grazed her shoulders. She wore her hair in a style that Lucy had never seen before: long, fuzzy cords, like the ones that used to be fashionable for French poodles.

Lucy sat down and introduced herself.

"Name's Mamie," the woman said. "How you doin', honey?"

"To be honest, I'm tired. It's such a long ride, and I have the whole day to go."

"How far you going?"

"All the way to New York."

"Ah, the Big Apple." Mamie patted Lucy's hand. "You'll like it there,"

Lucy sighed. From the Church of the Orchard to the Big Apple—what had she been thinking? Suddenly she was sure that she should have bought a ticket for someplace—anyplace—else. But she was being impolite.

"And you?" she asked Mamie. "Where are you going?"

"Erie, Pennsylvania. Plenty of work in Erie for someone on her own who needs to make a lot of money. A body can always use more money, am I right?"

Lucy smiled and nodded.

"But you have bigger fish to fry," Mamie said. "I see that. My mama, she was an island girl, and she had the gift of seeing. I think I got some of that, too." Mamie shivered. "There's somethin' up, for sure. I felt it ever since yesterday. Somethin' not quite right anymore. Don't know what, but I sure feel it."

"What do you mean?"

"All last night, seems like I was havin' strange dreams. Rivers on fire. Forests explodin'. People dyin'."

Lucy said, "I had nightmares, too. I think it's the bad food."

That made Mamie laugh.

They chatted until the bus pulled into the Erie station. Lucy stood up so Mamie could get out. Mamie shrugged her shoulders to work out the kinks.

"Good luck to you, girl," she said. "You take care, you hear?"

"You, too."

As Mamie walked toward the front of the bus, Lucy heard her mutter, "Somethin' sure not copacetic. Don't know what, but something."

The second day of the trip was certainly more scenic than the first had been. The bus went south for several miles before turning east, past rolling farmland and eventually through the Allegheny State Forest, where Lucy was delighted to see the trees growing in unpruned abandon, the gold and orange of their leaves punctuated by the deep green of conifers. Their route wound through the passes in the Pennsylvania ridges, then turned south again. The bus stopped at Williamsport in late afternoon before continuing on to Harrisburg, with the wide, curving Susquehanna River just outside the windows.

All day the seat beside Lucy had been empty, but now that they were in a large city again, with only two more stops before New York, the bus became more crowded. Her new seatmate was a mousy, gray-haired man who merely nodded before opening his paperback book.

It was dark before they got to the next stop, Allentown, but Lucy had trouble sleeping this time. The monotony of the long bus ride was wearing her down. When she managed to doze off, she had strange dreams about guns and money, apple trees exploding into flames, voices shouting for help.

"Where are we?" she asked her seatmate when flickering yellow lights woke her.

"Lincoln Tunnel," said the mousy man, looking straight ahead. The interior of the bus stirred with sleepy people gathering their belongings. And then the bus pulled into the Port Authority Terminal in New York, the brakes squealing one final time.

Lucy was too exhausted to feel much jubilation at finally arriving at her destination. She'd been queasy almost the whole trip, and now she felt lightheaded when she stood up to pull her bag from the overhead shelf. She stepped off the bus and followed the crowd up a large escalator.

In the enormous terminal, she tried to figure out what to do next. She asked about places to stay at the information desk and was given directions downtown to the YWCA. She lugged her bag down the street. It was nearly nine o'clock, but the city streets were lit up with flashing neon signs, and crowds jostled her as though it were broad daylight. Back at the orchard, they would all be in bed by now. Whatever excitement she'd felt at the beginning of her trip had eroded to exhaustion by bus fumes, bad food, and fitful sleep.

When she finally unpacked in a rented room at the Y, she reeled from the scent of apples wafting out of her clothes. She scurried from her room to the shared bathroom at the end of the hall. After she upchucked in the toilet, she washed all her things in the sink, but it took a week of nightly scrubbing before she was able to get the smell of apples out of them, and another week after that before she realized that she was pregnant.

* * *

Bare buds, exposed to November rain. Rain dripped from every twig. Thirty-nine degrees and raining in the dark of the year. It only seemed as though it had been raining ever since October, that this waning of the sun's light had been a deliberate act of theft: Lucy left, and she took even the sun.

Goddard sat before the fire, wrapped in a plaid blanket. He couldn't get warm no matter what. No respite, no comfort, not even from a full fireplace, pruned branches piled on the andirons, snapping. He sat with the lights out, only the fire glow flicker on his face, but it was cold fire, all flash, no heat.

He saw it coming; he couldn't have seen it coming. Neither one mattered. She was gone, and nothing felt right anymore.

He didn't have time to dwell on it at first. There had been the last of the crop to get in before frost turned the crisp fruit mealy. The cider presses had squeezed out every drop; the last bushel basket sold, accounts paid, migrant workers set free for the winter.

Now the trees were dormant, settled into their seasonal slumber, juices withdrawn, life force sucked back into the earth, only dry bark and sealed buds left to face the snow and ice. That's how Goddard felt, too. Dry as bark. No juice.

Damned snake.

That wasn't all of it, he knew, that was just the last of many reasons, or no reasons, what does any of it matter? The cycle would go on and spring would eventually return, but it was going to be a long, dark winter. Goddard's morning star would shine no more. The light was gone, and with it, completion.

He wasn't used to this feeling, would never get used to this feeling. He sat in the dark and licked his wounds like an injured bear, salivating at the fragrance of honey a second before the hive erupts and soldier bees sting and sting. He sat in the dark with nothing to do, had no words for his congregation—dwindled to a few local farmers now that the harvest was over—except words of ice. He wrapped the blanket closer and bent his nose to the wool, hoping for a remnant of her smell—the shampoo she used, her lotion, her sweat—but he smelled nothing more than musty wool gone too long unwashed.

It had been perfect, his vision for their life together. She understood that. What misplaced desire made her want to destroy it—simply pride? Nothing would ever be right again. She opened a fissure in the universe, she poured her light into the fissure until it widened into a fracture, and then the whole of it burst asunder, and all he could about it was to pull the blanket around his shoulders and throw another branch of applewood on the counterfeit fire.

"I brought you some mulled cider, boss."

Goddard reached for the mug and wrapped both hands around it. He inhaled the fragrant steam. He knew exactly what proportion of Red to Golden Delicious was in there, how much Macintosh to offset the other apples' sweetness and how long it has steeped; he could tell to a grain how much cassia and clove wafted from the liquid.

"Thank you, Jesse."

"Shall I open the drapes? It's dark in here."

"Is it any lighter outside?"

"Well, no, but if it stops raining the stars will come out."

"It won't stop raining, so what's the point?"

Jesse squatted down in front of the fire and held his hands to its warmth. "The point is to stop sitting in the dark by yourself."

"How are the trees?"

"The trees are fine. Everything's fine, everything's finished. Pruned, raked, mulched, all the rotten wood burned. Tools oiled and put away. Cider press sterilized and lubed and ready for next year. Refrigerators cleaned. Barns swept. It's all done. The orchard's been put to bed for the winter. There's nothing to do but wait for spring."

"Deer hunters will be along soon."

"We've posted new signs. It's all done, I mean it. Maybe you should head south, too, like the boys. Get out before the snow hits. I can keep an eye on things for you here."

"Jesse, I don't know what I'd do without you. You're the perfect foreman."

"I'm just trying to help, boss. I'll do anything I can to make it better. You just tell me what needs doing, and I'm your man."

Goddard sipped at his cider. "Thank you, Jesse. I'll keep that in mind."

* * *

Lucy got a job at the Automat, working there from November until the sunny day in late April when her water broke. She stood at the counter as usual, spooning macaroni and cheese into bowls, putting the bowls onto the little shelves behind the little glass doors that customers could open once they put a nickel in the slot. She had been spooning macaroni and cheese for a whole month. The month before that was Salisbury steak and the month before that chicken à la king.

It was hardly the life Lucy had expected on reaching New York, but it hadn't occurred to her that she was qualified to do very little, professionally speaking. She knew how to play the organ, but had no music degree, so she couldn't play in a church or teach. She didn't want to be a cook, or a maid, her only other skills, but she was certainly capable of spooning food into serving dishes.

All through the long, cold winter—the coldest on record, everyone said—Lucy took food from stainless steel pans and put it into serving dishes and put the serving dishes on the little shelves behind the little glass doors. She had started with desserts, spooning Jell-O and pudding into small dishes, which hadn't been too bad, although she was woozy from morning sickness most of the autumn. By the time December rolled around and Lucy had moved to vegetables, the sickness had been replaced by backaches and sore calves and swollen feet and varicose veins. She spooned creamed spinach and sliced carrots and buttered corn into small dishes and put the small dishes on the small shelves behind the small glass doors.

As the months went on, she had to lengthen her apron ties, and by the time she was on main dishes, Lucy was having trouble reaching the small shelves. She stood catty-corner to the counter, which gave her extra reach, but the twisted posture made her back ache even more. Her supervisor was understanding, to a point, and let her take potty breaks more often than the other girls, but still, she wondered, as she spooned out the macaroni and cheese, how would she make it through this last month without peeing every fifteen minutes?

Just then she felt warm liquid flowing down her thighs. Oh, no! She'd been to the bathroom on her morning break not ten minutes before, and here she was, wetting her pants already.

Lucy waved to the supervisor, who rolled his eyes but nodded okay, and then she headed for the ladies' room, trying to stem the flow by tucking her uniform skirt between her legs. The first contraction hit just as she opened the door. Now she understood why her back had been aching so much more last night and this morning, and what all the warm liquid was, puddling on the floor beneath her.

Marge, who did apple pies, bless her heart for that, came out of a stall just as Lucy doubled over. Marge had three of her own so she recognized Lucy's state and took charge. She sat Lucy on the vinyl couch, stuffed a wad of paper towels up her crotch, and wiped the floor with another bunch of paper towels.

"I thought you weren't due for another three or four weeks," said Marge.

"So did I."

"Let's get you to the hospital. Which coat is yours?"

"The brown one that's missing all the buttons below the waist."

"I'll be right back." Marge was already out the door on her way to the cloakroom when another contraction grabbed Lucy's middle. She gasped with the force of it, fighting it until Marge came back with Lucy's coat and purse.

"I flagged a cab and he's waiting outside. Can you walk?"

Lucy nodded.

It took three tries to get her off the couch but finally Marge had her upright. She helped Lucy put on her coat and put an arm around her waist. "Lean on me and let's go quick before the next one hits."

They waddled out the door like creatures from a world with heavier gravity. Outside, the Yellow Cab blazed in the sunlight; reflections from the chrome door handles and bumpers made the women squint. The rear door was already open and Marge shoved Lucy onto the back seat.

"Take her to the Women's Hospital, and hurry," Marge said. She put Lucy's handbag on the seat next to her. "Good luck, honey—I'll come see you when I get off shift."

Lucy nodded her thanks and Marge shut the door. Lucy grimaced as the cab accelerated and another contraction took her breath away.

"You turn blue if you hold breath like that," said the cabbie.

She could just see his pale eyes in the rearview mirror.

"Come on, lady. Do not want you dying in my cab."

"I'm not dying." Lucy took a shuddering breath. "I'm in labor."

"Da, is obvious. In old country, my mama is midwife. She say always to breathe for baby. In, out, in, out, very slow, very deep. Supposed to help, she say. I do not know such things, myself, but what you have to lose?"

Lucy tried to breathe slowly and deeply as the cab wove in and out of traffic with the cabbie alternately blowing the horn and shaking his fist out the window. But she didn't time it right and couldn't manage this strong contraction that made her feel like she was being turned inside out. Her abdomen tightened so hard all she could do was curl around it like a dried leaf. When it was over, she leaned against the back seat, trembling.

But when she felt the next contraction building, she breathed in and out, in and out, and the pain didn't slam into her so hard this time. She rode it like a swimmer cresting a wave. When it released her, she looked at the nameplate on the back of the seat.

"Yuri," she said. "You're right. Breathing that way helps. Thank you."

"Sure. You just sit and breathe deep, and Yuri will get you to birthing place."

She leaned to one side to get a better look at him.

"Where do you come from?" she asked.

"I am from Ukraine."

He had a round face and high Slavic cheekbones. His hair was like frost, his skin so pale she could see the blue veins beneath it, and his eyes in the mirror were the palest blue of all. He looked like skim milk.

The taxi swerved as another contraction began. She saw a flash of taillights and closed her eyes, trusting Yuri to avoid the impending crash. Her sole focus now was internal.

Lucy put her hands on her belly. She felt the baby shift and settle lower. She took deep, slow breaths, watching yellow sparkles dancing on the inside of her eyelids. This was happening much faster than she expected. Each contraction crested and passed, like a run on the Cyclone at Coney Island. It couldn't have been more than 15 or 20 minutes to the hospital, but by the time they arrived, with Yuri leaning on the horn and white-suited orderlies rushing out with a gurney, she already felt a strong urge to push the baby free.

"Don't push," someone shouted, but she couldn't help it. She was no longer in control of her own body. She could have been a bystander watching from across the hall.

Lucy felt the baby's head push against the walls of the cervix, and the wonder of that released the last vestige of her *self*. She screamed—not in pain, but in animal strength. She became a roaring muscle, powerful and pushing until the head was in the birth canal. She felt the pressure of the baby's skull. She could feel her bones shifting to ease the passage. She felt her vagina stretching wide to welcome it.

Lucy pushed and felt the sting of her own flesh tearing but it was nothing at all. She pushed and smelled feces, she pushed and felt the baby's head emerge and retract, she pushed and pushed and pushed again.

And there it was, a rush of flesh sliding against flesh, a wet slithering emptiness, the smell of iron and salt, the baby's cry.

"It's a girl," she heard.

"Give her to me," Lucy said.

"In a little while," said someone, nurse or doctor, she didn't know or care. "We have to clean her up, and we have to get you to a room."

"I have to see her! Just as she is, give her to me!"

Eyes frowned at Lucy over the white mask but the baby was placed on her chest. The baby was a rainbow: blue veined and pink skinned, white with vernix and red with Lucy's blood. The baby cried and raised her tiny fists; her legs were folded like a frog's.

"Hello, my daughter. Hello, my lovely blossom, my new spring flower. Hello, my Lily."

A few hours later, propped up against pillows, Lucy shocked the nurse by pulling the hospital gown down to her waist and offering her breast to Lily.

"Doctor says bottle feeding is much better for Baby," said the nurse.

"Nonsense. If it were, I wouldn't have two of these." She smiled as Lily opened her rose-petal mouth and latched onto the nipple, suckling rhythmically. The pain and pressure in Lucy's left breast eased. She sighed. They were united again.

The nurse put the bottle of formula on Lucy's nightstand with a thump.

"It's 1961, not 1861. Modern women give their babies formula. No civilized woman does what you're doing."

"That's too bad for the civilized women. They don't know what they're missing."

The nurse drew the curtain across Lucy's bed, screening the primitive sight from people passing in the hall, and stalked out of the room. Lucy began to hum a lullaby and looked down at her daughter. She was rainbow no more, just every shade of pink imaginable. She was even wrapped in a soft pink blanket. Her eyes were shut tight with concentration as she suckled. Lucy touched her cheek with the back of one finger. She felt a wave of love pass like electricity through her whole body.

Her daughter—her daughter!—was a revelation. Though she had seen mothers touching their children, and holding them close, it had always been abstractly beautiful, not quite real, like a painting. Now she knew, with every nerve, every muscle fiber, every heartbeat, every breath: She was holding an entire world in her arms. The connection was visceral, a certainty that she would do anything to keep her baby safe and well.

This was why she had given up everything that came before. This is what she would live for from now on. Goddard was her baby's father, but he would have no influence over Lily, would not force her into his rigid way of life, would not indoctrinate her or give her orders. Whatever Lily wanted to do when she grew up, she would do.

Lily's mouth went slack against the nipple—she'd fallen asleep in mid-suck. Lucy shifted the baby onto her shoulder and began to rub her back. Lily burped and settled deeper into sleep. Lucy's nipple still oozed a few drops of grayish colostrum. She wiped it with her fingertip, tasted its sweetness, and smiled.

True to her word, Marge stopped by that evening. She held a bouquet of pink carnations "from all the girls" but she seemed more worried than pleased.

"What's the matter, Margie? Aren't you happy for me?"

"Well of course I am, but Luce—what are you going to do now? You can't come back to work and they'll never hold your job for you. How are you going to live?"

"Something will turn up, don't worry."

But Marge was right. Lucy had avoided thinking about it, and as long as she had Lily in her arms, she didn't care. Later that night, when another disapproving nurse took Lily back to the nursery, Lucy had time to think, and wonder, and worry, not just about a job, and taking care of Lily, but about bringing up her daughter in this city. In winter it was freezing cold and dreary; in summer it would be stifling. Its paved streets and towering skyscrapers had become as claustrophobic as the rigid rows of the orchard had been.

Worse, the people were not as nice as country folk. Not all of them, of course, but enough to make Lucy fret for their immediate future. She trembled with the knowledge that as soon as she left the hospital, she would be wholly responsible for her daughter's wellbeing.

The wail of an approaching siren increased in pitch and volume, breaking Lucy's train of thought. So much noise! At first, she had reveled in the clamor of millions of voices, hundreds of thousands of cars and cabs, dozens of subway trains, even the lowing of the Queen Mary's whistle as the ocean liner left the harbor every two weeks. Now she pulled the sides of the pillow up against her ears.

For the first time since leaving Goddard, she missed the country, missed the stillness of a summer afternoon so quiet all she could hear was the breeze ruffling the foxtails of meadow grass. For the first time since leaving Goddard, she felt lonely. She rubbed her slack belly. Already her uterus was shrinking into itself, emptying out the last bits of tissue no longer needed to nourish and protect. After so many months of being two-people-in-one, the idea of being a single individual again seemed almost ridiculous.

Lucy rolled over on the hard hospital mattress. Two-people-in-one described her life with Goddard, too. They had been more than a pair, more than a team; they'd been two sides of a coin. In the early days of the orchard and church, they'd worked in unison, building and grafting, inseparable, a single thing, like an apple. You couldn't slice an apple across and make two apples. You made two wobbling halves, neither of which could stand alone.

Standing alone was exactly what Lucy had thought she had wanted, but now that she had Lily, she was glad she didn't have to stand alone anymore.

Late the next afternoon, Lucy watched the play of sun and cloud on the windows across the street, where the shadows shifted and the sun sprayed the windows with golden light. Someone knocked on the door.

She turned her head. "Yuri!"

Her snowy-haired charioteer stood in the doorway, hesitating.

123

"Come in. It's all right. Please sit down."

"I hope I not intrude. I worry about you yesterday and today, all shift. Wonder if baby and mama okay."

"That's really sweet of you. I'm sorry I didn't thank you for bringing me here. I was a little preoccupied when we arrived."

"Is nothing." He handed her a small plush lamb, with a pink bow around its neck. "For baby."

Lucy petted the lamb's soft head. "You're so kind. Thank you very much. Did you see her?"

He nodded. "She is all pink, like bow."

Lucy smiled. "I almost had her in your taxicab."

Yuri laughed. "Would be something, that." He looked around the room, and then at her. "I know, is not Yuri's business, but, where is papa?"

Lucy shook her head. "Very far away."

"You go to him?"

She shook her head again.

He shook his head, too. "Where you go? What you do?"

Lucy leaned against the pillow and hugged the lamb to her chest. "You're the second person to ask me that, Yuri. I'd like to get Lily out of the city, but to be honest, I don't know where to go or what to do."

He patted his pockets and pulled out a folded piece of notepaper. "I have cousin, down Jersey shore. She has motel, very respectable, very clean. I call her after I see baby. She give you place to stay. You cook, clean, work what you can. Is good place for baby, very good. I write address and telephone here."

"Yuri, I—I don't know what to say. You're so good…I'll think about it, I really will. Thank you."

"Is not just for you. Cousin Maia need help, too. Is too much work for her. I would help, but must drive cab. So, go see. Be good for her, for you, for baby. Here."

He handed her the paper and stood up, rubbing his right eyelid. "You take care."

"I will. Thank you, Yuri." She frowned. "Are you all right? Is there something in your eye?

He stopped rubbing his eye and shrugged. "Glass eye. Gets dry sometimes." He grinned and left.

She stared after him. She had been driven to the maternity hospital by a half-blind cabdriver. Only in New York!

She looked at the name and address he had written down. Paradise Motel, Point Pleasant Beach, New Jersey. She looked outside again, as the sunlight withdrew from the windows across the street. So unexpected, and so kind, but she couldn't impose on his cousin.

Could she?

* * *

Spring came, and even the last snowdrift ceded its frozen heart to the sun. Goddard felt the warmth on his face, took off his jacket and opened his shirt collar as he inspected the trees. His lungs filled with soft air, verdant with the fragrance of the living soil, of moss spores. He heard sweet sap running through the veins of each trunk and twig, he caressed the soft sepals that cradled each swelling bud. Normally his heart would fill with the pure beauty of his apple trees. Not this spring.

He sighed, still midwinter inside.

He had walked the orchard all morning, half expecting each tree to show signs of rot, but if anything, this spring the trees were healthier than he had ever seen them. No doubt Jesse had taken extra care with them, thinking this surely would bring him out of his despair. Goddard acknowledged a small pang of gratitude for such loyalty, but even this faded like sunlight obscured by a cloud. He walked back, inspection complete for the day, and strode toward the top of the small rise where the Church of the Orchard stood, its white clapboards gleaming against the clean blue sky. Even this, the soul of the entire orchard, offered Goddard only an echo of the stirring that once gripped him.

He reached the bottom step, feeling a little short of breath, and looked up at the gray-painted stoop. Someone had left a basket there. How kind. People sometimes did that, in thanks for whatever burden he had lifted from their hearts. An apple pie, perhaps, or a cream cake

125

with fudge frosting. They had covered the basket with a small blanket to keep off the flies from nearby pastures. Goddard sat down heavily on the stoop and lifted a corner of the blanket to see his unexpected gift. He gasped, his whole body shuddering.

He opened the blanket fully. A baby boy opened its eyes and yawned, looking up at Goddard with dark brown eyes and a mildly puzzled expression, as if trying to place him. Then it smiled, as if to say, "Oh yes, I know who you are."

Goddard stared at the child, then looked around, wide-eyed, wondering if the mother might be peering at him from behind an apple tree, but there was no shadowy movement; there were no dusty footprints coming up the steps except for Goddard's. No one was here except for Goddard and the foundling, as though the baby had materialized from the earth itself, a wildflower in the middle of a row of peas. Goddard reached out a tentative finger, and the baby, clearly delighted, matched his gesture. Their fingertips touched, and the ice finally began to melt.

* * *

Point Pleasant Beach was exactly what Lucy had hoped for. The broad blue-green sweep of the Atlantic Ocean, with the horizon miles and miles away, was indeed both restful and dynamic, soothing in its eternal thrumming of wave against sand, wildly exciting when it frothed and swirled in a storm. Lucy felt a kinship with the mutable water that she had never felt with the orchard. Staring down the length of the featureless beach, seeing the sky reflected in the wet strand, watching sanderlings chase each wave as it retreated, she felt at peace.

Maia turned out to be much like her cousin in temperament and appearance, although she dyed her hair a shade of bright vermilion that was so obviously from a bottle it raised a few eyebrows in the small beachfront town. Maia didn't care one bit what anyone thought of her, and her breeziness was contagious. She welcomed Lucy and Lily as if they were relatives. She treated every day as a new delight, and each of Lily's baby milestones as an achievement: the first tooth, the first step, the first word. *Mama.*

Lucy wasn't sure at what point their relationship had shifted from employer-employee to friendship. She realized with some surprise that she'd had very few woman friends before. Almost all the help at the orchard, both the year-round hands and the seasonal workers, were men. The few wives who came with their husbands during the harvest season spoke Spanish, and although Lucy would have welcomed their company despite the language barrier, the social barriers between them were too strong. Their rural neighbors were occupied with their own farms and families. And the nearest small town was just a place for commerce that couldn't be done through mail order.

She and Marge had gone out for drinks on occasion after work, to the movies, and once to hear the New York Symphony, but Marge was bored by classical music. They had little in common beyond working at the automat, more pals than friends.

Lucy wondered whether she might still be at the orchard if she'd had a friend like Maia to confide in when the rows of apple trees began to feel like impenetrable green walls. Maybe it was just isolation that made her leave, an isolation she had not recognized because she'd never experienced anything else.

She was far from isolated now. Except for those first few months in New York, she'd never lived in a place with so many people. In the off season, the town merchants worked together to make sure the coming season would be a success. Homeowners who lived in the beach town year-round came out, as if from hibernation, to frequent the shops and restaurants that were too crowded for them in the summer.

From Memorial Day to Labor Day, the population tripled. Families came from all over North Jersey to spend a week or two at the shore. On weekends, traffic on Route 35 backed up for miles as day trippers drove over the Manasquan Inlet bridge to spend a sunny afternoon on the beach.

Lucy worked hard to please the families that checked into the motel, cleaning their rooms in the mornings and waiting tables afternoons in the attached coffee shop. The work was humble but more satisfying than dishing up stewed tomatoes at the Automat, and Maia's workaday pride of ownership was easier to live with than Goddard's obsessive, malar passion.

Maia, who managed the front desk, handled all the yard work, too, and much of the maintenance herself. She was equally adept with a pipe wrench or a lawnmower. Where most motor courts had a swimming pool, she had planted a courtyard garden with a central fountain.

"If they want to swim, they have whole ocean right across street," she told Lucy. "Everyone gets tired of scratchy sand in toes and needs to walk bare of foot in soft grass. At the beach, all is blue and white, or gray and white: sky, water, sand. Heart needs green and yellow, heart needs pink and red."

On summer evenings, after Maia lit the "No Vacancy" sign, and Lily was tucked in her crib, the two women would sit in the garden talking. Even though both were tired from the long workday, they looked forward to chatting quietly, with the sound of the surf in the background. At first Maia instructed Lucy in the workings of a motel that had to do 85 percent of its business between two holidays. Later in the season, after they had become real friends, they talked about more personal topics. Maia's earthy good spirits made no subject taboo. It was a treat for Lucy to be able to talk about makeup, tampon brands, whether it was possible for any girdle to be comfortable, the best way to fold a diaper, whether either of them missed having sex, or whether they were too tired most days to even care.

Lucy liked the picture they made: two women sitting side by side, sipping Tom Collinses from brightly colored aluminum tumblers, dangling their feet in the fountain while they watched fireflies lift off from the stiff blades of zoysia grass. Lucy, the grass widow—orchard widow, she called herself—and Maia, the true widow, whose husband had been killed during the Siege of Leningrad. Although Lucy was always willing to hear Maia talk about her life before coming to the Jersey Shore, Lucy was more reticent about that subject. She preferred to keep their conversations grounded in the idyllic present, or contemplating Lily's boundless future.

* * *

Goddard held the manila envelope with work-roughened hands. He debated whether to open it or just throw it away. He had felt extraordinarily foolish to hire a private investigator to find Lucy, something only people in a bad pulp fiction novel would do, and the man always did it because his wife had been unfaithful. Goddard was certain Lucy had not been unfaithful. They had been two halves of the same being, intertwined souls, perfection. Or so he used to think.

He used one chipped nail to lift the small flanges of the brass clasp and then slid his thumb under the flap. The paper inside was cheap onionskin. The detective was frugal, Goddard had to give him that. He opened the envelope just enough to read the first words.

Gabe's report got right to the point. *I found her.*

Goddard had to sit down to keep reading. He let the contents of the envelope fall into his lap: four sheets of paper, two grainy black-and-white photographs. Goddard's eyes supplied the color the photos were missing. A deep green wall of arborvitae formed the background; in the foreground stood a fountain, very plain, just poured concrete, but the water from the single central jet shot up three or four feet, the drops sparkling so brightly he could almost feel cool mist on his face. The fountain looked like the centerpiece of a formal garden, divided into quadrants by narrow rectangular pools. He was sure the bottom of each pool had been painted sky blue. He saw pear trees, quince, a weeping cherry; rows of crocus and hyacinths, a small square of lawn scattered with violets and periwinkle; the green blades of iris leaves. Hanging baskets of jasmine depended from the gateposts that framed the photo.

And to one side, what his eyes had tried to avoid seeing, Lucy seated, her head tilted up to the sunlight, smiling. She'd let her hair grow. It cascaded like the jasmine flowers over the back of one of those cheap, old-fashioned metal chairs with tubular arms.

It was the second photo that made him gasp: Lucy, in the same chair, with a baby on her lap. Lucy was wearing shorts, but the baby was wearing a tiny dress. Goddard knew immediately the baby was his. She had his brow, his nose, his chin, his whole face in miniature, softened

129

by baby fat. Only her eyes were Lucy's. He knew they were the color of emeralds.

Now he read the full report, a tedious travelogue at first, an overly detailed account of Gabe following Lucy's path to the East Coast. It had taken longer than expected, of course it had, but Goddard didn't care whether Gabe was padding his daily expenses or not. Cost was irrelevant to knowledge. He turned the page.

My big break came in New York. I'd been showing her photo to hotel clerks, greengrocers, cabbies, all over Manhattan. Finally ran into a cabbie who had taken her to the hospital to have the baby. He said he didn't know where she went after that, but I could tell he was holding back. I made up a good sob story, and he gave me the address. She's at the Paradise Motel in Point Pleasant Beach, New Jersey. It's on the beachfront. It isn't much of a place from the outside. The photos show where she spends a lot of time, a good-sized courtyard with a lot of fancy flowers and a fountain and all. The kid is there, too, the spitting image of you, so no worries on that account. She must have been p.g. when she left.

Advise next step—Gabe

The final piece of paper was the list of expenses. Goddard shoved it in his pocket without even looking at the amount due.

Advise next step indeed. That was complicated, because Lucy was not Gabe's only current assignment from Goddard. He had also been tasked with discovering where the baby boy had come from. Based on the child's dark hair and eyes and olive skin, the mother was likely one of the migrant workers Goddard employed on a seasonal basis. But when the baby appeared on the church steps it wasn't picking season. Equally puzzling, the infant was not a newborn, so it was not a case of a mother giving birth and running away. But Gabe was at a rare loss, failing to come up with any kind of trail that could lead to the mother.

He and Goddard both knew that these workers, especially the ones who were not in the U.S. legally, had ways of disappearing when they needed to.

Reluctantly, Goddard had contacted the authorities himself. He offered to foster the infant, with the daytime help of a paid nurse, until the mother could be found. His standing in the community was such that no one questioned whether an orphan child could or should be fostered by an apple grower and his male farmhands. Besides, it was less paperwork simply to agree. Chances were slim that anyone would come forward to claim the baby at this point. The state police sifted through notices of missing children half-heartedly, but came up empty. It had been nearly a year, the deadline by which the child must be put into the adoption system.

Giving the child to the authorities was by far the most sensible thing to do. The orchard was entering the busy season. Goddard had his hands full enough with nurturing tens of thousands of fruits, let alone one human child. But the baby had endeared himself to everyone, and to Goddard most of all. Sitting at his office desk, he looked up from the paperwork that would release him from his obligations as a foster parent, and watched the child, whom they have up to now simply called "Baby," as he sucked on a teething ring the color of a Red Delicious. Baby made eye contact with Goddard, dropped the ring, and gave him a broad, toothy smile. "Da!" he said. "Da, da!"

Goddard knew that Baby was simply practicing sounds, not trying to say "daddy." He imagined how quiet the office would be without Baby. He imagined never again hearing him cry—and what fine lungs he had, the lungs of a future singer, perhaps; he imagined how much more pleasant his home would smell without the diaper pail; he imagined having a placid breakfast again without having to wash baby cereal from the high chair, floor, and counters.

He put down the papers, and picked up the phone. Baby watched solemnly while Goddard waited through two, three, four rings, until he heard the greeting at the other end.

"Hello," he said. "This is Goddard....fine, thank you. And you?...Yes, I have the papers here.... No, actually. No. I would like to start the adoption process myself."

Baby smiled and picked up the teething ring again in his chubby, perfect little hands.

* * *

Lucy adored the month of May, when the garden exploded with color and life. The delicate small flowers of spring were upstaged by the blowzy blooms of early summer—frilly yellow and purple iris, red petunias, azaleas the exact color of her shocking pink capris. Soon nicotiana and heliotrope would fill the garden with their sweet scent, competing with the fragile jasmines in the hanging pots that she brought inside on cool nights. The beach community was in the last quiet days before the seasonal onslaught of blue-collar refugees from the city. Many were regular customers, taking their two weeks' vacation there every year, driving down in a car so overloaded with beach umbrellas, blankets, picnic coolers and cases of beer that the rear end sat low on the springs. Lucy liked their customers' down-to-earth approach to life. Most weren't picky about the number of towels in the room or how much of an ocean view they had. They were just happy to be at the beach.

Maia and Lucy had spruced up the place during the most recent off-season by repainting the aqua trim, fixing leaky faucets, steam cleaning the carpets. Together they worked up a new item on the lunch menu, submarine sandwiches made with roast beef and provolone cheese, just like the ones served in the city, so vacationers would feel even more at home. Everything was shiny, clean, and fresh. Everything was ready.

Four-year-old Lily was with Maia, flying a kite along the beach where the surf was so calm that Lucy could hear her daughter giggle as the bright yellow kite swooped up and down like a dizzy sun. Giggles were much better than the crying that had woken Lucy last night. She'd held and rocked Lily until the bad dream—something about policemen shooting at her—faded away with the setting of the moon. No more evening television for Lily; the shows were much too grown up for a little girl more used to Captain Kangaroo.

Lucy listened to the happy beach sounds as she ran her toes through the coarse grass, savoring the last of the off-season lull. They were happier here than she could ever have imagined. Each season had its joys and its charms: the hectic, nonstop days of summer; the cool, restful fall; even the most frigid days of winter when the tideline was laced with spindrift and the water was gray as steel. But spring was, oh, so beautiful in this well-tended courtyard garden. She stretched and got up to stroll in the grass, stopping now and then to brush her fingertips over the iris blossoms.

Something lay in the path on the north side of the flowerbeds. She thought it was a snake, but what kind of snake had two small legs just beneath its head? Then she saw it for what it was, the front half of a toad protruding from a garter snake's mouth. The toad was still alive but made no attempt to struggle; the frothy secretions on its back, its only deterrent, had not worked this time. Lucy could see its throat pulse. Small drops of blood dotted the gravel next to it. Lucy was glad her daughter was not here to view a scene that would engender nightmares worse than any TV show. She turned around and was startled by a man leaning against the garden gate.

He touched the brim of his fedora but did not remove it.

"Afternoon, ma'am."

A cloud covered the sun, but that's not why Lucy shivered. Something about the man—maybe the hat brim that prevented her from seeing his eyes—made Lucy uneasy.

"If you're looking for a room, the front office is to your right. This garden is for guests only."

"I found what I was looking for. Name's Gabriel, but everyone calls me Gabe." He paused for dramatic effect. "Goddard sent me."

Lucy took a step backwards, too close to the snake, which released the half-swallowed toad and slipped between the irises. The toad lay bleeding on the path.

Lucy clenched her fists inside her pockets. "What does he want?"

Gabe raised his eyebrows at her question. "Among other things, he'd like to meet his daughter, now that she's growing up. What do you think about that?"

"I think you'd better get out of here before I call the police."

Gabe laughed and stepped out of the shadow of the gate. He put his right hand into the pocket of his suit jacket, as though he had a gun in there, and Lucy began to wish she had heeded Molly's long-ago advice about self-defense.

"I'm not going back there with her, no matter what you say or do," she said. "It doesn't matter whether you're really holding a pistol, or whether you're just a bully who tries to frighten women. It won't work. I'm not afraid of you and I'm not afraid of him."

He laughed again and took his hand out, spreading his arms wide in an exaggerated pose of surrender. "No matter. There's a phone booth on the corner, and I'm going to make an important call. I'll be able to keep an eye on this place while I'm talking, so don't get any ideas about a fast getaway while I'm occupied."

Lucy stood rigid until he was out of sight, then she slipped into the coffee shop and watched him through the window. He was a man of his word, it seemed; he stood in the phone booth, facing the shop. It must have been a long-distance call because the connection took several minutes. He stared at her while he waited.

Lucy could see the yellow kite out of the corner of her eye. She willed herself not to look toward the beach, even though she realized he must know that Lily was there. She could hear little girl's shrieks of joy even through the plate glass.

She watched Gabe begin to talk, and keep talking. Then he stood up straighter. She could see a puzzled look on his face, could see his mouth form the words, "Are you sure?" Then he hung up, shrugged, and stepped out of the booth. He faced Lucy again, touched the brim of his hat once more, and got into a white Ford Fairlane with rental plates.

When Lucy was sure that Gabe had really turned inland and gone, she ran to the beach. She was indeed afraid, no matter what she had told this stranger. Her fear gave way, somewhat, to relief when she spotted the two of them unharmed, Maia leaning down to help Lily hold the kite string. Lucy shaded her eyes and stood still until she caught her breath; she didn't want Lily to sense her anxiety. Lily laughed when she looked up and saw her mother. She pointed up to the kite.

"Look, Mama, look at our sun!"

Lucy walked over to them and knelt to take Lily in her arms. "It's beautiful, my sweet, but we need to go back inside now."

Lily's smile disappeared. "Now, Mama? Why?"

"I'll explain later, baby, but we need to go *now*. Maia will take care of the kite for you."

"It's not a kite, it's the sun," Lily said, refusing to let go of the string. Lucy could see a tantrum brewing.

"What's wrong?" Maia asked. She frowned as Lucy disentangled Lily's hand.

"Someone just came—a man—he threatened us. We have to leave. Now."

"I don't understand," Maia said as she wound the kite string around a piece of old broom handle. "What man?"

"I don't know him. He said his name was Gabe."

"That nice man who helped us launch the kite?"

Lucy froze. "He was here on the beach? He saw her?"

Maia nodded.

Lucy stood up and began to run back to the hotel with Lily sobbing in her arms. Lucy's stomach was churning with anxiety. Despite Maia's protests and Lily's tears, she tossed their clothes into her old suitcase.

"Maia, I'm so sorry. I don't know how he found us. Maybe because we stayed here so long." She sat on the suitcase to shut it. "You've been such a good friend, I hate leaving you alone like this, especially now, but I have to. She's my baby! She's my life! I won't let him take her from me."

Maia stood in front of the door. "I don't understand. Your Goddard, he hit you?"

"Of course not. He's not like that."

"Then why you so scared of him?"

"Not of him, exactly, but of what he would do. Lily is the only thing I have that is all mine. With Goddard, everything had to be his. I cooked what he wanted, served it when he wanted, wore what he wanted, even made love when he wanted. Everyone who worked for him did what he wanted. He wanted to control everything and everyone. He'll want to take her from me. If he does, he'll control her, he'll make her life miserable, and he'll turn her against me. I know him. He doesn't *love* Lily, he just *wants* her, like he wants everything. I can't let that happen. She's *my* baby—don't you see?"

Maia shook he head. "I still don't understand, but you must keep little one happy and safe. Mother knows best. So, I'll help. I'll drive you to bus station."

She carried the suitcase out to the car and got behind the wheel. Lucy held Lily in her lap, trying with no success to stop her sniffling.

When they arrived at the bus station Maia reached into her purse. "Here, you will need money. Take this. I wish there was more."

"Thank you, Maia, I will pay you back someday, I promise."

"You pay me back by taking care of little one." She gave Lily a goodbye kiss on each check. "Be safe, *zaichik*. Remember *Baba Maia.*"

Lily began to wail.

"Say good-bye to Yuri for me," Lucy said. "I don't know how to thank you both for taking us in the way you did. You've been wonderful to us, and we've been so happy here. I'm sorry. I'm so sorry."

Maia hugged them both again. "I already miss you. Send a postcard when you get where you go, so Yuri and I will know you both safe."

She drove off, leaving Lucy as tearful as her daughter. Within an hour they were on a bus heading south. With Lily finally asleep in her lap, Lucy had time to wonder how far they could go, whether even Mexico would be far enough away.

She looked down at Lily's tear-stained face and swallowed hard to keep from crying out loud herself. What a fool she had been to relax her guard, to think that she and Lily could settle down undisturbed. She should have realized that Goddard would try to find her—she had been incredibly naïve.

"Never again, Lily," she whispered into her daughter's soft, wavy hair. "You are *my* baby, *my* flower, *my* light. Not his. Never his."

* * *

Lucy didn't know that when Gabe was on the phone, Goddard told him, "Let her go." When Gabe protested that she was sure to hit the road, Goddard answered, "I know that. I still want to know where she goes, so make sure that you keep watch over her, but from a distance. Don't be confrontational. And don't approach the child again. When the time is right, well, we'll discuss how to proceed. In the meantime, I will send a check for services rendered to date. Consider it the first payment on a permanent retainer."

Gabe smiled as he drove back to his own motel, a cheap one on Route 9, miles from the beach in Lakewood. The room smelled musty but the bed was decent enough, the kind with a coin-operated vibrating mattress. The prospect of steady income had him considering something a little classier, maybe with a pool, for his next stop. The old man was getting soft, now that he'd adopted that kid, and that was fine with Gabe. Not that he'd ever minded spending so much time on the road—he was as loyal to Goddard as anyone who worked for him. But a little extra comfort never hurt.

He took off his hat and jacket, loosened his tie, and stretched out on the bedspread. He sipped long from his pocket flask, and unfolded the bus schedule, contemplating destinations that might appeal to Lucy.

* * *

Mexico turned out to be altogether too far. Lucy made it as far south as the Georgia-Florida border before her money gave out. She got a job at one of the tourist traps just over the state line, a place where the water smelled of sulfur. The shop gave out small cups of fresh-squeezed orange juice to entice vacationers into buying burlap sacks of oranges and grapefruits that would go bad long before they had the chance to eat it all.

137

Fruit again, but at least oranges had some compensations, like the astounding fragrance of their flowers. And they weren't living in the actual orange grove. They rented an old Airstream parked under the Spanish-moss-draped boughs of a red oak. Lucy and Lily played pretend that Lily's name was Edie.

While "Edie" attended kindergarten, and then first grade, in the local school, Lucy stood for an eight- to ten-hour shift behind the counter every weekday and every other weekend, doling out orange juice samples to bickering spouses and their cranky children. *We drove all the way down from Parsippany for this?* The kids would whine and fidget, appalled at the smell of the swamp beyond the rest area, sometimes screaming when a palmetto beetle ran across a sandal-shod foot. The tackiness of the place, so completely unlike Maia's neat-as-a-pin motel, was the camouflage Lucy hoped would keep Gabe from finding them again.

The rest stop had a reptile attraction to supplement the juice business. A shallow pit encircled by chicken wire held a pair of small alligators that El, the proprietor, would pretend to wrestle. The gators were called Fred and Ethel even though both were females. They were so well fed and docile it would never occur to them to bite El's arm off.

Once in the morning and once in the afternoon, whichever one was "Fred" that day endured being turned upside down and held. On a good day, "Fred" would open her mouth in a yawn that would frighten the small crowd. El, for whom gator wrestling broke up the boredom of pumping gas all day, would make the most of it and leap over the fence in feigned terror.

What really scared El were the two snakes he displayed in a pair of old rabbit hutches. They'd been there when he bought the place, and he would have let them slither into the swamp long ago if they didn't attract paying customers so well. One was a harmless six-foot-long black rat snake; the other was a small Eastern rattlesnake that was as well-fed and docile as the gators. It regarded El with undisguised lack of interest. El had to smack the cage with a stick to make the snake lift its head and rattle its tail.

Lucy didn't much care for the alligators, and she forbade Edie from going near them, but she felt sorry for the captive snakes, which she fed once a week with thawed mice. After a couple of months, El stopped drinking his warm Schlitz long enough to notice that Lucy not only fed the snakes, but she could handle them, too, even the rattler that he wouldn't get within six feet of if he didn't have to earn a living. So twice a day, for an extra five dollars a week, Lucy ducked under the juice counter to stand outside while El wrestled Fred. Afterwards, she would open the snake cages one at a time, spending most of the demonstration with the black rat snake draped around her neck, and then coaxing the rattlesnake into her hands for a few minutes.

It looked much more dangerous than it was. She could easily feel the rattler's muscles tense the second it felt threatened, and she always put it back in the cage before it got too nervous. The black was her favorite, a serene creature that liked to be petted. On a slow day, when there were no cars or buses in the gravel parking lot, Lucy would sit in the sun at the picnic table with the snake curled up in her lap, stroking its smooth, supple flanks. Or she would drape the snake across Edie's arms, making her giggle.

El spat in disgust every time he saw the two of them with the snake, especially when Edie would kiss its scaly head.

The first night that El knocked on the Airstream door, with wet hair slicked back and reeking of too much Aqua Velva, Lucy hesitated only a moment before letting him in. She was lonely again, missing Maia more than she wanted to admit, and it had been far too long since she had been with a man. So, she opened the door, and afterwards, she made El put his clothes back on and leave.

She relished the afterglow that she hadn't experienced in years. But she and El had nothing in common, and certainly no future together, so when El started acting like Lucy was his due, she would open the trailer door with the black snake around her neck. After a while, El didn't think it was worth the trouble to check whether she was alone or not. Lucy thanked the snake by making sure it always got the larger mouse.

Every day, she kept a wary eye out for Philip Marlow wannabes as she served cups of orange juice. Almost no one under the age of 50 wore a fedora anymore, but she couldn't rely on that clue anyway. If Gabe showed up again, he'd most likely be in some kind of disguise, or Goddard might have sent another investigator in his place.

Finally, after two years of scrutinizing every male who unfolded himself from behind the wheel of his car, she had enough cash saved to walk out on El, Fred and Ethel. The snakes she released into the swamp, hoping they retained enough serpent common sense to find their own prey.

* * *

Goddard sat on the front porch, waiting for the school bus to arrive with his adopted son, whom he'd named Alan. To Goddard, it seemed only yesterday when he found the baby on the church stoop. But it had been five years, four since the adoption went through. Alan had lost all trace of baby fat and had become an active little boy, riding the bus to kindergarten every morning at 7:30 and returning home five hours later.

Goddard smiled and waved when the bus stopped at the end of the hilly driveway and Alan ran up to him, jacket unbuttoned and shoelaces untied again. Even though Alan was not his flesh, Goddard saw much of himself in Alan. The boy loved the apple trees. Sometimes, on their Sunday afternoon walks through The Orchard, Alan would run to a tree and give it a hug, and then run back to Goddard and hug him as well.

Now he skipped up to Goddard, shouting, "Guess what! Guess what! Guess what!"

Goddard grabbed Alan to keep him from toppling over those shoelaces and set him on the bottom step.

"Before I guess, suppose you tie those shoelaces so you don't trip and fall," Goddard told him. Alan gave an exaggerated sigh but he bent down to tie his shoes, concentrating so hard he had to stick his tongue out while he maneuvered each lace into a loop and then curled one loop over the other. He repeated the process with the other shoe and then jumped up and down.

"There's going to be a play and I'm in it."

"Well, isn't that wonderful! What is the play called?"

"It's The Frog Prince, and I get to be a tree!"

"A tree? What kind of tree?"

"A apple tree!"

"AN apple tree."

"AN apple tree."

"Let's go inside and have lunch, and you can tell me all about it."

Lunch took twice as long as usual, because Alan told Goddard every detail about the play and how he would be one of five trees who are the forest where the princess meets the frog and how he and the other trees get to sing a song after that and how they get to sing again at the end of the play when the frog turns into a prince.

"And everyone will come watch, won't they, pretty please?"

Goddard listened and nodded, all the while peeling a Stayman with a paring knife, carefully, so the peel came off in one continuous, curling strip.

* * *

The late Sixties were an easy time for people to be on the move; easy to disappear for weeks or months at a time. Large cities would be the easiest places to stay anonymous, but race riots and anti-war protests made them dangerous places for a single woman with a little girl. They were too conspicuous in country villages, too, so Lucy tried to stick with medium-sized towns. At first she stayed close to the water she loved so much, moving along the Gulf Coast, but she realized that Gabe or someone else would be more likely to look for her there, so she reluctantly moved inland, gradually working her way west. She stopped anywhere there was a coffee shop or diner that could use another short-order cook, so work was rarely a problem.

Men, however, were almost always a problem. For Lucy, peripatetic and friendless, physical comfort let the isolation recede if only for a few hours. But any man who approached her could be another private investigator, for one thing, and for another, all of them wanted to be on top all the time. It was easy for Lucy to spot a drug-addled hippie to steer clear of, and the married ones were obvious in their own way, but there were some men who hid their love of violence until it was too late. The first time one of them hit her, she'd had to defend herself with the jagged edge of a broken beer bottle. She'd left him bleeding on both arms and doubled over from a kick to the groin. She vowed not to go through that again, and for certain would never expose her daughter to it. She would let loneliness close in on her again, until she couldn't bear it anymore and found herself once more in bed with a stranger.

Edie, however, was Lucy's biggest problem. Lucy could handle the succession of dead-end jobs and efficiency apartments, but it was hard for Edie to start over with a new school in a new town every year. She needed a real home, a place with knickknacks and photos on the wall. Even more, Edie needed real friends. She had spent more than half her life on the road. Lucy was running out of satisfactory answers to Edie's increasingly pointed questions about what—or who—they were hiding from.

The last time they'd moved, Lucy already had their suitcases packed when Edie had come home from the last day of school. Lucy's heart broke when she remembered the look on her daughter's face as she walked in the door and saw them. No little girl should look that old and that sad.

Communes were common as Quaaludes in the summer of love, but Lucy wanted no part of a life where the men smoked pot and debated politics all day while the women did all the work.

She had to find another way.

* * *

Alan walked into the kitchen after school and saw Goddard standing behind a frosted cake ablaze with candles. It was Valentine's Day, the day Goddard had chosen as Alan's birthday, the anniversary of the day he had signed the adoption papers. Goddard thought February 14 might very well be the actual date of his son's birth, judging by how old

Alan must have been when Goddard lifted the blanket and looked into his eyes for the first time.

Before he even tasted it, Alan knew the cake, beneath its whipped cream frosting, was an apple cake with chopped walnuts in it. Life at the Orchard held few surprises. On weekdays, it was all about the apples: tending the trees, growing the crop, picking, cidering, pruning, and starting all over again. On Sundays, it was all about church in the morning and then back to apples in the afternoon. But it was a pleasant routine, and routine is comforting for a young boy. He dropped his book bag on the floor and ran over to the table.

Jesse, the foreman who had become a surrogate older brother to Alan, walked in holding the cake knife flat on a white dishtowel, like a king about to knight a subject. He knelt in front of Alan and winked.

"Your sword, my liege."

Alan always liked this game. He bowed his head and accepted the knife with both hands. He walked over to the cake with as much decorum as he could muster, but the sight of the burning candles—ten of them, a double-digit age at last—was too much. He dropped the knife on the table, closed his eyes to wish, and blew the candles out.

"Are there presents?" he asked Goddard, who laughed and said, "Of course, there are presents." Jesse gave him a small pocket knife, sized for a child's hand, but with two sharp blades, one short and one long, and two screwdrivers, one flat head, one Phillip's head.

"Wow," Alan whispered. "This is neat! Thank you, Jesse."

"It's from me and all the guys," Jesse said, "so be sure to thank them, too, later on."

"And this is from me," said Goddard, who placed a rectangular box on the table. Alan could tell from the shape and heft that it was not the G.I. Joe he had wanted so badly, but he hid his disappointment as well as a ten-year-old can by ripping off the white ribbon and red wrapping paper. From inside the box he pulled a ten-year-old-sized work boot.

"It's a steel-toed boot, just like the kind Jesse and I wear when we are in the orchard," said Goddard. "Now that you are so grown up, you need a pair of grown-up boots, too, when you help us out."

"Thank you, Father," Alan said. He put his arms around Goddard's neck. He understood the old man meant his practical gift as a kind of compliment, but it was hard not to cry with disappointment.

Alan knew he was a lucky boy, because everyone at school told him he was, with graphic detail about how stark his life might have been without Goddard's kindness. Alan even understood, at some level, that everything Goddard did for him, he did out of love. And he loved his father back, with the deep, pure love of a child.

But he sure did wish he could have had that G.I. Joe.

* * *

That same Valentine's Day, Lucy was working at a luncheonette in Hobbs, New Mexico. Hobbs was a dreary place and as far from a seaside town as it got, with ugly black pump jacks bobbing up and down 24 hours a day, sucking out crude oil even in the center of town. A young hippie girl had been panhandling across the street from the luncheonette for two hours, and had finally collected enough cash for a meal. She sat at the counter and ordered a grilled cheese on wheat and a small Tab.

She was the only customer at that hour of the afternoon, and the counter waitress, Tia Sue, was on break, so Lucy took the order herself and brought it out to the girl, who didn't look more than 15 or 16 years old. They chatted and the girl—who said her name was Star—told Lucy she was hitching her way to the Pacific Northwest.

"I hear there's this place they call The Grove, near Vancouver," she said, licking the margarine off her fingers, "kind of like a commune, but it's just women. No guys to mess with your head or make you roll joints for them. I was getting really tired of my old man, anyway, so I left him in Odessa. I hope to get a ride to the coast, or at least Santa Fe, as soon as I eat this. It's real good, by the way."

Lucy couldn't stand the thought of a sweet girl like Star hitchhiking by herself, so she offered to help Star with bus fare.

The girl's face lit with pleasure. "Far out!"

"The bus doesn't leave until morning, though," Lucy said. "Do you have a place to spend the night?"

"Nope."

"You can come home with me, then. My shift ends in half an hour."

After Lucy had refilled all the salt and pepper shakers, and made sure the ketchup bottles were capped, she hung up her apron and led Star to the one-bedroom apartment she and Edie stayed in. Star seemed oblivious to the cowboys who stared at her when they walked by. Her hair was long, straight, and greasy. She wore a tie-dyed tank top, no bra, under a faded denim jacket. A crinkled skirt slung low on her hips, hanging down to her filthy feet. She wore no shoes, just sandals that seemed to be made from old car tires. She had a patchwork bag slung over her shoulder; Lucy hoped there was a change of clothes in it. Lucy knew that a girl who seemed as nice, and as vulnerable, as Star might be playing her, so she could slip out during the night with the money in Lucy's purse. But something about her made Lucy want to take a chance that Star was on the up-and-up. Maybe the way Star shivered and crossed her arms when a cold breeze blew.

Edie was coloring at the small kitchen table when they got home. She'd met so many new people that she accepted Star without a trace of shyness.

While Star soaked in the tub, Edie helped her mother make burritos for supper.

"How long will she stay here?"

Lucy flipped a soft flour taco over a burner on the stove. She had to watch them carefully to make sure they didn't burn, but she glanced over at Edie before she answered. "That depends. She wants to go to a place in Canada that sounds really nice."

Edie didn't stop slicing tomatoes, but Lucy saw her face close down, saw the wary look in her eyes.

"You want to go there, too," she said, not a question, but a statement with years of resignation behind it.

Lucy turned the burner off. "I'll tell you what—this time, I'll let you decide. We'll have dinner, and we'll get to know Star a little better, and then we'll sleep on it. Tomorrow, you can let me know whether you want us to go or not."

"What if I decide we should stay here?"

"Then we'll stay."

Edie looked up. "You promise, Mama?"

"I promise."

"Why?"

"Why what, sweetheart?"

"Why would you be willing to stay this time, if that's what I decide?"

"Because I can see how much you don't want to go right now."

"But I never wanted to go anywhere. And you never really explained why we have to move all the time."

"Sure I did, sweetheart."

"No. You never did. You only said something about bad people finding us. You mean my father, don't you?"

"Your father? What makes you say that?"

"Because he isn't here. Because I've never met him. Why? Is he a criminal?"

"No, no, nothing like that. Sweetie, it's complicated. He acts nice, but inside he really isn't nice at all. He likes to control people. Everyone always has to do what he says, what he wants, when he wants it. It's hard to live like that day after day. And he's sneaky. He sent a man to spy on us, don't you remember?"

"No. What man?"

"The day we left New Jersey. You were only a little thing, barely four years old. Don't you remember that day? You were on the beach, flying a kite."

"The yellow kite? I remember that, and I remember Maia. I had fun. I don't remember any man."

"Well, that's good. Because he wasn't a nice man, either, and he scared me. That's why we had to leave."

"Is he still looking for us, after all this time?"

"I don't know, baby, but I don't want to take the chance. Your father—if he found us, he would want you all to himself. He wouldn't let me see you anymore. That would break my heart. You wouldn't want that, would you?"

"Of course not."

Star came out of the bathroom with a towel wrapped around her. She grinned at them, which made her look no older than 12. "It's been so long since I had a real bath. Thanks. It felt so nice, but all my clothes are dirty, so I washed them in the sink. I hope you don't mind—I hung them up on the shower rod."

"I don't mind at all, Star. I'll get you a nightgown."

When she was dressed, Star helped set the table. She ate more burritos than Lucy and Edie put together, which they pretended not to notice. Aside from telling them that she was from Iowa, she didn't volunteer any more information about her origins or past, nor did they ask for any. It wasn't hard to infer why an underage girl would be a runaway. Maybe that's why they both felt so easy with Star, and she with them. All three were in flight from something, or someone.

After supper, Edie combed Star's long brown hair, and then the two of them sat over Edie's coloring book, like sisters. Lucy sat down to read the newspaper, but she couldn't concentrate with Edie asking Star about Canada.

When Lucy tucked Edie in for the night, she whispered, "I like her, Mama."

"I like her, too, sweetheart."

Lucy made up the couch with a sheet and pillow for Star. "It's a bit lumpy, I hope you don't mind. It came with the place and I can't afford a better one."

"Oh, no, man, this is just great. Last night I slept outside, at least I tried to—those oil wells squeak a lot, don't they?"

Lucy gave her a quick hug. "Pleasant dreams."

In the morning, Edie announced that she wanted to go where Star was going, and that was that. Lucy gave her notice at the luncheonette, collected her pay, and the following day the three of them left together for The Grove. Lucy and Edie were old hands at bus travel, but this trip was a pleasant contrast to all their previous journeys. This time, they were leaving by choice. This time, Edie didn't sit on the waiting room bench, sullen and fidgety. She and Star played cat's cradle and chatted as though they were best friends. They sat together on the bus, with Lucy across the aisle. From old habit Lucy scrutinized every man who seemed to be traveling alone, but she was more relaxed than she had been in years.

It was a long, tiring trip across the desert, mile after mile of red rocks and red sand interrupted by shabby trading posts that all looked alike to Lucy: a sagging porch, a hitching post with one or two mules napping alongside a couple of dust-coated, dented pickup trucks of unknown vintage. They changed buses late at night in Los Angeles, and began the ride up the Pacific coast. By dawn, the southern California smog and sprawl had given way to soaring pine trees and grass-covered slopes that plummeted toward the blue sea. Edie, excited to see the ocean again, grabbed Star's arm and pointed each time the bus rounded a curve that afforded a glimpse of deep blue.

But once, when Lucy dozed off, she dreamt of smokestacks and flaming towers, long fingernails, red neon, harsh laughter. She woke up with a shudder, saw Edie and Star safe beside her, asleep with Edie's head against Star's shoulder, and leaned back, taking slow breaths to relax. She hadn't had that old dream in a long time, and hoped she would never have it again.

The bus pulled into a rest stop somewhere in Oregon, and they got out, stiffly. Even with fluorescent lights shining, Lucy could see stars in the night sky. The air around them was chilly but smelled fresh and piney. Inside, the dining area was surprisingly clean and welcoming. Lucy's sandwich was stuffed with bean sprouts and avocados. She threw off the last remnants of the dream and joined Edie and Star, who were already biting into their sandwiches with gusto.

They had to change buses again the next morning in Seattle. Crossing the border into Canada was no problem for Lucy or Edie, who showed Social Security cards. She had never used their cards before—no one ever asked for ID for the kind of jobs she took, and she was always paid in cash. She didn't think they could be traced with these numbers; surely not even a private investigator had access to government records like that. She held her breath when Star produced a driver's license that was surely a fake. But the laconic border guard let them pass without a second glance. When they got to Vancouver, a local bus took them within ten miles of The Grove. After that, they hitched a ride. The last mile, they walked.

The Grove was like no other commune Lucy had seen or heard of. It was situated in a narrow valley beneath hills of Douglas Fir. The clearing, 15 or 20 acres, held a big cedar-sided building, small cottages, and animal pens, surrounded by fallow fields and greening pastures. There seemed to be a lot of women Lucy's age or older, women who may once have been married, or perhaps still were. There weren't many children Edie's age or younger, but there were many long-skirted teenagers like Star. They met The Grove's nominal leader, whom everyone called Nana, a gray-haired, solidly built woman who welcomed all three of them with a hug. She showed them to a cottage that was furnished simply. Everything in it was made by hand, even the beds, table, benches, pottery, and blankets. There were also wreathes of dried herbs and flowers for wall hangings. Every woman who stopped in to say hello brought a small gift: a bouquet of wildflowers, a tin of tea leaves, a bar of goat's milk soap. One older woman gave Edie a hand-knitted sock doll with button eyes and an embroidered smile.

That first day they were free to stroll around and meet other residents, to explore or rest as they desired. They shared the evening meal with everyone else in the large dining hall, and went to bed not long after dark, glad to sleep in real beds under warm blankets after such a long journey.

The next morning, they received a brief orientation from Nana. "We're not a commune, we're a community," she told them. They learned that The Grove supported itself through farming. The benevolent Pacific Northwest climate let them grow enough food and herbs to feed everyone who lived there, with a good surplus to sell in a nearby farmer's market. The only males on the property were a rooster, named Randy for obvious reasons, and a Billy goat named

Baldy. The female goats provided milk for the children and for making cheese, soap, and lotion.

All decisions were made by the group, and, so Nana said, they achieved consensus with remarkable harmony. It was as if they were individual women who shared a common soul. Not so different from a beehive, Lucy thought. She felt as though safety and security had wrapped themselves around her like a crocus blossom around a honeybee.

Lucy's experience as a cook made finding work for her an easy decision, but because The Grove's cuisine was lacto-ovo vegetarian, she was apprenticed to the head cook, Aurora, until she learned to use the more unfamiliar ingredients. She made bread from amaranth, learned to grind rye and spelt in a hand mill, and soon was skilled enough to take charge of all the baking. Edie discovered that she had a green thumb and divided her time among the gardens, her lessons, and playing with the baby goats. She was mothered and taught by everyone else, including Star, who turned out to be only 14 years old. True to her persona, Star knew the names of all the constellations. On clear nights she and Edie would climb to the roof of the main house, where she showed Edie the wonders of Cassiopeia, Virgo, Draconis, Serpens.

Lucy was relieved to see how quickly Edie adapted to life at The Grove. Freed from the necessity of hiding and lying about her background, Edie blossomed. Lucy had wanted to call her daughter Lily once again, but Edie had grown so used to her once-pretend name that she decided to keep it. She grew to like all of her "sisters," and to love a few of them, especially Star. She was always happier to be outdoors among the plants and animals than in the schoolroom, but she applied herself to traditional subjects if only to finish quickly enough to do the fun work of milking the friendly Saanen goats.

All three settled easily into The Grove's annual cycle of sowing, tending, harvesting, and lying fallow, an ancient rhythm that was second nature to Lucy. But instead of the row-by-row cultivation of The Orchard, with its pesticides and pruning, The Grove grew all its food organically, in tidy raised beds with a variety of vegetables, herbs and flowers mingled together. Weeds were pulled out only if they were invasive. Lucy discovered that most so-called weeds had their own place in the growing season: a tasty rhizome for roasting, or leaves and tender stems for salads. Even the inedible ones were appreciated for their flowers, in part for the sheer beauty of them, but also for the nectar that The Grove's bees converted to honey.

What irony that Lucy should find tranquility at last, not alongside the sea, but among the towering trees and fields of The Grove.

As with any group of women living together, inevitably their monthly cycles coincided. Their periods were not disdained as "the curse," but celebrated in the ancient way as a reminder of the gift of life. It was not a gift without its problems, though, even in The Grove, and Lucy thought it funny that so many of them grew short-tempered in time with the phases of the moon. She was glad the older women were there to act as a buffer, and hand out cups of relaxing herb tea or mildly alcoholic mead when needed. She thought it must have been this way at the dawn of time.

When Edie was twelve and had her first period, the event was celebrated by the entire community. In accordance with The Grove's neo-Pagan ritual, Edie spent the night alone in the forested hills in a womb-like place called The Sanctuary, a low structure shaped like an egg, with a short tunnel leading into it. The Sanctuary was probably built centuries before, by a First Nations people, but no one knew for sure. While Edie was inside, the rest of them surrounded The Sanctuary, playing music, talking, sleeping, or making love, wrapped in blankets beneath a crisp winter sky.

The lovemaking had surprised Lucy, but it made perfect sense given the makeup of The Grove. She had felt incredibly awkward the first time Nana kissed her. But Lucy learned more about her own body that first night with Nana than from any of the men she'd been with previously. There was more give than take with Nana, a real sharing of love, without demands, without expectations. In a short time, Lucy felt with Nana the same emotional companionship she'd cherished during her long talks with Maia years before, with physical intimacy as an added bonus. Her life was perfect, at last.

The next morning, Edie emerged, tired, happy, and different. She refused to talk about what her experience had been like. Lucy knew that the hours in The Sanctuary were supposed to be a young woman's private retreat, but she and Edie had always shared their experiences with one another. It hurt to have Edie keep a secret from her, no matter how benevolent. To Lucy's dismay, that night was only the first thing Edie refused to talk about. As winter turned to spring, Edie spent more time with Star and the other girls, and less with her mother. The bonds between mother and daughter were shattered by the onrush of teenage hormones.

* * *

One morning, Alan was sitting on the porch, whittling. The ground had had a dusting of snow during the night, but the sun had warmed the earth and air, so now he sat on the top step with his jacket unzipped and the sound of meltwater running down the rain gutter. It was that brief time when the earth is balanced between two seasons: too early to be astronomical spring, although the trees were ruddy with nearly opened buds, and the winter hazel next to the porch was a mass of yellow blossoms. The ground was still frozen in the shade, but in sunny patches he could see the minute, bright blue flowers whose name he didn't know, which mean that meteorological winter was over. The orchard was about to burst out of its long dormancy. When he took a deep breath, he smelled the living soil for the first time in months.

Jesse came out onto the porch, stretched, and then plunked down next to Alan.

"That's enough bookkeeping for today," Jesse said. "What are you up to?"

"Just whittling."

"You still use that old knife we gave you?"

"Sure. It's a good old knife, and I keep it sharp."

"So how was school today?"

152

"Nothing special."

"Don't you have a junior prom coming up?"

Alan looked sideways at Jesse. "Yeah, so?"

"So, are you going to ask anyone to go to it?"

Alan felt his face and neck heat up. "No one to ask."

"You mean you don't have a crush on a single girl in that whole high school?"

"I don't ever see you with a girl," Alan said, "Or Mike, or Rafe. Or Goddard."

"Well, we do our flirting in town."

"Does Goddard?"

Jesse picked up a chunk of whittled scrap and turned it over in his hands. "You know how it is with Goddard," he said, finally.

"Tell me about her."

Jesse tossed the wood chip into the yard and wiped his hands on his jeans. "Shouldn't you be asking Goddard instead of me?"

"I try, but he clams up as soon as I ask. What was it? Did she leave him for someone else?"

"No, I don't think she did. That's the strange part. I don't think she had anyone else, or anyplace to go. She just lit out one day, no notice, no big argument, just up and packed her bags and walked down the road."

"She didn't give any reason at all?"

"No reason that makes any sense. She said the rows of trees were too straight and she couldn't take it anymore."

Alan whistled. "That's weird. I mean, it's an orchard."

"Well, I don't think she meant it literally. I think she just wanted another kind of life."

"What's wrong with this one?" Alan asked. "I love The Orchard. It's so neat the way the apples start out as nothing, just the middle of a flower, and then they grow and get big and sweet and red. The trees look so pretty in the spring when they're all flowers, and in summer when they're full of apples. And the smell of cider in the fall. And

153

burning the old wood in the fireplace in the winter. It's just about perfect."

" 'Just about' perfect? What else does it need?"

Alan stopped whittling, and sighed.

"It needs a mom."

* * *

One morning Lucy realized that The Grove had been their home for nine years, half of Edie's lifetime. Aside from the emotional excesses of Edie's early teens, their time at The Grove had been one of exceptional harmony for Lucy. The women here had become her family. The world outside the boundaries of The Grove almost didn't exist for her, except when she took her turn at the farm stand along the county road that led to town. For the first time in her life, she felt completely whole and completely safe.

For Edie, too, The Grove had been a true home. Once she realized they were there to stay, Edie flourished. The closed-faced little girl with the slouching shoulders became a tall young woman with a quick smile and an easygoing manner.

Lately, though, Lucy could see her daughter grow increasingly wistful. The bright intelligence that shone in her face had been dulled a little, like a fire that was tamped down, ever since her eighteenth birthday. Lucy tried to find out what the problem was, but when asked outright, Edie would simply smile and say, "There's no problem," and continue to wrap goat cheese in waxed paper, or to infuse ginger into a tea for one of the other girls. But the smile no longer reached her eyes, not even when she tended the goats.

As the growing season progressed, others began to sense that something was amiss, a tiny ripple of serious disquiet—not merely adolescent caprice—that Nana had to address, lest it gather strength and tear the tranquil fabric of The Grove. After the noon meal, one day not long after midsummer, Nana walked into the gardens, where Lucy was helping Edie pinch flower stalks off the basil plants, and squatted down to join them. Three pairs of hands made the work go quickly. When they were finished, Edie poured mugs of iced herb tea, and the three of them sat in the shade, watching bees rummage through the yellow and purple clover at the garden's edge.

Nana broke the silence first.

"Edie, is there something you'd like to tell us?"

Lucy's daughter shook her head and arranged her lips in a counterfeit smile. "No, Nana, everything's fine."

Nana and Lucy exchanged a glance.

"You know, child," said Nana. "One of our guiding principles is to be honest with one another. Tactful when the occasion warrants, of course, but truthful at all times."

"I know."

"Then why do I get the distinct impression you aren't being truthful when you say that everything is fine?"

"Because she's trying to be tactful," Lucy said. She tilted her head to one side and looked at Edie. "That's it, isn't it, sweetheart? Something's bothering you, but you don't want to say what, because you don't want to hurt someone's feelings?"

Edie stopped smiling and nodded without meeting her mother's eyes.

"My feelings?"

Edie nodded again.

Lucy took Edie's hand. "Why, my dearest love, whatever could you say that would hurt my feelings? You're my life, my breath, my heart."

Edie yanked her hand away. "Oh, Mama, that's exactly why I haven't told you. When you say things like that, it makes it so hard for me."

Lucy sat upright, holding the mug of tea with both hands, as if the cool mug would protect her from the sting of Edie's words.

"Go ahead, then," she said, working to keep her voice steady, because Edie looked like a rabbit about to bolt. "I promise to listen, no matter what you say."

Edie wet her lips and sniffled. She took a tissue out of her pocket and wiped her eyes and her nose. She looked everywhere except at the two women who waited for her to gather her courage—one with infinite patience, the other with anxiety, trying to make a mental list of the things that could possibly have upset her daughter this much, and failing utterly.

Finally, Edie let out a long breath.

"I want to leave The Grove. At least for a little while."

"Whatever for?" Lucy asked.

"Because I want more than this."

"More what?" Nana asked.

Edie sighed. "Boys, for one. I'm eighteen and never had a date."

Lucy looked nonplussed.

"Nana, Mother, I love it here, you know I do. But look around! It's all women, and mostly older women. That may be all right for the two of you, and the others, but I'm young and I don't want to settle down. I need to get back into the world and make my own way."

"You used to hate moving," Lucy said.

"Sure, when I was a little kid. But I'm grown up now. And I haven't had the chance to do anything. Go to dances. Watch TV. Be with people my own age."

"She has a point, Lucy," Nana said.

"But where would you go?" Lucy asked.

Edie took a deep breath. "I thought I'd start by meeting my father."

Lucy's hands contracted around the mug so hard she broke the handle off. The ceramic cracked with a sound like a rock face shearing off into a deadly landslide, with Lucy trembling in its path. Of all the things Edie could possibly have said, this was the one thing Lucy had never, ever anticipated.

Nana leaned over and took the shards out of Lucy's shaking hands. She wrapped a handkerchief over the blood. "Surely you knew this day would come," she said.

Lucy couldn't speak. She shook her head. She literally could not recall the last time she had thought about Goddard. It had simply not occurred to her that Edie would ever want to leave her and go to him.

But Nana was right. Of course, she would want exactly that. She would want to see for herself why her childhood had been spent in

156

flight. Lucy understood Edie's need to confirm that her mother had made the right decision. She understood the curiosity. What terrified her was that Edie might prefer Orchard to Grove, that Edie would never come back.

"She's eighteen, Luce. She has the right."

Lucy closed her eyes and nodded. "I know," she whispered. She stood up. She heard the trees begin to swirl with the outflow from a dark cloud behind them. Her heart was beating so hard she could see the blood pulsing behind her eyes. The air turned livid with her fear. She heard flames crackling. She heard someone scream. She heard cracks like trees sundered. Her heart was pounding.

She opened her eyes. The trees were whole and steady. The air was still. The light was the clear gold of late afternoon. She took a deep breath, just as her daughter had done a moment before.

"How long do you plan to be gone from us?" she said, the words slicing her tongue into pieces, shredding her heart.

"I don't know, Mother. I thought a while, at least. Maybe a few months. Maybe more, depending on how things go."

"With him?"

"Maybe."

Lucy shook her head. "It's a mistake. You won't like it. He's so—"

"He's 'so controlling,' I know, I've heard it all before. Well, maybe he won't be that way with me. I'd like to find out for myself."

Lucy practically sputtered with anger. Nana raised her hands. "Enough, both of you. Lucy, I understand how difficult this is for you. Edie, I also understand your eagerness to make your own way. But I will not have disagreements like this disturb the sanctuary of this place. I want the two of you to stop, take a deep breath, and make a reasoned, calm decision."

"So be it," Lucy said. "Go to him. I won't stop you."

* * *

Edie arrived at the Orchard one evening at the beginning of cidering season. She had written ahead, asking permission to visit. Goddard was so elated when he received her letter that he replied by telegram, wiring her funds. Jesse met her at the train station.

Goddard strode from the barn when he heard Jesse tap the pickup's horn. His feet slid on the gravel drive and his daughter—*his daughter*—took his arm to keep him from falling. He brought her inside, to drink in the face and figure denied him for eighteen years. For his daughter to come stay with him of her own free will was more than he had ever hoped.

She was quite simply the most beautiful woman in the world. Her waist length, honey-colored hair drifted across her shoulders like a cashmere shawl. She was as tall as he, with bright green eyes (he knew it) and clear tanned skin that glowed without a hint of makeup.

"My daughter," he said, laying his hands on her head. "Welcome home."

He had question upon question to ask her, but she was weary from the journey, so he contented himself with pouring her a glass of cider from the season's first pressing, and offering her a slice of apple cake, and basking in her pleasure at the taste of them. It was unimaginable to him that she had never tasted apples before—what perverse upbringing had that woman given her?—but he held his tongue about that, and chatted only about the train ride and trivial matters before showing her the room that had been waiting for her as long as he had.

In the morning (the first morning!), Goddard awoke inside a halo of joy. After breakfast he took her on a tour of the orchards, the cider mill, the converted barn where they sold cold cider and warm donuts. Though she knew nothing about apples, this strange daughter of his, she was clearly learned about plants in general, and the intelligence of her questions made him proud.

"Where did you study horticulture?" he asked, forgetting what she had told him in the kitchen not an hour ago.

"I'm here on one condition," she had said, pouring his coffee and buttering an apple muffin for him. "I won't talk about where I've come from, or what I've done before this. I want this to be a real beginning, for both of us."

He'd agreed, of course; he would have agreed to give her the sun and moon if it meant she would stay with him. But it was hard not to ask for answers when the questions had been forming for eighteen years. The last positive report he received from Gabe, she'd been traveling north along the Pacific Coast; since then, nothing. It was as though she had dropped off the earth for the past nine years.

After the tour, they went back to the kitchen where the orchard managers ate their noon meal at the large trestle table. The three men were already there, passing a pitcher of cider from one to the other. All three stood up as Goddard ushered Edie into the room. Two of them looked alike enough to be brothers, which they turned out to be, although one of them had fiery red hair while the other was more of a strawberry blond.

"Hi, I'm Rafe," said the redhead, extending his hand. "I'm in charge of the cider operation."

"I'm Mike," said the strawberry blond. "I'm retail."

The third man was younger, darker, more slender than the other two, and more shy.

"Alan," he said, with a sharp little bow of his head.

Edie smiled at him. "And what do you do here, Alan?"

"I'm still learning the trade."

Jesse walked in and heard how Alan described himself. "Don't fall for the modest act, Miss Edie. Alan thinks he works harder than the three of us combined."

"Alan is my adopted son," said Goddard. "He's the assistant foreman, helping Jesse oversee the orchards: grafting, pollinating, spraying, harvesting, shipping. He is learning every aspect of the business."

"It's very nice to meet you all," she said.

Edie acted more self-possessed than she felt. This place was very different from anywhere she had lived before. It was neither beachfront nor desert. She missed the crisp, fir-scented air of the Pacific Northwest. She missed her herb garden, and the goats. Most of all, she missed her mother and Nana and Star.

159

It was awkward to be the lone woman at a table full of men. Edie hadn't seen so many men in one place since she was a child. Almost all of the apple pickers were men, too, though she saw a few women and older children among them. They had waved but otherwise continued picking apples this morning when her father led her on a tour of the huge orchard.

"They don't speak English, most of them," he told her. "They're Mexicans who come for the harvest, migrant farm workers. They're only here until cidering is done, then they go back home and work their way north again as the growing season progresses."

Now Goddard passed her a steaming bowl. "It's stew, made with pork and apples. Eat hearty."

Edie looked at the hunks of meat in the brown gravy and felt queasy. "I'm sorry, Father, but I don't eat meat."

The men had been eating steadily and silently. Now they stopped, and she blushed to feel five pairs of eyes staring at her.

"Would you mind passing the bread, Jesse?" she asked.

He handed her a plate filled with slices of soft white bread. She thanked him and took two slices. "Wonder Bread. I haven't had this since I was a little girl."

Mike and Rafe looked at each other. Rafe raised one eyebrow; Mike shrugged. They continued eating, as did Jesse and, after a moment, Goddard. Alan put down his fork.

"You have to eat more than bread for your lunch," he said. He stood up and opened the refrigerator. "We have the best cheddar cheese in the country." He cut a slice from the wheel of cheese and handed it to her. It was covered with red wax, like an apple skin.

"Thank you, Alan," she said, peeling off the wax and placing the white cheese between the slices of bread. She took a bite, and smiled. "Delicious."

After lunch, the men stood up to go back to the orchard. Edie sat at the table, unsure what to do next.

"I can help you clear that," Alan said.

"I'm sure Edie can take care of it, Alan," Goddard said. "A kitchen should properly be a woman's domain."

"I'm happy to help out however I can," Edie said.

After clearing away the food and washing the dishes, Edie explored the kitchen and pantry, dismayed to find very little produce aside from apples. There were no fresh herbs, or dried ones for that matter, not even lettuce for salad. At dinner that evening, she offered to do the grocery shopping and cooking. Goddard beamed at her.

"I can't drive, though, so I'll need a ride to the store."

"Rafe drives into town every Tuesday," Goddard said. "He can drop you at the supermarket while he does other errands. That will save him a lot of time and trouble."

Although Edie had to cook meat for the men, she made sure there were vegetarian alternatives at every meal. Alan was the only one brave enough to try her hummus, and he developed a preference for the whole grain bread she baked twice a week. The bread was nowhere near as good as her mother's, but it was certainly better than the white fluff the men had been eating. It was too late in the growing season to start a kitchen garden, but she began to plan for one. She found a patch of rhubarb that would be fine for making pie in the spring, and, although for reasons she couldn't fathom Goddard would not allow peaches, pears or cherries at his table, she bought pomegranates, dried figs, and dates.

She knew that her efforts pleased Goddard, especially because they meant she was planning to stay with him longer than she had originally thought. Although she'd arrived with only the vaguest of plans for the duration of her visit, she knew now that she wanted to stay long enough to experience a Wisconsin winter, and to see the apple blossoms that Goddard so lovingly described.

She understood he did all he could to make her feel truly at home. She had to endure a few uncomfortable hours in his church every Sunday morning, but as long as she had a good night's sleep the night before, she was able to stifle her yawns and listen politely. Goddard had his eccentricities, for sure, with this apple obsession, and his preaching.

One Sunday she tried to suggest that leading by example was more effective than merely telling people how to behave, but he seemed so offended that she apologized and dropped the subject.

He also had a strange need to maintain the hierarchy of the orchard, with workers reporting to Mike, Rafe, and Alan, and Alan to Jesse, and Jesse to Goddard, who made all decisions regarding the harvest, the cidering, and the store. She was beginning to see what her mother warned her about.

She talked with Alan about it during one of the long walks they were in the habit of taking when work stopped for the evening.

"Don't you mind that you always have to go to Jesse with your ideas, and then Jesse to Goddard and back down the pipeline again?" she asked.

"No, why should I? Goddard's system works fine. The orchard runs smoothly, and it's a huge success. Besides, Goddard is my father. Children are supposed to obey their parents."

"Well, most of the time. My mother didn't exactly want me to come here, but I did it anyway."

"I can't imagine leaving home the way you did. I mean, I understand you'd want to meet your father, and that's a good reason, but I don't think I could ever defy Goddard just for the sake of doing it."

"Well, that's not what I was doing by coming here. At least, not entirely. It just felt like time I did something for myself, made my own decision about what to do next. Don't you want to have a life of your own? Don't you ever wonder what else is out there?"

"Nope. I have everything I need, right here. Especially now."

"What do you mean?"

"Nothing," Alan said, blushing. "It's getting chilly. Are you cold?"

"I never notice the cold when I'm talking with you," Edie said.

Alan blushed even more.

"Did I say something wrong?"

"No, Miss Edie. You said something nice."

"Would you mind not calling me 'miss'? It's so formal, and kind of sexist. No one has ever called me that before."

"Goddard wouldn't like it if I didn't call you Miss Edie," said Alan. Edie sighed. "Of course, he wouldn't."

Alan could pinpoint the exact moment he fell in love with Edie: the first time she walked into the kitchen, the very first time they met. She was like a bright butterfly in a group of dingy moths. He'd been struck dumb by the sight of her long, blond-highlighted hair, which she plaited into a single braid when she did chores, and by her soft skin, her smile that lit up her green eyes. He was amazed he had managed to say "hello" without stammering.

It was as though he hadn't known himself at all until she walked in. And now that she was there, what he wanted more than anything else in the world was to be with her. He imagined what her lips would taste like, what it would feel like to press close to her. He knew he should feel nothing more than brotherly affection, but she wasn't really his sister, not a blood relation, and that opened all sorts of possibilities. At least, it would if she could possibly feel the same way toward him. But of course, she couldn't. She was perfect, a self-possessed girl who knew who her parents were, and he was just an adopted orphan who worked in an orchard.

It was bad enough during the harvest season, when there was work aplenty to keep him occupied all day and then some, and even after the hard frost, when there was still a lot of cleanup and maintenance to distract him. But in the heart of winter, when it was too cold most days to even go outside, and they were often in the same room together, playing three-handed rummy with Goddard, or just reading, or watching TV, he had to concentrate hard on anything except Edie, or his pants would get tight in the crotch and he would have to leave the room abruptly in embarrassment.

"I don't know what's gotten into that boy," Goddard said as Alan scurried away yet again from the fireplace and slammed the bathroom door. "It seems like anything he eats disagrees with him anymore. Too many vegetables, maybe."

Edie ignored the comment.

163

As winter progressed, Alan became curt nearly to the point of rudeness, the only strategy he could think of to deal with the problem. In this unsatisfactory way, he made it to the spring thaw, when he could attack the grafting and pruning chores with the pent-up energy of unrequited lust.

Alan was so wrapped up in his own misery that he didn't realize Edie was as attracted to him as he was to her. Instinctively, she understood that it would be up to her to make the first move. She was as inexperienced as Alan, but she'd had the benefit of adolescence in The Grove, where the women were open about sexuality, answering her questions frankly, and giving her a copy of *Our Bodies, Our Selves* when her period began.

And so, on an unseasonably warm first day of spring, Edie found Alan making a brush pile of dead branches on the far side of the hill from the cider mill. Goddard and Jesse had gone to the local extension station for updates about treating fire blight and black rot. Rafe was helping Mike get the store cleaned up for the coming season.

Alan saw Edie strolling down the hill, graceful and soft as an apple blossom. Her borrowed field jacket was unbuttoned, and the light breeze made her unbraided hair flow out to the side, where it sparkled like sunlight on water. It seemed to him that each tree she passed bowed in tribute to her beauty. He took off his leather work gloves and tucked them into his belt. Edie walked right up to him, put her arms around his neck, and kissed him on the mouth.

He put his arms around her and they fell to the ground in the shade of the brush pile, tongue to tongue, pulling at each other's clothes awkwardly. Alan groaned and slid his hands over her flanks. He scarcely had time to unzip his fly before Edie was kneeling astride him. She pulled him inside her, and it was over much too fast for either of them.

When they caught their breath, Edie just said, "Again." This time they kissed and caressed more slowly, at least at first. This time Alan was on top. This time they climaxed together, Alan arching his back. Over the treetops he saw shooting stars blazing in the blue morning sky.

Lunch was more than a little awkward for the two of them that day. Alan and Edie sat on opposite sides of the table, as always. In Goddard and Jesse's absence, Mike sat at the head of the table, Rafe sat next to Alan. After the soup and sandwiches were passed around, the four of them ate in silence. Mike, preoccupied with the tasks of readying the store, wolfed down a couple of peanut butter and jelly sandwiches and went back to work in less than twenty minutes. Edie, not really hungry at all, stirred a bowl of reheated lentil soup, but after a few sips, she covered the bowl with plastic wrap, put it back in the fridge, and excused herself.

Alan felt hungry enough to eat everyone's lunch. He devoured several slices of Edie's homemade bread; cut a quarter-pound hunk of cheddar; slurped up his soup and retrieved Edie's from the refrigerator; and finished by crunching up one of the last Golden Delicious from the winter hoard.

Rafe eyed him and shook his head. "Don't do it, kid," he said.

"Do what?" Alan asked, biting the last of the apple's flesh from the core.

"Her."

Alan felt his face get as red as a Winesap. "What are you talking about?"

"Mike may have his head too full of inventory to pay attention to you two, but I don't, and I'm not blind."

Alan was silent for a moment. "I'm not sure it's any of your business, Rafe."

"Come on, Alan, don't take offense. We're all family here. That's the problem."

"Edie and I aren't related."

"That's not how the old man sees it. In his eyes, you're her big brother."

"We're the same age, Rafe."

"The point is, you're both his kids, to him. You're as much his kid as she is, more, even, because he took you in and raised you."

Alan stood up. "I don't need you to tell me how good Goddard has been to me, Rafe."

Rafe stood up, too, and took their dishes to the sink.

"I know, I just don't want to see him hurt, is all, and it would hurt him a lot."

"How can it hurt him? I love her, Rafe. I've never seen anyone as beautiful as Edie. I love her, and she loves me, too."

"Don't confuse love with screwing around."

"No? What do you know about love, Rafe? I don't see you with a wife and kids. And why wouldn't it make him happy, if Edie and I are together? You'd think it would make his day to have the two of us fall in love, get married, and give him grandchildren. A real legacy, not just words on an adoption paper."

Rafe turned around and leaned back against the sink, folding his arms across his chest.

"Maybe it would have, if *she* hadn't left him. He's a lonely, lonely man, Alan, and he's going to want his daughter for himself. Not that way—sheesh, that's not what I meant. And no offense, but Miss Edie *is* his flesh and blood. He missed her whole growing up, so now it's his turn to be her dad. And that bitter streak that's been eating at him ever since *she* left—Miss Edie's able to soothe it like no one else, not Jesse, not you. He needs her. He's happier now than I've seen him in years. If you two get together right now, he'll feel like somebody put a big piece of apple pie in front of him and then took the plate away before he even picked up his fork. She may be hot, but she's the boss's daughter, and that's always forbidden fruit. That's all I'm saying."

"I don't want to argue with you. She's a grown woman and free to do as she pleases. And I'm a grown man, free to do as I please, too."

Rafe shrugged. "Yeah, you're free all right. Don't say I didn't warn you, kid."

Edie slipped into Alan's room slowly, feeling her way to the bed on this moonless night. Somewhere in the orchard, a screech owl whinnied and trilled. She touched Alan's hand. He lifted the covers for her.

Goddard's bedroom was right next to this one, so they tempered their urgency with silence. This stealth seemed wrong, but what if Rafe was right? Alan had even oiled the bedframe to prevent the smallest squeak from giving them away.

Deprived of sight and sound, they became a tangle of texture, taste, smell. They were still discovering the foreign territory of each other's body; they could not get enough of each other's skin. Their tongues tasted of apples and cinnamon. The floral silk of Edie's hair made Alan moan; she shushed him by guiding his face to her breast. Too much. He entered her for those glorious moments of reaching, straining to become one animal, one life, one soul. When they climaxed, Alan buried his face in the pillow; Edie pressed her mouth against his neck, and somehow they managed not to cry out.

They dozed, and woke, and made love again. They knew Edie should go back to her room, but Alan wouldn't let her go, and she didn't want to, so they lay together like spoons, half dreaming, listening as the owl's love song was answered from the far side of the orchard.

"We need to tell him, Alan," Edie whispered.

"Shhh" he whispered into her luxuriant hair, breathing in Lily-of-the-Valley.

"I don't like hiding it from him."

She turned her head toward him to keep her voice low. "We aren't doing anything wrong, and he has a right to know."

"All right. In the morning."

"I should go."

"Stay. Be my evening star for a while longer. It's nowhere near morning."

Edie loved when he called her his evening star. She closed her eyes, relaxing against Alan's firm, warm body. "Okay, just for a little while."

Whether she had been asleep for moments or hours she couldn't tell. The sun shone strong this morning, making her squint, but it wasn't the sun in her eyes, it was the ceiling light. And Goddard was standing in the doorway.

His mouth worked but at first no sound came out. He seemed to be trying to catch his breath. He managed to say only "I am...."

Edie pulled the sheet over her breasts; Alan sat upright, squinting, with a hand shading his eyes.

"Father," he began, but Goddard raised his hand to silence him. Then he pointed at Edie.

"You. Get out of my house."

"But Father—" she said.

"I SAID OUT! You—are—just—like—your—mother. Sluts, both of you."

"That's not fair!" Alan said. "We love each other."

"This isn't love, son. But it's not your fault she seduced you. They do that."

"No one seduced anyone," Alan said.

"She sneaked into your room, didn't she? And now she's getting out." He pointed at Edie again. "I want you dressed and out of this house at once."

"Then I'm going with her," Alan said, reaching for his jeans. He pulled them up as Goddard stood dumbstruck.

"Don't be foolish. You'll put this infatuation behind you soon enough. I'll help you."

Alan zipped his jeans. "I won't let you throw her out on her own. She doesn't deserve it."

"She doesn't deserve you."

Alan stood eye to eye with Goddard, and the open defiance on his face slammed into Goddard with a physical shock. "Don't say that. I don't know what happened between you and her mother, but don't take it out on her. I love her. Can't you remember what that feels like? If you force her to leave this place, then you force me to leave, too. Do you really want to make me choose between you and Edie?"

168

They stared at each other, then Goddard lifted his chin. "So be it." He turned his back and slammed the door.

Alan sat down on the bed and took Edie in his arms. "Don't cry, love. There's no reason to cry." He didn't believe his own words. Irrevocable things had been shouted in this room.

"I can't let you leave because of me. This isn't my home, but it is yours."

"It's all right."

"No, it isn't. I'll get my things together and leave right away. I'll be all right. I have my own home to go back to. Stay here and make up with him. He's more your father than he is mine. And he needs you."

Alan kissed the tears from her cheeks. "You're my evening star, and my morning sun. I need you more."

They took very little with them, just enough clothes to fill one suitcase. Alan put it in the back of the pickup. Mike was at the wheel, sitting tightlipped, waiting. Rafe stood in the kitchen doorway.

"Where is he, Rafe?" asked Alan.

"With Jesse. I've never seen him like this, man. I told you. You should have listened."

"I'm listening to my heart, Rafe. I just wish it didn't have to be like this." He held out his hand, but Rafe kept his hands in his pockets.

"Goodbye, kid."

"Goodbye, Rafe."

Rafe watched Alan help Edie into the truck. He narrowed his eyes, staring at them, as the truck peeled out in a cloud of dust and gravel. Rafe spat the dust out of his mouth and went inside.

Mike drove them to the bus station without saying a word. Alan squeezed Edie's hand, but he also remained silent. She looked straight ahead, trying not to cry.

When they reached the station, Mike stayed behind the wheel. Alan lifted the suitcase out of the truck while Edie walked inside. He looked up at the sky.

"Smells like rain, Mike. I hope it doesn't hail."

Mike shifted the truck into reverse and looked directly at Alan for the first time.

"You broke his heart." Then he put the truck in a K-turn and drove away.

Edie was waiting at the ticket counter. "Where shall we go?"

Alan flipped through a schedule. "I don't know."

"Help you?" asked the ticket agent in a tone that clearly said she was not a morning person.

"Let's get married, Edie. Today. As soon as we can," Alan said, ignoring the ticket agent.

"Most people wantin' to get hitched go to Vegas," she said, popping her gum.

Edie nodded.

"Two tickets to Las Vegas, then," Alan said.

They were in luck. The next westbound bus was leaving within the hour. They had time to get breakfast, although neither was hungry, so they just had coffee and split a glazed doughnut. They waited on a bench facing the street, holding hands, not talking much. Neither knew what could be said to make this situation better. The wind picked up a bit, swirling candy wrappers and pages of a newspaper across the street.

"There's no telephone at The Grove. We should send my mother a telegram," Edie said, when the bus pulled in. "She might be able to meet us when we get to Las Vegas."

"That's a good idea. Maybe there'll be a Western Union office at the next stop."

The bus pulled next to the curb, raising a nimbus of dirt and diesel fumes that spiraled past as Alan handed the driver their tickets. A gust of wind rocked the suitcase and the three of them looked up at the sky. A spreading anvil cloud, high enough to be lit by the sun, stretched wispy fingers to the north. Beneath it, the dark cumulonimbus began to shadow the ground. The underside of the cloud looked like it was boiling. Alan didn't like seeing weather like that so early in the day. Lightning flickered in the cloud. Thunder followed a few seconds later.

"Let's go folks," the driver said. "I'd like to be miles away from here when that storm hits."

* * *

Lucy woke from the old nightmare with a jerk that startled the young garter snake that had been curled up in her lap, dozing in the morning sun. It slid off her thigh and curved its way down the leg of the chaise to make itself small and safe under a rhododendron.

She sat up, placing her hand over her belly as though she still carried life there. She had not had this dream since she first came to The Grove. It brought a familiar, sweaty panic she had hoped she'd never experience again.

That first bus ride away from Goddard. Flames in the night sky. Soot-filled air. The bus racing out of control down a two-lane road. "Now it's your turn!" she hears. Mamie, standing in the aisle of the bus, muttering, "Somethin' not right. Not right at all." Lucy turns toward the window, sees her reflection: she's wearing a filthy stocking cap, wisps of pale blue hair poke out from under it, and she begins to moan, "The end, the end, the end...." Her moans are punctuated by gunshots.

A soft breeze stirred the firs. Lucy inhaled their sweet scent, like butterscotch, taking deep breaths to calm down, reminding herself that she was safe in The Grove, that the journey from The Orchard was many years ago, and nothing like her dream. Everything was fine now. It had been an easy transition from winter. The earth, fully thawed, smelled sweet with mud and pine needles. Fiddleheads poked up, and the first violets bloomed. The herd of goats nursed a half-dozen new, healthy kids. A surplus of preserves and winter vegetables lay cool in the root cellars. No problems here. And didn't she get a postcard from Edie just last week, saying how happy she was?

But disquiet stayed with her for the rest of the morning, like a chill she couldn't shake off. She made a cup of tea with lemon balm and mused about something she hadn't thought of in a long, long time—the apple trees, how old they must be now, and whether they still bore fruit. And she wondered for the umpteenth time how her daughter could possibly have found happiness among their rigid alleys.

* * *

The bus to Vegas sped from the storm. Hail pellets jostled up and down in the swirling clouds. The storm sucked warm air into itself and spit the air back out, freezing cold, almost eight miles above the fields where wild onions showed green against the thatch. Pushed by an April cold front, the cloud shadow raked across the countryside, expanding as it moved north and east. Lightning flashed from the edge of the cumulonimbus, where the many-layered hailstones, too heavy to rise any more, plummeted down through the green and yellow sky. The hailfall obscured the view of the lowering cloud, whose dark heart began to circle counterclockwise. Within minutes a wide funnel drilled its way earthward.

From a distance, the funnel's first contact looked delicate, like a ballerina that spins on her toes in an open music box. But the swirl of brown chiffon that billowed up around the funnel was sharp as harrow blades. It swirled and danced, gathering speed, strength, and debris, on a course that led it straight to Goddard's orchard.

Mike sounded the alarm as soon as the hail started falling, so everyone made it into the storm cellar in time. The bolted steel doors rattled and squealed as the tornado approached, exploding the transformer on the edge of the property and snapping the power lines. The storm cellar went dark. They all held hands then, their ears popping from the sharp drop in air pressure, and not one of them felt like a grown man when it hit.

The mile-wide funnel's core swirled at more than 200 miles an hour. Like a hungry giant it devoured everything Goddard loved. The apple trees that held the ground secure for half a century were ripped up like weeds; grass and topsoil flung themselves into the tornado's voracious center. The tendrils at its base zigzagged across the property, chewing up fences, imploding the cider mill and the store, inhaling the pickup and spitting it back to earth a quarter mile away. Goddard's church disintegrated in an instant. Keys from the organ would eventually be found more than three miles from the foundation slab.

It felt like eons before silence returned.

It took the strength of all four men to push open the Bilko doors against the weight of broken branches. They walked up the concrete steps, blinking in the sunlight, and stood back to back, scanning in all directions, their work boots slipping in five inches of golf-ball-sized hail. To the north, the black thunderhead and flashes of lightning dominated the horizon; to the south, east, and west, they saw a white and brown rolling plain. Not a building was left; not a single apple tree was unscathed. The ones that weren't uprooted altogether had twisted and snapped, leaving jagged stumps. Their bud-filled branches lay scattered across the countryside. Some were still swirling in the tornado that would gouge the landscape for another fifty miles, topping the list in the record books for many years to come.

Part 2

On the first of May, Alan and Edie were married by a minister of dubious pedigree in a wedding chapel on a side street two blocks from the neon casinos of Las Vegas. Their only witnesses were Lucy and the minister's yawning wife.

Lucy had arrived that morning, and she took the two of them to the local Goodwill store, where Edie found a white broomstick skirt and a white gauze peasant blouse, Alan a pair of avocado-colored chinos, a white shirt and a green string tie. They had bought their rings in the wedding chapel storefront, the cheapest the establishment offered: thirty dollars each, two for fifty bucks.

When the minister began filling in the marriage certificate, Lucy pointed out that Edie's legal name was Lily, so that's what he wrote down.

"It's fine," Alan whispered. "You'll always be Edie to me."

The minister gave them a coupon for lunch at the MGM Grand.

They went to the Grand, where each picked what looked edible and relatively fresh from the salad bar. The dessert table was much more appealing, with a vanilla seven-layer cake that made an adequate substitute for a tiered wedding cake. Lucy could see how much they loved each other, and it gave her some comfort to know that Edie had chosen a good and kindhearted young man, but the sad little ceremony and dismal luncheon seemed a poor way to start life together.

After lunch, Lucy said goodbye. She felt exposed and vulnerable outside of her beloved Grove. She couldn't stay in this garish, nutty town any longer, and she wanted to give Alan and Edie a semblance of a honeymoon. Alan hailed a cab for her while she hugged Edie one last time. She got inside the cab with a mixture of relief and sorrow that would stay with her during the long journey home.

That afternoon, during the matinee at the Grand, Edie caught one of the Elvis impersonator's scarves.

* * *

Goddard was slumped on the straight-backed motel-room chair when Jesse, Mike, and Rafe came back with pizza and news. Mike and Rafe sat on one of the beds and passed out bottles of Old Milwaukee while Jesse opened the pizza boxes.

"Pepperoni or sausage?" he asked Goddard, who ignored him.

Jesse put a slice of each on a paper plate and set the plate on the small round table, which had a matchbook shimmed under one leg to level it. He divvied up the rest among the other men and himself, then sat down opposite Goddard and began to eat. Goddard stared in front of him at the paper plate that slowly grew translucent with grease.

"Boss, eat something, please," Mike said. Goddard picked up the slice of pepperoni and took a bite. He put the slice down again.

Jesse finished his second slice, burped, and wiped his mouth on a napkin that he balled up and tossed overhand into the empty pizza box. He sighed, watching Goddard chew mechanically and slowly. At least he's eating, Jesse thought. That's progress.

"I talked to the FEMA man, Boss," he said. "He told me your claim is 'in the system', whatever that means, and that we can expect a check sometime in the next four-to-six weeks."

"Isn't that what he said six weeks ago?" asked Rafe. He folded a piece of paper into triangle and tried to pick a piece of oregano from between his teeth.

Jesse frowned at him and inclined his head slightly toward Goddard, as if to say, you idiot, I'm trying to make the old man feel better.

"What about the property insurance?" asked Mike.

"It doesn't cover so-called Acts of Nature," said Jesse. "It won't cover anything FEMA doesn't, but it's paying for the motel, at least."

"Oh, yeah, we're living the high life in the Super 8," Rafe said. "Couldn't we at least have stayed in the Red Roof? It has a Friendly's right next door."

"Until we know how much the FEMA settlement will be, Goddard is right to economize as much as possible," Jesse said. His tone was so placating he sounded like he was talking to a child.

Rafe rolled his eyes, but he looked at Goddard, who sat with his shoulders sagging.

"I guess you're right," he said. He tossed his empty bottle into the wastebasket and stretched. "Anybody for a game of Liar's Dice?"

"Not me," said Mike. "I think I'll take a walk. I'm not used to all this sitting around."

Jesse shook his head. "I'll stay here. Why don't you go with Mike, Rafe? Get some air."

Mike jabbed his elbow into his brother's ribs and inclined his head toward the door. "C'mon."

"Uh, sure," Rafe said.

After they left, Jesse folded the empty pizza boxes in half and stuffed them into a trash bag. "I'm going to toss this stuff, Boss," he said. "I'll be right back."

He walked over to the dumpster, where crows were shredding plastic bags with their beaks and rummaging for food. They flew up when Jesse got close enough to throw the pizza trash onto the pile, cawing with annoyance, seven dark forms against a pale sky just showing a little sunset color. They settled down again as he turned back toward the room. He rubbed his neck muscles and stretched. They were all getting stiff and flabby from not working. Jesse had probably put on ten pounds from all the junk food they've been eating, as had Mike and Rafe, but Goddard was losing weight. Jesse hadn't seen him this bad since *she* split nearly twenty years ago. He tried to think charitable thoughts about Edie but he wished she had never shown up. Not that she'd had anything to do with the "twister of the century," as the newspapers called it, but the timing couldn't have been worse.

If only the check from FEMA would come through. Their claim was just one of thousands, he knew, and it wouldn't cover everything, he was sure, but if they could just rebuild the cider mill, and plant some trees.... He kicked a chunk of loose pavement. Who was he fooling?

They couldn't plant any trees, not there, anyhow, because the soil was gone. The rich loam that had given them the sweetest, crispest apples in the state had been scattered like ashes across six counties. The hardpan scar left by the tornado would take decades to fill in naturally, and they couldn't afford to truck in that much topsoil. Even if they found a new site, and planted new trees, it would be years before they harvested enough fruit to break even, let alone turn a profit. It wasn't going to happen. However much money FEMA ended up giving them, the check never could be used to replace The Orchard.

Jesse kicked the pavement shard again, and it thudded against the back wall of the motel. He stared at the wall, made of dented aluminum siding over a cinderblock foundation. Money couldn't replace The Orchard, no, but it just might replace its church.

He opened the door to their room. Goddard had not moved. The cold, half-eaten pizza had soaked through the paper plate, and the beer bottle had dripped a ring of condensation onto the wood-grained plastic table top.

"Boss," Jesse said. "I have an idea."

He talked about rebuilding the church, not sure whether the old man even heard him, or if he did, whether he was actually listening, and if he was listening, whether he thought it might be feasible, and if he did, whether it was enough to light a fire in his eyes again. Jesse finished his pitch, and sat back, a little out of breath with his own enthusiasm.

Goddard turned his head and looked out the window at the parking lot and the strip mall across the street, where they got the pizza. There was also a Chinese restaurant, a dry cleaner, an adult bookstore, and a tattoo parlor over there. Traffic passed slowly along the highway with many utility trucks from as far away as New York, returning home after weeks of making repairs. He noted semis hauling building supplies moving in the other direction. Between the trucks were a few happy families starting their summer vacation, towing RVs.

Goddard finally looked at Jesse. He started to speak, but could only say "I am" because his mouth was so dry. He picked up the beer, looking at it as though he had never seen beer before, and took a sip, grimacing because it was warm. But he guzzled half the bottle before setting it down.

"I'm not so sure I want to do what you suggest."

Jesse tried not to look disappointed at Goddard's words, but focused instead on the positive: the old man had finally spoken a complete sentence.

Goddard continued speaking, slowly, thinking aloud as he went. "I'm not going to try to rebuild what I had before. I couldn't bear to set a new structure in the old place. To look out on that scene of desolation...no."

"You could sell the land. We could set down roots someplace else. Michigan, maybe. Or someplace where they don't have tornadoes. Back East. Out West."

Goddard thought about that, playing with the wet label on the beer bottle.

"I don't think I want to sell that tract of land, not yet, anyway."

"But do you think the FEMA check, if it ever gets here, will be enough to buy land and build a new church?" asked Jesse.

Goddard snorted and finished the beer.

Jesse saw a small twinkle in Goddard's eye, not enough to call a spark, not nearly enough to call a fire, but definitely a sign of renewed interest in life. Long after Mike and Rafe returned, said good night and went to bed in the room next door, Jesse and Goddard talked, and worked out a plan.

Mike and Rafe were on board with Goddard's idea as soon as Jesse filled them in. No longer were they bored by an endless succession of idle days. They had purpose again, they had plans to make. They had research to perform and shopping to prepare for, so when the FEMA check finally arrived—exactly seven weeks after the FEMA rep said to expect it—they got right to it with the enthusiasm and energy of the inspired.

The four of them walked onto the lot of RV Heaven not half an hour after Goddard deposited the check. The lot was three solid acres of new and used Winnebagos, Airstreams, MCIs, pop tops, hard tops, and fifth wheels. The salesman recognized the difference between buyers and browsers when he saw Goddard stride purposefully to the Class A Motor Coaches. The man was more than happy to show them the latest models. He was overjoyed when they inquired about optional equipment. He was ecstatic when they inquired about customizing a top-of-the-line Bluebird Wanderlodge left over from the previous year's models.

"Let me tell you about this baby," the salesman said, and he whipped through a list of features so fast they couldn't keep up with him. "...tilt wheel, spotlight, power bath vent, day/night shades...two recliners, four bunks, shower AND tub, coffee maker...power inverter, generator, 200-gallon fuel tank, 100-gallon water tank, leveling jacks, Allison tranny and wait until you hear this sweet Caterpillar diesel start up...."

Later on, in the showroom, while Jesse, Mike, and Rafe flipped through the catalogue of interiors, debating such crucial matters as upholstery fabrics and curtain colors, not to mention who would get which bunk, Goddard patiently explained to the salesman exactly what his plans were for the land yacht he was purchasing.

"I am"—he cleared his throat—"I am bringing our church to the people, instead of bringing people to the church. I am going to build the biggest church there ever was, not with wood and nails, or bricks and mortar, but with people, people coming together in the great outdoors. I will reach far more souls than I could ever crowd into any clapboard church building. I will drive every interstate, every US highway, every county road, every city street, every country lane to bring this church to the people. Well, Mike will do the actual driving, but you get the idea." He sat back, smiling.

"Well, hallelujah," said the salesman. He pushed a stack of papers toward Goddard and handed him a ballpoint pen. "Sign here, here, and here."

They took to the road six months to the day after the tornado changed everything. The Bluebird Wanderlodge gleamed in the morning sunlight. Jesse and Rafe had painted "Church of the Orchard" on the sides in candy-apple-red letters. The interior was furnished with a kitchenette and living room; a bunk room for Jesse, Mike, and Rafe; and a small private bedroom for Goddard. During the day, his bunk stowed up and a shelf swung out so he could use it as an office as well. The single bathroom was a little tight for space, so Jesse decided to grow a beard instead of taking up room with a razor and shaving cream.

"Where to, Boss?" asked Mike, who sat behind the wheel in the comfortable bucket seat that swiveled when the Wanderlodge was in park. Goddard sat next to him in the companion bucket seat with a new Rand McNally road atlas—a lagniappe from the salesman—open in his lap.

"I've always had a yen to see Bemidji, Minnesota," he said. "Let's see what autumn looks like up there."

"You got it, Boss," Mike said, and he turned the key.

Autumn in Bemidji looked a lot like autumn back home. The trip north was uneventful, and not much happened when they arrived. The response to their church on wheels was lukewarm at best in cool Bemidji. They headed farther north into Canada, but there the response was merely mild puzzlement. The Canadian people were unfailingly polite, but their utter lack of interest in the church was harder to combat than outright hostility, so they came back into the United States, racking up mile after mile on the Bluebird, from Fargo to Laramie to Denver to Salt Lake City to Portland to San Francisco to Los Angeles to Tucson to Taos to San Antonio, with less than stunning results.

Northern California was hopelessly New Age. If a kindhearted woman there made them zucchini bread, it likely had marijuana baked inside. In the Southwestern deserts, Goddard's orchard metaphors fell flat. In Southern California, the bus was pelted with bottles and trash. They headed east, and found the warmest reception in the Rust, Corn and Cotton Belts, places where the recession was hitting hardest. Mortgage rates were nearing record highs. Steel mills were closing, family farms were in foreclosure, fabric mills were shutting down. People were losing the only way of life they had ever known.

At last, Goddard had found the perfect audience.

* * *

Alan and Edie couldn't follow Lucy back to The Grove, of course, because Alan couldn't live there, but when Edie got pregnant right away, they set up housekeeping outside of Vancouver to be as close to her mother as possible. Despite the stunning scenery of mountains and pines and the proximity of the Georgian Strait, Edie was unhappy there. The water was too cold and the currents too treacherous for swimming. It seemed to her that the sky was cloud-covered or raining for her entire pregnancy. Now that she was alone except for Alan, she realized it had been the company of Star and the other women of The Grove that made the rainy falls and winters bearable.

It was hard for Alan to live in Canada, too. There were few jobs for Americans outside of the city, and those few more often than not involved fishing boats, something Alan had neither the desire nor the talent to attempt. His concerns about supporting a wife and child intensified when Edie gave birth to fraternal twins after a grueling, 48-hour labor. They named the older son Ken, because he seemed to understand everything they wanted of him, and the younger Alan, Jr., because of the way he grasped Alan's fingers.

"You'll be able to do anything you want, AJ," Alan promised him. "Both my sons will."

The boys were two when Alan and Edie decided to move to New Jersey, because Edie's earliest memories were of the Jersey Shore. Except for her time in The Grove, she had been happiest there.

"I want our boys to run on the wet sand and fly a yellow kite on the beach," she told Alan. "And you need to get back to the States where you can get a decent job. It's just not working out for us here."

181

For Edie, saying goodbye this time was even harder than when she had first left The Grove. For Lucy, it was almost unbearable. Mother and daughter went for a long walk on the last day, ending up at the labyrinth at the very center of the property. They walked along the spiral path bordered by small white stones and clamshells. At the center was a stone bench carved with a pattern of fish and frogs, where the women sat for a while, watching a V-shaped flight of trumpeter swans overhead. Their calls sounded both musical and melancholy.

Lucy spoke first. "I know it's part of a mother's job to say goodbye to her grown children. We raise you to be strong and self-sufficient, to prepare you for life in the world. But it's a hard thing when the day comes. You'll find out soon enough how that feels."

"I wish you weren't always right," Edie said. "I think of it already, the day when the boys grow up and make lives of their own."

"They'll be just about your age when they do," Lucy said. "The years will fly for you, like they did for me. Oh, Edie! I was able to let you go before because I was sure you would come back to me. But you haven't really, you live Outside. And now—all the way back to the East Coast. When will I ever see you again?"

"You can come with us. Alan would like that. You're the only mother he's ever had."

"Poor Alan! No, I can't leave, Sweetheart. It will be all right. The Grove has always been more my home than yours. This is where I belong, not where you belong. I never intended my sanctuary to keep you from finding your own happiness. No mother wants that. Alan is your sanctuary, and the two of you have a wonderful family." She stood up. "Besides, my sisters need me here. I'm the eldest now."

"You will visit us, though, won't you? I'll want you there when our next baby is born."

"I promise I will."

They spiraled their way out of the labyrinth and through the clearing, into the woodland path bordered with mountain laurel and mahonia. They paused near a flat stone set beneath an ancient Douglas fir. A depression in the shale held water for birds, and dates carved into the border of the stone marked the tenure of the former mistress of The Grove.

"I miss Nana," Edie said.

"So do I. I miss her wisdom and love every day of my life."

"Maybe she is watching over you right this moment."

"I hope not. I hope she is reborn somewhere and rediscovering all that life can be."

* * *

Goddard dozed in the soft bucket seat on the passenger side of the Bluebird, until the right front tire dipped into a pothole.

"Sorry, Boss," Mike said, when Goddard sat up and looked around, trying to place where they were.

"We're in Indiana," Mike said, anticipating Goddard's question. The old man stretched and yawned. "It doesn't look much different from Ohio," he said. He watched as the mile marker flashed by, then checked the map to see how far they'd progressed. "We'll be in Gary, soon."

"Yep. Couple of hours."

Goddard folded the map and placed it in the seat pocket. He saw a skein of geese high overhead. The season was changing; after Gary they'd have to head south again. He smiled to think that his life now was not much different from those of the migrant workers he used to hire. He still wasn't used to being on the road, though, not after what seemed like an eternity rooted to the ground in The Orchard. He had to remind himself every day that he and his men were doing good wherever they went.

In one of the oncoming lanes. an old Volvo station wagon approached, trailing a stream of bluish smoke. Mike said, "Looks like they need a ring job." Goddard nodded, although he had no idea what a ring job was. Mike was the mechanic among them. He put on the left turn signal to pass a truck full of manure. The lane change brought them momentarily opposite the Volvo, and as Mike eased back into the right lane, Goddard was startled to see that the driver looked like Alan. The same dark, curly hair; the same light brown skin.

He shook his head, dismissing the vision. He saw Alans everywhere these days.

* * *

Alan and Edie's cross-country trip was as uneventful as any 3,000-mile car ride can be with twin toddlers in the back seat and an engine with 150,000 miles on it under the hood. Edie was relieved to see that Alan had planned a route that angled well away from The Orchard. The only disquieting part of the journey occurred in eastern Indiana, when they saw a private bus in the westbound lanes of I-80 with the words "Church of the Orchard" printed on the side in candy-apple red.

"It couldn't be," Alan said, and Edie agreed that it must be a coincidence, but the sight of the bus made her vaguely uneasy. She wondered about it until Ken distracted her by losing his favorite binkie under the car seats. They had to stop to search for it, or he would have howled all the way through Ohio.

Two days later, when they crossed into New Jersey at last, they took a diapering break at the Delaware Water Gap State Park. Alan bought ice pops, splitting the blue one in half for the boys, and sharing the red one with Edie. The Delaware Water Gap was very different from the mountain passes their old Volvo had struggled through in the Rockies. The long, ancient ridge of Kittatinny Mountain was forested, sloping roundly down to the arched bridge that connected the Jersey side to Pennsylvania. The river here was narrow, fast and shallow. Cloud shadows played across the surface. High above, a yellow glider circled beneath one of the cottony white clouds that dotted the sky. As pretty as it was here, Edie couldn't wait to see sand and waves again.

After each of their sons had chosen his perfect souvenir rock from the riverbank, they resumed their trip and turned southeast toward the Jersey shore. Edie was eager to arrive in Point Pleasant before sundown, so she could show Alan where she had lived as a little girl and introduce him to Maia. To her disappointment, the Paradise Motel was gone. In its place stood a high-rise condominium.

An elderly woman stopped to admire the babies. Edie asked her about the Paradise Motel.

"That old place? It burned down one winter, a couple of years ago," she said. "The Russian lady who owned it moved away, to Brooklyn, I think. She had a brother or some other relative there she went to live with."

"Well, at least the ocean is still here," Edie said, as though she half expected it to have disappeared as well. They walked onto the sand and Edie took off the boys' shoes. They chased sanderlings and made the herring gulls fly off screaming. Alan and Edie strolled hand-in-hand along the jetty that marked the Manasquan Inlet, watching party boats returning with the tide. Edie leaned against Alan's shoulder, relieved to be home at last.

Alan thought he would have a better chance of finding work if they were within easier commuting distance of New York, so the next day they drove up the coast to Sea Bright. They had no trouble finding an off-season, month-to-month rental while Alan looked for a job. There were no openings at Delicious Orchards; the foreman there was sorry but they had already hired for the fall season. The beach shops were closing for the winter, and the few remaining truck farms, like the orchard, already had a full complement of seasonal workers. Their first winter in New Jersey was so bad they seriously considered moving one more time, but Alan didn't think their old station wagon could make another long road trip, especially at that time of year. Road salt had eaten a hole in the muffler, and more smoke spewed from the tailpipe every time Alan started the car. The tires were dangerously slick on streets that were often wet from rain or melting snow. Edie was pregnant, too, so they couldn't risk traveling before the baby was born. She applied for food stamps while Alan took a succession of low-paying janitorial jobs.

True to her word, Lucy traveled East when Edie had their baby girl, Anna. Although Edie was glad to have her help, she could tell that her mother was uncomfortable being away from The Grove. The noise and people of the beach town seemed to make her as skittish as a white-tailed deer. After two weeks, Edie said she would be fine on her own, and sent her mother back to her sanctuary.

185

After Lucy left, Alan took a second job as a dishwasher at a waterfront restaurant in Highlands. Then their luck finally changed. The manager, Sol Dial, liked Alan's good manners, his neat appearance, his promptness even when the weather was bad. He promoted Alan to waiter, and with tips Alan made enough money during the summer season to quit his night job as a janitor. Sol let them refurbish the second-floor apartment over the restaurant during the slow winter season, and now they lived there for nominal rent in exchange for having done all the labor themselves. It was a good thing, too, because by the time the twins were in kindergarten, Edie was pregnant again. After Sheila was born, Sol gave Alan another promotion, this time to manager. He also hired Edie to bake fresh rolls and make desserts.

One Wednesday evening not long after Labor Day, Alan was working on the restaurant's accounts. School had resumed, and the beaches were nearly deserted during the week. Boaters were winterizing their cabin cruisers, and the restaurant trade was slowing into the off-season, when locals could once again get their favorite table by the window. Although the restaurant did the majority of its business in the crowded summer months, Alan much preferred this time of year. He was able to spend more time with his family once the pace slowed down, and that was always a good thing, especially now that Edie had given birth to their third daughter, Irene.

He was tapping out numbers on an electronic calculator when Sol walked into the back room they used as the restaurant office.

Sol was almost as wide as he was tall, and he wasn't very tall. The short walk from his parked Cadillac into the restaurant had left him sweating and breathing hard. He wiped his face with a monogrammed handkerchief.

"I gotta get out of this racket," he said to Alan as his way of saying hello.

"You're always saying that, Sol," Alan said, moving stack of receipts out of the way.

"Yeah, but now my doctor agrees with me, the old quack." He sat down with a grunt, leaned sideways so he could stuff the handkerchief into his pants pocket, and put one elbow on the desk. "You should get one of them new computers, Alan."

"No, Sol, you should get one of them for me."

"I don't understand what people see in the damn things anyway," Sol watched Alan for a moment. "I meant what I said, you know."

"Hmm? About what?"

"About the doc saying I should quit already."

Alan stopped entering numbers and looked up at Sol. They'd known each other now for almost ten years. Sol was not much fatter than he'd been when he first offered Alan a job, but he was a lot balder. He'd recently replaced his bad comb-over with an even worse toupee. His neck was wattled with fat, and his stomach was so pendulous it hid the white patent leather belt he had grown fond of in the 70s and would not stop wearing, no matter how much Edie teased him about it. He wore plaid polyester pants in which the colors fought one another, maroon winning out in some places, pine green in others, and a banana-colored polo shirt that showed damp spots under the arms. His breathing was still labored.

"You're serious, aren't you? What did the doctor say?"

"See, that's what I love about you, kid. I drop a bomb that could maybe affect your future but you ask about my health. I knew you were one of the good guys the minute I laid eyes on you. I told my ex, when she was still speaking to me, that you were a good guy if I ever saw one."

"Sol, what did the doctor say?"

"The old quack says if I don't lose weight, I'll wake up someday dead from a heart attack or worse. He says I should retire all the way and go someplace where I can play golf and get myself back in shape, and to lay off the Lobster Newburg, quit smoking cigars, and stop drinking bourbon. Good thing he didn't say anything about giving up women, too, or I'd just slit my wrists and get it over with. I'm thinking maybe Scottsdale."

187

Alan could feel the pulse in his neck throbbing in time to his thoughts: *Five kids. Five kids to feed. Five kids.* "You're going to sell, I presume?" He congratulated himself on getting the question past his lips in a neutral tone.

Sol nodded and slapped the desktop. "Bingo! I am gonna sell this place. To you!"

"Very funny."

"What?"

"Sure, I can support my family on what I earn here, with Edie's help, but I have five children to put through college now. Every penny we manage to save goes into their college fund. I can't use that money on a down payment for this place, and no bank will give me a mortgage on a commercial property without at least 20% down."

"So what? I'll hold the mortgage. I'll give you a better rate than the bank and you won't have to fork over all those fees and points. You get the restaurant, I'll have a steady monthly income, and in, say, 15 years you'll own it free and clear. And everybody's happy."

"Even you need a down payment."

Sol waved his hand.

"How do you know what I need? We'll work out the little details later. I'll make you an offer you can't refuse, ha, ha." He laughed at his own bad joke until he had to wipe tears from his eyes. Then he put the handkerchief back in his pocket again and sighed. "Alan, in all seriousness, you and Edie and the kids, you're the closest thing to a family I got. Mine are all gone, fifty years ago this year, did you know that?"

Alan shook his head.

"Fifty freakin' years ago. Gassed and thrown in the ovens. Every last one of 'em. I'm the only one that made it. I think about them every time I look at this damn tattoo on my arm." The numbers were faded but still legible.

"I figured there was no point keeping kosher if that's your reward for doing it, and I've been eating Lobster Newburg ever since. Well, since the postwar years, anyway, after I came here and started this place and could afford it. Maybe the doc is right and it's time to go back to plain old gefilte fish." He stood up and reached into the file cabinet for a bottle of bourbon and two shot glasses. He sat heavily, poured the shots, and gave one to Alan.

"Can't let my last bottle of bourbon go to waste. To family," Sol said. They clinked glasses. Sol downed his in a single gulp. Alan took a sip and put the glass back down. The warmth of the bourbon began to relax the tense muscles in his jaw.

"Your kids call me Uncle Solly. I love it when they call me that." He pulled out his billfold and opened it up. "Look here. Your wife gave me a copy of their school pictures last June. Ken, AJ, Anna, Sheila, and this new one of your precious little baby Irene. They're your kids, but I carry their pictures like they're my own. Uncle Solly they call me. Don't you worry from down payments—we're gonna work things out so you can keep taking care of these five beautiful kids, and so my ex doesn't get a red cent." He put the billfold back in his pants pocket and stood up again. "Unless you don't want the place. But you're a good man, Alan. I can't think of anyone else I'd rather see owning it."

Alan stood up, too. He bent over to give the old man a hug and kissed the top of his bad toupee.

"You're the good man in this room, Sol." And they shook on the deal.

* * *

After a few years on the road, a town was a town and a bar was a bar. It didn't much matter what the name was, or the population, or whether it had a two-lane main drag or a U.S. highway running through it. Whether the bar proprietor was a good old boy or second generation Irish/Italian/Jamaican/Puerto Rican. Whether the bar itself was oak or Formica, polished smooth or sticky with spilled whiskey sours. Whether the place was full of booths or tables, with or without billiards. As long as the beer was cold, Jesse and the guys were satisfied.

It had been a fine idea to take the ruined church on the road. They've been making more than enough to cover expenses and, in fact, were squirreling away a percentage of the tithes, in hopes they would maybe even settle down and rebuild someday. Most of the people they met were good at heart and sorely in need of guidance. Goddard's new fire-and-brimstone sermon style was a winner every time, now that they were secure in their niche and knew their audience. It wasn't a bad life at all.

They'd settled into a routine just as they had once done at the orchard: Rafe handling publicity and bookings, sometimes going on ahead for two weeks at a time; Mike doing most of the driving and routine upkeep on the Bluebird; Jesse greeting the churchgoers and taking care of Goddard; Goddard preaching and taking care of the donations; all of them helping to set up the chairs, the folding pulpit, the meeting tent, and afterwards, putting it all back in the storage bins of the Bluebird and the small trailer they now towed behind it.

There were enough orchards around for them to keep a supply of apples on hand, and they were usually pretty good, even if never quite as tasty as the ones they used to grow. In winter they had to resort to the waxed and often mealy-textured supermarket apples, which none of them could stand to eat raw, so Jesse often baked cobbler or made applesauce in the Bluebird's small but efficient galley.

And always, after their day's work was done, the guys went to the local gin mill and spent an hour or two getting mildly buzzed. Generally, Rafe and Mike shot a game or two of nine ball while Jesse kept to himself, chatting a little with the bartender, munching on peanuts, enjoying the crisp tang of a freshly opened bottle of brew. Jesse always drank the first bottle fast, before condensation had a chance to form on the label, but he let the second or third last a long time.

If anything troubled Jesse it was that Goddard rarely joined them at the bar afterwards. Goddard said he wasn't worried about how it would look for a preacher to indulge, he just preferred to stay in the moment of grace and relax with plain apple cider or, at most, a sip of Applejack. He said he liked to work on his sermons when the boys were out, but Jesse wondered how much time he could spend polishing the preaching that didn't change much from burg to burg. He thought the old man still brooded too much for his own good, even though it had been years since his rift with Alan.

He also wondered about the envelopes Goddard received every two weeks no matter what town they were in. They were plain manila 9x12s, with no return address, and Goddard always read the contents in private. Jesse suspected that he burned them afterwards, because there was no room in the Bluebird for Goddard to store them, and stacks of manila envelopes, sometimes thick envelopes at that, would be hard to keep out of sight.

Jesse, who always collected the mail, would never go as far as opening them without Goddard's permission, but he often held them up to the light, or gave them a gentle shake, and felt them to see if there was anything in them but paper. The only clue was the postmark, but aside from their being on or near the Jersey shore, he couldn't imagine what towns like Sea Bright, Long Branch, Rumson, Keyport, Colts Neck, Eatontown, Red Bank, Farmingdale, Neptune, and Port Monmouth possibly had in common.

* * *

The downside of running a popular waterfront restaurant was the difficulty of closing for vacation. With five future college tuitions to accumulate, neither Alan nor Edie could see any sense in closing for two or three weeks during the off season, and Alan was unwilling to trust their investment to anyone else even for a short time. So they fell into the habit of taking separate boy-girl vacations, after school ended but before the hectic July 4th long weekend, Alan and the two boys alternating each year with Edie and the three girls.

Alan liked to take the boys to historic battlefields and forts while camping in state parks. Living on the shore as they did, these trips inland were a treat. Mountains provided relief from muggy heat, and the green of their forests comforted Alan, for whom the everyday seascape was a little bleak. They worked their way south from Fort Ticonderoga down to Fort Sumter. They spent two vacations on the Revolution and two on the Civil War; they caught and cooked trout for breakfast and dinner; they acted out Washington's Crossing in a rented rowboat. The boys had their pictures taken with the costumed Rebel troops who mustered at Harper's Ferry. They spent long hours searching fruitlessly for minié balls at Manassas and Gettysburg. One year they splurged on Williamsburg, buying Edie handmade bayberry candles, adventurously trying peanut soup, country ham and spoonbread.

In the off years, when the boys stayed home to bus tables, they had as much of the Jersey shore to play in as they could reach by bicycle, or in the battered old aluminum johnboat they found one summer. They scavenged local boatyards for a small outboard, did all the repairs themselves, and spent whole days exploring creeks and coves off the Navesink and Shrewsbury Rivers, sometimes solo, sometimes together, sometimes with a buddy of AJ's tagging along. There were marshes and mudflats to investigate, fiddler crabs scuttling along the creek banks, clumps of mussels adhering to rotting piers.

In the spring they might come upon a Canada goose hunkered down on a feather-lined nest. If they went too close, the gander would come charging out of the marsh grasses, hissing and flailing his great wings at them. In the summer, there were cattails to break off so they could light the brown punks and smoke them like cigars. By the time school started, short days and homework limited their free time, but at that point the state park no longer charged admission and the beaches were free, so they hauled the boat for the season and instead took their bikes across the river to Sandy Hook, or down Route 35 to the sea wall.

For the girls, summer vacation meant only one thing: a welcome trip to see their grandmother. They would leave from Newark Airport in the morning and by evening they would be with Nana Lucy and her friends, sipping fresh lemonade under the great Douglas firs of The Grove.

In addition to the fun of visiting Nana Lucy, The Grove offered respite to each girl in her own way. Sheila's favorite place was the goat pen. She loved the way a nanny goat would rub its head against her legs for petting, or nibble at her sleeves when it thought she was ignoring it. If she was lucky, there'd be a late-born kid to play with. Nothing was sillier or more fun to watch than a baby goat hopping around the pen like it was wearing springs on its little hooves. She learned how to feed the goats, to clean their barn, to milk them, and even to help make the chèvre sold to local restaurants.

Irene, the youngest, stayed close to her mother in the kitchen learning to bake bread. Once she was old enough to do more than play with the flour sifter, she developed a natural touch for making sweet breads with dried fruits and honey, hearty amaranth loaves for dinner, and flaky pie crusts. She would take her skills home and help Edie at the restaurant after school.

For Anna, the best part of The Grove was that no one there teased her about the things she liked to do. If she wanted to spend the whole afternoon in a hammock with a book, no one stopped her. Once her gardening chores were done, she could climb trees, or lie face down on the moss-covered log that bridged one of the streams to watch silver-sided minnows swim by. She could catch frogs or butterflies, roll down a grassy slope, pick flowers; in short, she could be a young girl. She didn't have to worry that her hair was not cut the right way, or that her clothes were not fashionable enough, that she was not wearing a bra or makeup yet, that she hadn't kissed a boy, or fondled his you-know-what or let him touch hers.

No one here talked about any of that. No one made her feel stupid, even though she knew she was one of the smartest girls in her class.

Here, all the women, especially her mother's best friend Star, were like favored aunts who welcomed them with hugs and laughter and warmth she couldn't identify as anything else but love. She almost never heard anyone quarrel. Any real conflicts were brought to Nana Lucy and settled amicably over glasses of iced herb tea. The serenity of the compound was infectious; even Anna and her sisters stopped bickering when they were there. As soon as they passed through the hand-carved gate, with its arch shaped like birds' wings, they felt at peace.

How three weeks could pass so quickly when they didn't even do anything, or so it seemed, the girls couldn't understand. They hated leaving The Grove so soon, even though they missed their father and brothers.

The year Anna turned 14, Nana Lucy called to ask if the girls could spend the entire summer with her.

Edie hesitated. "A whole summer? I've never been away from my girls for so long."

"You can stay all summer, too, you know. But your daughters are growing up, and they should know more of our Way. For Anna especially, this is the right time."

Edie told her they would discuss it at dinner. But the girls needed no persuading. They were excited at the first mention of it.

"Mom, a lot of girls go to summer camp every year," said Anna.

"If you spend that much time there, it won't be like summer camp," said Edie. "It won't even be a vacation, because they'll want you to help with all the chores, not just the ones you like."

"I always take care of the goats anyway," Sheila said. "It would be fun to see them grow up over the summer."

"Won't you miss your brothers and your Dear Old Dad?" Alan asked. Ken and AJ rolled their eyes.

"Of course we will, Daddy," said Irene, "but a whole summer with Nana Lucy would be fun."

"More fun than helping in the restaurant?" Alan pretended to be shocked. Irene made a face, and Sheila said, "Oh, Daddy!" with all the scorn that a 12-year-old can pack into those two words.

He shrugged, and punted to Edie. "It's okay with me if it's okay with you."

"Please, Mom?" the girls begged. "Please?"

Of course, the answer was yes. When school ended, the girls were sent on ahead so they would arrive in time for the Summer Solstice. Edie planned to join them for a week at Midsummer. The Grove kept to the ancient way of dividing the year into eight seasons, marked by two solstices, two equinoxes, and the halfway points between them. Edie envied the girls. The ancient calendar had been a central feature of her life from the day she and her mother first arrived there until the day she left. She still acknowledged the eight-fold year with decorations in the restaurant and changes to the dessert menu, but these were faint echoes of the fun she had once shared with the other women, especially Star.

As much as she hated being apart from Alan for even one night, and as much as she missed her sons every time she was away, Edie was eager to join her daughters at the Grove. She remembered her own Coming of Age celebration, that exhilarating, very personal night when she was inside The Sanctuary, and the rest of the women were outside. Now it was Anna's turn to mark the passage from child to woman. She'd already had her period for several months, so it wouldn't be quite the same as celebrating the very first one, but it made Edie feel good to know Anna would still feel the support of the entire community.

A girl's First Night was always held as close to the full moon as possible, Edie explained to Sheila and Irene that morning at breakfast. Anna was fasting for the day, drinking only herb tea and a little fruit juice. She was to spend the day any way she wished as long as she kept apart from the others. "It's a kind of spiritual journey, a coming-of-age celebration of Anna's new womanhood. It's an ancient ritual, they say."

The ritual for Anna was a holiday for everyone, with food prepared the day before, so no work would need to be done, except care of the animals. Sheila showed her mother and sister two alpacas that were recent additions to The Grove's animal husbandry; their soft, light wool would make excellent shawls. Sheila was a little jealous that her sister would be the center of attention all day, even when she wasn't in sight. She didn't understand why Anna would want to be alone for a whole day and night, or how it was possible to go 24 hours without eating, nor did she see why it was such a big deal that Anna had her period. Irene, less moody than her older sister, was enjoying every bit of the festive day. She laughed when she got too close to the brown alpaca, prompting it to spit at her.

195

Anna, for her part, was happily wandering her favorite parts of The Grove. She spent some time lying on the mossy log that still leaned out over the creek. She wandered among the old growth forest, looking for whitewash and pellets to show her where owls were roosting. She lay down for a nap in the afternoon, knowing that she would be expected to stay up much of the night. She didn't rejoin her mother and sister after everyone had eaten dinner.

They were waiting for the sunset.

When it was time, Anna bathed and put on a long, red silk dress. She slipped on sandals and came out of the house to see everyone else waiting. Lucy handed a garland of flowers to Edie, who placed it on Anna's head without saying a word, though she smiled and kissed Anna on the forehead. No one would speak to Anna for the rest of the night; this was her time to think, to meditate, to experience whatever Mystery might come.

With Lucy in the lead, followed by Anna, then Edie with Sheila and Irene, the women of The Grove walked to The Sanctuary where Anna would spend the night, just as her mother had done many years before. The Sanctuary had a central fire pit, where Anna would light a small fire and tend it. That was her only task. She would experience whatever she was destined to. Maybe nothing at all would happen; maybe she would spend the whole night dozing. There were no rules, except to tend the fire. The experience was hers to define, hers to know, hers to keep.

As they walked, the musically inclined women, Lucy among them, played softly on guitar, tambourine, small drums, flutes. At the entrance to The Sanctuary, they fanned out to encircle the small building. Lucy kissed her granddaughter one more time, cradling Anna's face in her hands. Anna knelt to crawl inside the short tunnel. The rest of the women arranged themselves in couples or small groups, with Lucy in front of the entrance, Edie and the girls directly opposite, behind the structure. Everyone watched the roof. When a wisp of smoke appeared, almost exactly on time with the sunset, the music stopped.

"What happens now?" whispered Sheila.

"We lie down and watch the stars come out," Edie said. "And then we go to sleep."

"That's it?"

"For us. It's as close as we get to sharing Anna's night."

"What if I have to go to the bathroom?" Irene asked.

"For tonight, you get to go in the woods, like a raccoon."

Irene and Sheila giggled, and settled down to look at the stars, but the rising moon soon lit up the night, making all but the brightest stars fade away. The trees cast long shadows, and deep in the woods, a spotted owl called. The girls and Edie slept, but Lucy stayed awake. Around the protective circle, the women lay down and slept or made love. Lucy smiled as she kept vigil, alert, enjoying her role as Guardian, listening to the sounds of love fade like the stars as the moon slowly arced overhead.

Inside The Sanctuary, Anna congratulated herself on lighting the fire with only one match. She looked around as the firelight played against the walls, first highlighting and then throwing into shadow what looked like ancient pictures of stylized birds and frogs, people's hands, geometric shapes like ovals and triangles, and swirls like tumbling water. It was surprisingly comfortable in here. She had expected it to be spidery and scary, like a cave, but The Sanctuary was well-kept, with a clean stone floor and lots of comfortable red cushions for her sit on. Whoever had built it placed the entrance facing east, and they had designed it somehow so that the smoke from the fire rose straight up. There was a pitcher of cool water and a ceramic mug so she needn't go thirsty, and an old-fashioned chamber pot just in case.

Her stomach had stopped growling hours ago, so she wasn't hungry anymore, although she was the tiniest bit lightheaded. Strangely, she wasn't the least bit sleepy. She thought she should be doing something, but Nana Lucy had made it clear that there were no rules, except to keep the fire going and the suggestion that she stay awake. It was up to her whether she chose to simply lie down and go to sleep, or sit and twiddle her thumbs the whole night long.

Or "explore her body" as Nana Lucy had so quaintly put it. As if she hadn't already done that. As if half the girls in her class hadn't already gone all the way. Sex was no big deal anymore, and if they'd had TV in The Grove they would have known that, although she guessed it was no big deal here, either, since it was common enough to see two women go off together arm in arm and not come back for a while. Maybe this ceremony had meant more to young women in her mother's era than it would to her tonight.

Funny that she and her sisters were the youngest ones here. According to their mother, sometimes a young woman would leave The Grove for a while and come back with a girl child, but that hadn't happened in a while, apparently. Nana Lucy often talked about Star as though she was a young girl, but Star was even older than their mother. How long would The Grove last if no one new came along?

She put another branch on the fire and watched the flames catch on the dry bark. They flickered along the branch like the glowing scales of a snake. As Anna watched the snake, it grew brighter, and longer, and lifted out of the fire pit, swirling around her, spinning itself longer and longer until it encircled the room. She put her arms out and touched it, but was unhurt by the dancing flames. They were like stage fire, the kind that couldn't burn you. And then she understood that she was having an honest-to-gosh vision. She heard chanting, too, lots of women's voices chanting, as the red spiral tightened into a pillar shooting up through the smoke hole. She knew it couldn't be real, but she couldn't help reaching toward it, wanting to feel that energy course through her. Just as her hands touched it there was a sound like thunder, and a flash like lightning, followed by red rain, which faded into the blood red light of dawn.

* * *

Goddard's men were weary. He saw it in the circles under their eyes, he saw it in the stoop of their shoulders, in the slow way they hauled themselves up the steps of the Bluebird. When they had started on their peripatetic rounds they had stepped on board with energy. Now their reluctance was apparent to Goddard, even though his loyal team would never say a word to him.

Goddard was weary, too. He thought that by now he knew every two-lane road in the country by heart. Blue highways, they were called, and though he knew this referred to a color on a map, the sameness of these roads could make any man feel blue. Even the Bluebird was having a case of the blues. The motor coach was getting shabby, with scratched cabinets and worn patches on the furniture. They'd had to replace the transmission twice, the engine once, the brakes more times than he could count, and who knew tires could be such an expense?

Still, Goddard had put aside a pleasing amount of money. They'd lived frugally for long enough, he thought, and that may be part of the ennui that he observed in everyone, including himself. When the passing mile markers put him in a near trance, he found himself daydreaming about solidity: wall studs, lath and plaster walls, slate shingles on a roof.

A bump in the road jostled him out of his reverie. He started to ask Mike the usual question—*where are we?*—but he remembered crossing into Tennessee from Bristol, Virginia, miles and hours ago. No matter where they went, they always seemed to end up crossing Tennessee. Whether they ventured up into the old coal-mining towns of Pennsylvania or the towns that clung to old steel mills in Ohio, or homes strung along weed-filled roads where fabric mills used to be in Alabama, they ended up here in Tennessee. And if they'd been preaching to sorghum farmers in Missouri or cotton farmers in Arkansas, they passed through Tennessee on their way back to the Appalachian villages tucked into "hollers" and along river valleys.

Tennessee, apparently, was in the middle of Goddard's flocks. And what a pretty state it was, especially in these rolling hills west of the mountains but east of the Mississippi's flood plain. It reminded him a little of the verdant countryside around The Orchard, where he once had a home and a church on a hilltop. He remembered the sound of the church doors clapping shut, the heft of the big old iron key in his hands, how steady the floor felt beneath his feet. He could almost smell the floor wax on the wide pine boards, and felt a wave of homesickness wash over him that he hadn't experienced since they first boarded the Bluebird.

Suddenly he sat up. "Pull over, Mike."

"What's wrong?" Mike braked and looked for a wide patch of shoulder to stop in.

"Nothing, just stop. Up there. Up there a little ways."

The Bluebird halted with a huffing of its pneumatic brakes, and Mike opened the door. Goddard went down the steps; the rest of them followed.

"What's up, Boss?" Jesse asked. He'd been sleeping, and he rubbed his eyes, squinting in the noon sunlight.

Goddard was staring at several acres of overgrown pastureland. The fields were in a shallow bowl of land, which rose on the other side to a low ridge, where a run-down rancher and a decrepit barn sat at the top of the rise. Even from here, Jesse could see daylight between the boards of the barn. The rail fence was once white but now showed more bare wood than paint. There were big gaps in the fence line where rails had come loose at one end and lay diagonally with one end on the ground, or had broken off altogether.

"Well, there sure haven't been any horses or cows around here in a long time," said Rafe. He, like Mike and Jesse, wondered what the old man saw in this abandoned wreck of a farm.

What Goddard saw was a For Sale sign.

* * *

Edie didn't like the new name of the restaurant.

"It's been Dial's Restaurant for years, Alan," she said.

"It's a waterfront place. It needs a nautical name."

They stood together, watching the workmen put up the new sign.

"We have the nautical atmosphere," he said. "We use fishnet curtains, and we have shells in the base of the table lamps. We have fish and shrimp and fried clams on the menu. The name needs to reflect that."

"I know all that, but couldn't you have called it 'Dial's Seafood Restaurant' or something? I hate to think we're losing Sol's name."

"Not catchy enough. We have to compete with every other seafood place between Keyport and Asbury Park. Besides, 'Tide Tables' fits better on a sign. Sol would like the joke."

Edie knew she would never get used to serving fish and meat at their restaurant. She'd been trying for years to convert her family to a vegetarian lifestyle, but she'd succeeded only with her eldest daughter. Alan had reverted to eating meat years ago out of practicality, when his dinner was one of the perks of working at the restaurant, so he had no qualms about cooking it, either. Sheila wouldn't touch tofu, which she called "solidified snot," and Irene had to copy her big sister's taste. The boys, who were growing so fast she could hardly keep them in blue jeans that fit, were confirmed carnivores.

Food was just another of the compromises of family life, she supposed, that made marriage such a complicated arrangement sometimes. It made her sad to know how many of her children's school friends came from broken homes. Because she came from one herself, and because Alan was orphaned, and because they didn't know where their children's grandfather was, or whether he would ever accept them, they had made their nuclear family the central truth and delight of their lives. Maybe that was why she and Alan loved each other even more than when they had first met.

Her husband was still as handsome as he had been in their apple blossom days. He was a bit too thin then, but he had filled out in the past few years, just enough to feel snuggly over a core of firm muscle. She had been captured by the depths in his eyes from the very first day. They were like dark chocolate, rich and sweet, and she had melted like chocolate at the sight of them. How hard it had been to go to bed every night back then, knowing he was just down the hall. How hurt she had been when he all but stopped speaking to her, until some instinct told her why, and then she knew it was just a matter of the right time, the right day, before they would surrender to one another and become one.

Her body still responded to those memories. Every time she saw how he looked and felt when he was aroused, she literally ached with needing him. He could never get inside her deeply enough. She wanted their bodies to meld into one being, no more he, no more she, just that blessed, fleeting moment of unity. She tried, each time, to hold onto the oneness, but it was like trying to keep a wave from washing back with the tide.

She felt it now, the delicious hunger for him, right here on the street at 10:30 on a Tuesday morning. She placed her hand softly on the small of his back.

"It looks as though the sign men have this job under control," she said. "You don't need to supervise every second of the process, do you?"

Alan didn't take his eyes off the men. "I suppose not," he said in a distracted voice. "Do you need me for something?"

Edie slid her fingers inside his belt. "Need is exactly the right word."

He shook his head, smiling, and turned to her. "Your timing is a little odd, my love, but I think we can leave them alone for a while."

He looked up at the two men, who were adjusting the sign's position with a level.

"Looks great, guys. I'll come back outside when you're done."

One of the men nodded. "No problem."

Edie and Alan went inside. He led her into the back office, since the ladders were right in front of their bedroom windows.

When she locked the door behind her, he grinned and asked, "Carpet, chair or desk?"

She leaned against the wall and pulled him closer, yanking his shirt out of his jeans as he bent to kiss her. She loved the way he responded to her. She loved feeling tenderness flow seamlessly into passion; she loved knowing they connected at this fundamental, animal level, not just as two bodies; they became one mind, one heart, one soul, every single aspect of them melding together in an act whose absolute rightness filled them with joy. They came together like cymbals crashing.

Afterwards they clung to each other, Edie still pressed against the wall, her arms and legs wrapped around Alan. She loved his breathlessness and his beating heart, loved how clenching her muscles made him shudder and groan, how easily she could make him hard again. She even loved how comical they must look as they slid down to the floor trying not to separate, loved how his need matched hers, how there were no words for this desire, just lips, tongues, limbs, hips, and love.

It never occurred to either Edie or Alan that having parents who were crazy in love with each other might be a bit tough on their kids. The twins were already suffering through high school traumas of confidence. At least, Ken was. AJ, with his abundant natural talents—including good looks, superb eye-hand coordination, and an innate sense of leadership—played shortstop on the varsity baseball team and was running for senior class president. He had his father's warm brown eyes and his mother's wavy, abundant hair. Teachers loved him for his sweet manners as much as his good looks, even though his grades were just average.

Ken was older than his fraternal twin by half an hour, but somehow AJ acted like the big brother. In junior high this had been a clear advantage, so Ken sheltered in his brother's aura, but when they entered the large regional high school, the differences between them became downright awkward, at least in Ken's eyes. He didn't realize how much of his father's handsomeness he had also inherited. But he had absolutely no talent for team sports. As president of the chess club, he would have been branded a geek if it were not for his brother, whose popularity protected Ken from the worst of the teasing.

AJ loved his brother unconditionally and was as unaware of his effect on him as people were of second-hand smoke. He knew Ken was moody, but AJ so easily sloughed off adversity that he could not conceive of how jealous his brother might sometimes feel.

AJ's natural lack of imagination was insufficient, however, on nights when he and Ken would lie in bed knowing their parents were having sex in the next room. Not that their parents made the walls shake, but the boys were old enough to read the looks their parents gave each other after dinner. They were pretty sure their sisters were still young enough to be oblivious, and at any rate their room was down the hall, so they missed the occasional muffled shout after everyone was in bed, and the more frequent laughter. For the brothers, however, neither situation was easy to bear when certain body parts were becoming more assertive every day.

Their mother changed their sheets almost daily without saying a word, except to think to herself how fast they were growing up. Their father had assured them that wet dreams were perfectly normal, but they weren't just having dreams anymore. The mere thought of anyone having sex—even one's parents, an image not to be dwelt on by any means—was enough to make a teenage boy's penis leap erect like a jaunty little jack-in-the-box. To overhear them actually doing it, while lying in the dark on a school night when one couldn't help thinking of a particular cheerleader, in AJ's case, or Miss February, in Ken's, caused a throbbing so embarrassing there was only one way to take care of it.

Secretly, Ken thought his parents were pretty cool, at least about sex, considering his friend's parents, like the divorced ones who used their kids as weapons to get back at the former spouse, and the ones who stayed married but who fought so much they should have divorced, the few who were violent, the majority who were boring at best and at worst so old and uptight they criticized their children's hair, clothes, music, eating habits, television watching, skateboarding, language, attitude, and personal hygiene. Not to mention the clueless teachers who were always passing out pamphlets about abstinence while the school nurse kept a supply of condoms on her desk. Ken couldn't deny that his parents loved each other and their kids. That his mom and dad were still horny at their age was a minor trial to bear, all things considered.

His parents had other annoying quirks, though, like his mother's meatless Mondays, and his father's inability to cope with computers. Ken often wished his father weren't such a technophobe. They could have put terminals in the restaurant a long time ago, and simplified not

204

just ordering but inventory, too. Ken had to set up their old IBM PC just so his father could do basic bookkeeping. Ken, in fact, used the computer more than his father, or anyone else in the family, and was the only one interested in exploring its potential.

He often thought about that potential after school, while sitting on his favorite bench outside the Twin Lights Museum. It was a killer bike ride up the hill, but worth it for the view over Sandy Hook to Long Island. He liked to catch his breath there while standing on the concrete pad where Marconi had sent his wireless radio messages into the air over the Atlantic long ago, back when the Twin Lights were still working lighthouses and many of the ships entering New York Harbor still had sails.

He came up here often, sneaking onto the grounds when the museum was closed, to think about ways to upgrade the computer without freaking out his dad. He was wondering whether there was a way for him to make money with hypertext when his brother biked up, scarcely out of breath at all.

"Hey, big brother," AJ said, leaning his bike against the bench.

"Hey, little brother." They enjoyed making fun of the half-hour difference in their ages.

AJ sat down and looked at the water, where the container ships waiting to enter New York Harbor looked like matchbox toys. "Mom sent me to find you. It's almost dinnertime."

"What are we having?"

"Kasha, I think. Or maybe vegetable chili. One of our usual Monday meals. Here. I stopped at Mickey D's."

He pulled a cheeseburger out of his jacket pocket.

"Thanks, man." Ken devoured the burger in three bites, crumpled up the wrapper, and shoved it in the pocket of his jeans.

"I've got something else." AJ held out an envelope with the Rutgers University logo in the return address.

Ken didn't take it right away. "Did you get yours, too?"

"Uh-huh."

"And?"

"I got the baseball scholarship."

"That's great, man! Congratulations." They high-fived.

"Yeah, well, it makes things easier on mom and dad."

Ken nodded. "Sure does, but still. Way to go."

"Thanks." AJ watched his brother rotate the envelope counter-clockwise in his hands. "Are you going to open it?"

Ken sighed. "I guess." He slowly slid his thumb beneath the flap.

"You're going to get in, with your grades. Don't be worried about that."

"Everyone says that, but they don't take so many in-state kids. They make a lot more money on out-of-state kids. And two from the same family..."

"First of all, it's a university, not a company, so it's not like nepotism or anything. And second of all, would it bother you?"

"What?"

"Me and you going to the same college."

Ken shook his head and pulled the letter out. "No, why should it bother me?" He unfolded the letter, read it, and nodded. "Yeah, I'm in. I get to skip freshman algebra."

They high-fived again. "Nice going, big brother. Which campus?"

"Main campus."

"Me, too."

AJ blew on his hands as a gust of wind kicked up. Dried leaves and candy wrappers skittered past their feet. "So what do you do up here all the time?" he asked.

Ken shrugged. "It's a good place to think."

"About what?"

He shrugged again. "Anything. Nothing. Doesn't matter. I like the view." Off in the distance, a cruise ship was heading toward the Hudson River. Closer in, the beach of Sandy Hook curved off to the north. Lights came on along the bridge that spanned the Navesink River. They could just make out the roof of their father's restaurant almost directly below.

"The view's better from Scenic Drive," AJ said. "At least there you can see the City."

"I thought you only went there to make out with Jennifer."

AJ grinned. "Yeah, I like her twin towers better than New York's."

"You taking her to the prom?"

"I guess so. You asked anyone yet?"

"Who'd go with me?"

"I'll bet a lot of girls would, if you ever got off your butt and asked them."

"Easy for you to say."

"It's easy enough to do if you'd stop talking about computers long enough."

Ken stood up. "We'd better get going."

"Don't get mad. I'd just hate going if I knew you were home having a crummy night."

"Don't worry about me, little brother. If I go, I go and if I don't, I don't. But I don't feel like talking about it. Come on. Our tofu-sprout-whosis casserole must be getting cold."

Ken ended up skipping the prom, of course. Asking a living 17-year-old girl to the senior prom was entirely different from imagining a fantasy date with Miss Anymonth, and he just plain lacked the chops to do it. That was the only real difference between what Ken saw as his own meager abilities and those of his gifted brother. Maybe before they were born, they swapped self-confidence back and forth between them like a beach ball, and the day of their birth he had passed it all back to his brother just before they were squeezed into the world.

AJ had seemed secure in his own mind and body for as long as Ken could remember. When they were climbing the monkey bars in the kindergarten playground, it was as though the bars shrank to fit AJ's small hands and shifted to place themselves under his feet. The first time AJ held a baseball glove, it was as though he were a magnet and the ball made of iron. It would nestle into his glove with the solid thump of the perfect catch. He knew the trajectory of every ball he threw, and when he held a bat, his hands seemed made of the same, fine-grained ash. His swing was fluid and powerful, not only because he practiced for hours, but precisely because he expected it to be fluid and powerful. Whatever he attempted—the lead in the senior class production of *Long Day's Journey into Night*, the electric slide, a double play—if it involved his body, AJ did it with ease. That made him the darling of every coach and gym teacher he and his brother ever had. Leading the baseball team to a state championship was all it took for D's and F's to be converted to C's or C plusses in algebra, biology, French, history, even English.

Ken, who worked hard for his straight A's, could sometimes barely stifle his frustration at having a brother who could do no wrong.

So, Ken stayed home on prom night while AJ was crowned king and afterwards had sex with Jennifer in the back seat of their father's car, parked on the side of Scenic Drive with the lights of Manhattan shimmering on the horizon. AJ breezed through the last weeks of senior year with the baseball scholarship in his pocket. Depending on when the minor league scouts came to visit, AJ had no doubt whatsoever that within a few years he'd be wearing Yankee pinstripes.

Ken, too, had little doubt about his future success, although he knew it rested more on bits and bytes than anything else. That is, it would, if he could earn enough over the summer, working the frozen custard stand on his days off from the restaurant, to finance a used car for commuting back and forth to Rutgers.

Edie smiled as one of their regular customers walked in the door.

"How are you tonight, Mr. G?"

"Mezza-mezz," he said, kissing her on the hand. "You look like a buttercup in that fetching dress."

"Thank you, Mr. G. Yellow has always been my favorite color."

She led him to the corner table by the window, handed him a menu, as if he still needed one after all these years, and said, "I'll make sure your beer comes pronto." She nodded her head at Anna, who came over to the table with pad and pen in hand.

"What can I get you tonight, Mr. G?"

The customer pretended to study the menu, then he laughed and said, "The usual."

Anna nodded and wrote "half rack, half chick, bb, slaw."

She reached for the menu but he took her hand in his.

"You are becoming a beautiful young lady," he said. "With those eyes I'll bet the boys are falling all over themselves for you."

Anna smiled a neutral waitress's smile and forced herself not to roll her eyes, because she'd heard it all before from a dozen other customers just like him, and she wanted a good tip. She pulled her hand away, went in back to place the order, and then went into the rest room to wash her hands. She didn't like Mr. G. nearly as much as her mother did. For some reason her mother didn't realize he was just a dirty old man with creepy, staring eyes who wore a cheesy bucket hat in the summer and an old-fashioned fedora over his eyes in the winter.

Meanwhile, Edie placed a frosted mug on the table in front Mr. G. and set a cold lager next to it.

She turned to go, but he put his hand on her arm.

"Would you do me a favor?" he asked, pulling two envelopes from his jacket pocket. "Please give these to the boys, with my congratulations on their commencement."

Edie looked down at the long, narrow envelopes. She had a feeling they held more than graduation cards.

"Mr. G., you shouldn't have!"

"Why not? Yours are the nicest boys I know. Whenever I see them on the sea wall, they always say hello, very politely, and talk to an old man for a few minutes. Allow me to honor their achievement with a small gift. Please. It would make me very happy." He placed the envelopes in her hand.

She shook her head, but she patted his hand and said, "You are very sweet, Mr. G. Thank you. And I'll make sure they each write you a nice thank you letter."

Gabe smiled. Goddard was going to love getting those letters.

209

AJ's trajectory at Rutgers was everything he'd expected it would be, mediocre grades counteracted by stellar performance on the ball field. At the end of their junior year, AJ was elected captain of the baseball team. His reputation was growing, and the following spring, minor league scouts were in the bleachers to look him over. They would have done so even sooner, but AJ's coach had told them his star pitcher had promised his parents that he would stay in college until he graduated.

"You never know, son," Alan used to say. "You could blow out a knee or shoulder in your rookie year, and then what would you do? Get the degree first, then turn pro. Because you just never know."

Nor can you know how much another child might blossom once he got into college. Ken had become the star of the Comp Sci department and was thinking seriously about graduate school. He was sufficiently insulated by the size of the school population from his brother and his baseball buddies. AJ was a resident, too, thanks to his scholarship, while Ken commuted every day, which also kept them in different social circles.

What really surprised everyone, especially Ken, was not just that he joined the university bicycle club in the spring of their freshman year, but also that he had developed a real talent for biking from years of almost daily trips uphill to the Twin Lights. In the spring of his freshman year, he completed the Bike-Down-the-Shore race, speeding downstate from High Point to finish on the beach at Cape May over one long weekend, and two years later he finished in the top twenty.

"Come on," he coaxed his brother during spring break their senior year. "Ride with me this time. Your playoffs will be over by the race, and we'll have nothing to do until commencement. It'll be fun. It'll help you get in shape for the Yankees."

"It's not the Yankees yet, it's their farm team," AJ said. "They'll be pretty pissed off if I fall and break my throwing arm."

"We don't have to go all out and race," said Ken. "I can win it anytime, if I want. I can do that next year. But by then, you'll be a famous ballplayer, and they won't give you time off in the middle of the season. Let's do the ride together, this once, just for fun. We can stay in the touring pack behind the racers and enjoy the scenery. It will probably be the last thing we do together before graduation. I'll even let you use my new bike. Mom and Dad and everyone can meet us at the finish line. What do you say?"

In the end, AJ said yes, as Ken knew he would. His brother was too sentimental not to. Even though they weren't planning to race, they still had to train to build up AJ's leg muscles for the pace and the hills. AJ had a game or practice almost every afternoon, so Ken got in the habit of rising before dawn to pick his brother up at sunrise. They trained at the Piscataway campus, riding past the stadium and golf course, or on the main campus, down Hamilton Street into the farmland of Somerset County. Every ten days or so, they drove north to Bedminster, and unloaded the bikes for some uphill and downhill work. By the time of the event itself, AJ was good enough to challenge Ken in a sprint.

Their mother and sisters drove up to High Point for the start of the race, and would follow the route of the contest while their father minded the restaurant, planning to meet them at the finish line. They were joined by Barbara, the latest love of AJ's life. She was the prettiest and blondest in a long series of pretty blonde or brunette cheerleaders and prom queens that AJ had dated since junior high. Ken knew that Edie tolerated her only because she knew it was just an infatuation, at least from AJ's point of view. No one, not even someone as pretty as Barbara, was going to distract him from achieving his baseball dreams. Ken also knew that Edie was worried that AJ might hurt himself in this race, but he reassured her that it was basically just cross-training and no more than a tiny detour on the critical path that would lead AJ, in twenty-five years or so, straight to Cooperstown.

They met up in the crowd at the start of the race, jostling among the well-wishers and cyclists at the top of the Garden State. The day could not have been better for racing, with temperatures barely into the sixties. Edie shivered a little as a cool breeze flipped all the leaves upside down, but Ken turned his face into the wind and smiled. A year ago the weather had been sultry, causing some of the racers to collapse with heat exhaustion. Today the breeze would be at their backs for much of the day's route.

The brothers didn't leave as soon as the starter's pistol went off. Since they were touring, not racing seriously, they stayed well behind in the pack, letting the gung-ho competitors cycle ahead. Ken grinned as they went, thinking that one more year of training would have him in peak condition to win. Then he focused on the pavement beneath his wheels. This first leg had the steepest uphill climbs and the fastest downhill runs. It was the shortest one of the race, and the most grueling, but the most exhilarating, except for the final sprint to the finish at Sunset Beach.

They ended the day in Clinton, in the back third of the remaining contestants, having run a clean leg. That evening they took turns massaging each other's calf muscles before Barbara knocked on the door of their motel room. By prearrangement, Ken spent the next hour in the coffee shop, where the decaf was mediocre and the blueberry pie was gummy. Ken picked out as many of the fruits as he could recognize and then made abstract designs in the purple goo with his fork. He nursed his lukewarm Sanka while watching an infomercial about a face cream for only $19.95 that was absolutely positively guaranteed to make you look like you'd spent a fortune at a spa.

"But wait," the announcer said. "There's more."

There was always more, Ken thought, and he was sure his brother wanted more time, but they had a lot of miles to cover the next day and they both needed sleep. He left a dollar on the counter and walked back to their door, knocking quietly, although he wanted to barge right in and hit the sack.

A moment later the door opened just enough to let Barbara slip out. She was completely if hastily dressed in athletic pants and a T-shirt, with sandals in her hand.

"Thanks, Kenny," she whispered. She stretched up on tiptoe to kiss his cheek, then jogged barefoot to her room.

AJ was already asleep, curled around a pillow with his butt hanging out of the covers. Ken pulled the blanket over him, and AJ settled into its warmth with a small grunt. Ken went over to his own bed, kicked off his shoes, tossed his jeans in a pile on the floor, and got under the covers. He closed his eyes. He was exhausted but wide awake.

He could still feel the precise spot on his cheek where Barbara had planted her dry little kiss. She had smelled sweet, like the cheap motel soap, and musky with sex. The whole room smelled of sex. It wafted over from the next bed like his brother's snoring.

It reminded Ken so much of the nights when they were kids and his parents made love, and sometimes babies, in the room next to theirs, that he had a kind of flashback erection. Only this time, he was not imagining some anonymous airbrushed playmate. He pictured how the light over the door had cast shadows emphasizing the curve of Barbara's braless breasts, how her nipples, erect under the T-shirt, had just brushed his sleeve when she leaned up and in to give him the sisterly kiss. Like a hormone-befuddled teenager, he grabbed himself under the covers while his imagination turned that innocent kiss open-mouthed, tongue-filled, and wet.

The next morning, Ken was thankful that the coffee shop lacked a table big enough to hold everyone. He ate breakfast with his mother and sisters, while AJ and Barbara were seated on the other side of the crowded restaurant. Barbara, of course, had scarcely noticed him. Her casual "Morning," aimed in their general direction, included his mother and the girls and probably everyone else in front of the "Please Wait to Be Seated" sign. She was wearing a Rutgers sweatshirt that almost completely obscured her figure, and in the harsh fluorescent light he could see bumps on her face imperfectly covered by flesh-colored acne cream. None of it made any difference.

Ken tried hard to keep all his attention on a tall stack of pancakes with a double side of bacon. He ignored the breakfast conversation as his sisters compared the physical charms of various racers; they were so self-absorbed he wasn't sure they knew he was even at the same table.

For her part, Edie was used to both her son's morning moods and her daughters' preoccupations, so she calmly ate oatmeal and only once in a while looked over toward AJ and Barbara with an expression both wary and resigned.

At the start of that day's leg, Ken tried to forget Barbara and focus on the task at hand, as he did when he was racing. At the sound of the starter's pistol he shot off at a fast pace, leaving his brother off guard and far behind within moments. Ken pumped his legs so hard it took AJ a few miles to get caught up. He pulled alongside his brother, pedaling hard to keep up with him.

"I thought we weren't racing?" he asked.

"We're not," said Ken.

"Well, then, can we cool it a little? At this pace I'll never make it to Asbury Park."

For a long time afterwards, Ken would feel guilty knowing that "I'll never make it to Asbury Park" were his brother's last words. Irony piled on irony that awful day, since they had already coasted through the most dangerous leg of the race the day before. In contrast, these gentle central Jersey hills were supposed to be no big deal. A final irony was the guardrail, placed alongside almost every county road in this litigation-crazed state specifically to keep you from going over the embankment, which turned out to be the very agent that launched his brother over the edge.

How it happened he was never quite sure. After he slowed down for AJ, the race leaders pulled away from them, but because AJ had sprinted to catch up, the rest of the pack was out of sight behind them. Briefly, the brothers were abreast and alone on a downhill stretch. They were accelerating through a curve when a small bird flew across the road in front of them—a sparrow, maybe, or a robin; they were going too fast to tell. Out of the corner of his eye Ken saw some huge bird, a hawk or eagle, coming straight for him, so he raised his arm to protect his face from the outstretched talons. Doing so put him off balance, and he leaned too far to the side. Whether his own front wheel caught AJ's, or whether the hawk itself smacked into them, he would never be sure. Stunned by the impact, he lay face down on the ground with bloody knees and elbows and a gash across his forehead where his helmet had hit the pavement and cracked.

The rest of the riders came around the bend and saw Ken lying in their path. They swerved and slid into one another, some riders swearing, others shouting. Some avoided the pileup, but many more ended up in the tangle. Ken tried to stand up but his leg muscles shook with adrenaline. He took his helmet off and wiped road grit off his stinging forehead, leaving a blotch of blood on his riding glove. He was so dazed it took a few minutes for him to realize that some of the riders who'd been caught in the mess were pointing at something over the embankment and waving the chase vans to pull over.

He got up stiffly and limped over to see what the paramedics were running toward. At first all he saw was his good bike, the new racing bike he'd worked all summer to earn the money for, lying twisted in the crotch of a tree, one wheel missing, the frame bent but maybe repairable, although it would never be a top racing bike again. Then he saw what looked like two leafless branches holding his bike at that crazy angle. He blinked away a bead of sweat, and the bare limbs resolved into his brother, upside down, legs broken around the bicycle frame, his head lying against the trunk at an even crazier angle than the bike.

None of the other riders had seen a small bird being chased by a hawk. No one had seen Ken collide with AJ. His story was weird but plausible, said the state trooper who questioned him about it; stranger things had been known to happen. There were no witnesses and there was no evidence of bad blood between the brothers, so the officer submitted a standard report about a freak accident. The local tabloids, which interviewed their classmates and other racers and even Barbara to try to turn it into a juicy love triangle murder, had to give up on their banner headlines and buried the accident story in the local news column on page 6.

*　*　*

When word got to Lucy, she was helping Star splint the broken leg of a spotted towhee. She waited until Star had put the injured bird safely in a small cage before collapsing to the floor in tears.

* * *

Goddard opened the manila envelope with no expectations. The first thing he read was the obituary from the *Asbury Park Press*. Aside from the clenching of his jaw, he didn't react. He made a quick phone call, instructing Gabe to send flowers. He went back to dicing apples.

* * *

The next day, the first racer to cross the finish line at Sunset Beach dedicated his victory to AJ's memory. Both Rutgers and the Yankees sent large flower arrangements to the funeral. There was an empty seat at commencement that year. The Yankee scouts called up the next young star on their list. A sympathetic upswing in customers at the restaurant lasted most of the summer. The public vacuum left by AJ's passing filled in as smoothly as grains of wet sand fill a footprint when a wave recedes. The private vacuum left in AJ's family expanded like a chasm.

* * *

Grief is a solitary endeavor. Two people can be in each other's arms, sobbing in exactly the same way, but grief lies between them, an unseen and unwelcome guest, stealing away all appetites, aging the body. Those who mourn stand up with effort, lean against one another, walk slowly toward the casket, as though their joints are arthritic.

Grief blurs the vision. Eyes might as well have milky cataracts, because they cannot accommodate the sight of the beloved "in repose," as the funeral director calls it.

Grief numbs the hands. They reach out but cannot feel a son. They smooth the lapel of the gabardine suit, adjust the collar of the cotton shirt, straighten the knot of the silk tie. They brush living fingers tenderly across what look like folded hands, but the digits are rock-hard facsimiles and cold, their scratches and cuts filled in with modeling compound, broken bones realigned, bruises covered by foundation.

216

Someone has tucked a fielder's glove between the gabardine suit and the white silk lining of the casket.

Grief robs all the senses. People speak, but in what language? What words can comfort? What words can share? *Here is a cup of tea.* The tea gets cold.

Family become strangers. You are surprised to see them when they walk in the living room where you are sitting, pretending to read the *National Geographic.* Aren't they supposed to be somewhere, you wonder? But people who grieve have no place to go. Not school, where they make other students uncomfortable. Not work, where no one lets them do anything. Not to the grocery store, because they will leave with a list of ordinary needs—milk, bread, bar soap—and come home empty handed, because once among those brightly lit aisles, faced with four shelves of soap with aloe, soap with oatmeal, soap with lotion, soap with antibacterial properties, soap in two sizes, soap in many colors, and they can't remember whether spring rain smells better than mountain fresh, and there are so many people, which isn't too bad at first because everyone leaves them alone, but then here comes the neighbor, who wants to say yet again how sorry she is, who wants them to talk about it, because they need to let it all out one of these days and if they do so here in the soap aisle it will make the neighbor feel so much better, but there is no way the laws of physics will let the floor tiles open up so the grieving can tunnel out of sight, and so they endure it as long as they can before finally escaping for home, shattered and soapless.

How long does grief go on like that? How long can it go on like that? A month, a summer, a lifetime?

* * *

After a while they had enough practice at pretending to be all right to function in public again.

"And how are you folks, tonight?" Edie asked as though she cared. "Party of four? Follow me, please."

"I need to increase my order of shrimp for next week," Alan told his supplier as though he was glad business was so good.

"I'm going for a drive," Ken said, now that he'd donated his bike to Goodwill, along with his helmet, gloves, and water bottle.

"I wish I had more time until school starts," Anna said, although she knew this statement was an outright lie. She couldn't wait until school started, because she could take only so much sadness before she exploded, and she'd been simmering in sorrow all summer.

"I'm going to miss you," Sheila said, because she was supposed to say that when her sister talked about going to college, but for her, too, this had been a long dreary humid summer and she just wanted life to get back to normal. Once she got past the first few days of junior year, when everyone would feel obligated to say something awkward, she'd be able to focus on something important to her for a change, like losing her virginity as soon as possible.

"I'm going to bake some cookies," Irene said again, because she couldn't sit still and brood anymore, even though they had stacks of cookies in the freezer: chocolate chip with pistachios, her brother AJ's favorite.

* * *

For Alan and Edie, normal had to be redefined. They hadn't made love since the accident. The one time they tried, a few weeks after the funeral, Edie couldn't stop crying, so they decided to wait, even though neither one knew exactly what they were waiting for.

It turned out they were waiting until the World Series was over. Then, they could pick up the Sports section or watch television news with no brutal reminders. Their shoulders could begin to relax.

* * *

One late October morning, Edie actually noticed the warm water when she took a shower. She felt it tumble down the nape of her neck and her back, watched it bounce off her breasts and stream down her legs. She felt that she inhabited a body again. She felt the glide of the soap, smelled the sweet froth of the lather. She shaved her legs and felt the smoothness of her skin. She asked Alan, who was brushing his teeth, if he would wash her back, and she felt his fingertips massage her shoulders, the palm of his hands at the base of her spine.

She turned around.

They looked each other in the eye for the first time since the accident. Alan turned off the water. Edie stepped out of the tub and stood on the bathroom rug, the one shaped like a yellow cockleshell. The wet, tangled hair that she had never cut lay over her shoulders and down her back. Her stomach was round and wet. Gooseflesh raised her nipples. Alan knelt and drank the water from her navel. He licked the droplets from her belly, he pulled her down and sucked the water off one breast, then the other. They kissed like starved newlyweds, tasting each other for the first time (again), feeling one another for the first time (again), simply fucking for the first time ever, letting the anger of loss fuel lust, both of them thrusting and contracting as hard as they could, and their climax was not enough. They moved from the bathroom floor to the bedroom floor, to the bed, and back to the floor again. They knocked over the table lamp, they shoved pillows aside, they screamed, they swore, they lay quiet, finally, on top of a pile of magazines, arms and legs still wrapped around each other, weeping for the loss of their second born, for the wholeness their bodies once used to convey to their souls. But they had lost that, too, and they were too weary to try to find it again.

* * *

Ken's wedding was simple, and a mistake, although it was not a simple mistake on Ken's part at least, but a complex one, born of blindsiding grief.

It had started simply enough, when Barbara showed up at his college graduation, staying just long enough to congratulate him. The week after, she found Ken slumped on a bench at the Twin Lights, staring out at the water.

"I stopped by to see how your mom was doing. She told me you were up here."

He didn't respond.

"I've never been up here before."

"Sorry, did you say something?" His voice was as flat as his expression. He scratched at his forehead, where the stitches were out and the swelling was down, leaving only a thin red welt.

"I said I saw your mom, and she said you were up here. It's a pretty view."

"Yeah, I guess it is." He didn't look at her, even though she was dressed in a pair of very short shorts and a tank top one size too small.

"What is this place?" she asked, and slowly but surely Ken began to tell her about Marconi and his wireless. She leaned her elbow on the back of the bench, nodded and made comments like "Hmm" and "How about that" at appropriate times. When he seemed to wind down, she said, "Wow, you sure are smart, Kenny." She stood up and then bent over to brush a stray hair from his scar. "I'll see you around, okay? Bye-bye."

"Bye, Barbara."

She watched his eyes move blankly from her face down to her bust line.

"Hey, call me Barbie, why don'tcha?" She flashed her cheerleader smile and walked back to her car. "Call me," she shouted just before she disappeared down the hill.

He did. Ken was equipped with a normal amount of testosterone, which has a way of asserting its influence regardless of what the intellect or heart have to bear. One evening not long after, when they were sitting on the seawall, she comforted him with a tentative hand on his thigh, and then he was kissing her, just like that.

Things progressed quickly from then on, especially after the condom tore. From the get-go, Barbie was sick every morning and most afternoons. Edie would not hear of any course of action except keeping the baby, which shot down both grad school for Ken and the extravagant black-and-white wedding Barbie had been planning since the fifth grade.

* * *

The Church of the Orchard bus was now parked, permanently, inside the central hall of Goddard's mansion, erected on the site of that rundown farm outside of Nashville. It was almost an exact replica of the White House, except it was painted pale green, like an overripe Granny Smith. The huge central hall, as big as a ballroom, was in the public part of the mansion. Goddard's private living quarters were in the North Wing, while Jesse, Mike, and Rafe each had apartments in the South Wing. The mansion was open to fans and followers. Admission was only $20 for adults; $12 for children age 12 and under.

Mike and Rafe took turns leading the tours. They began in the equivalent of the oval office, where visitors were shown a diorama of The Orchard, in exact detail down to every tree. A miniature Rafe waved from the cider mill, a miniature Mike from the store, and a miniature Jesse from a tractor. You had to peek inside the church to see the miniature Goddard. The church interior contained tiny pews and a pulpit, but no one sat at the organ. There was no miniature Lucy anywhere in the display, no Alan, no Edie.

Next, the tour moved to a small theater where a 15-minute film showed Goddard and the men on the road. It ended with a 60-second trailer for Goddard's TV show. Then the tour group proceeded to the studio where the live weekly shows were broadcast and taped for future syndication. (If it was a show day, they could pay an extra $10 to be in the audience.) Then it was on to the old Bluebird, where in single file they walked through the front door of the motor coach and out the back. The coach was set up as though it was at a rest stop, with a map open to Nashville on the passenger seat and four mugs of plastic apple cider on the dinette. The final stop on the tour was the gift shop, where they could buy die cast Bluebirds ($12.99), T-shirts ($16.99), baseball caps ($11.99), key chains ($3.99), signed photos of Goddard in his pulpit or Goddard and his team on the front lawn ($19.99 unframed; $34.49 framed), videotaped sermons ($9.99), bags of dried apples ($6.99), apple cider mix (just add water, $1.99), apple-shaped light switch covers ($2.99 each or two for $5.49), dishtowels with a picture of an apple and "Church of the Orchard" embroidered on them ($4.99), and new this year, Goddard bobble-heads ($14.99).

Goddard no longer appeared in person on these tours. So many people wanted to see him, touch him, and get his autograph that it wreaked havoc on the tour group schedule. He sent Jesse in his place. Jesse, when he wasn't talking to publicists and accountants, stood on the second floor landing for five minutes, waved, and sometimes got his picture taken holding a small child. At the end of the day he made his daily report to Goddard while the boss, sipping a glass of cold cider, soaked in his deep Jacuzzi with shiny brass faucets. Goddard always grimaced at the first sip—no cider will ever be as good as theirs had been—but it remained his drink of choice. Only on Sunday evenings would he allow Jesse to add a splash of applejack.

One weekday, Jesse was standing unobtrusively in an alcove, watching the tourists on the floor below. He wasn't entirely happy about how things were going. Of course, it was a relief not to be on the road anymore, and he had no complaints about his nice apartment in the South Wing. It had a sizable living room, bedroom, office, and kitchen, although the four men still ate together in Goddard's kitchen more often than not, sitting around a replica of the old trestle table. Jesse's bathroom also had a marble countertop, even a bidet, and his own Jacuzzi with shiny brass faucets, although it wasn't as spacious a tub as Goddard's. After so many years in the cramped Bluebird, Jesse was enormously grateful for Goddard's generosity. But he was more than a little uneasy at the tone of Goddard's sermons lately. He was having second thoughts, too, about the vow of celibacy Goddard recently made them all take. He wasn't at all convinced that abstinence was an essential cobblestone on the road to salvation.

What really gave him pause were some of the creepy fans in the studio audience and here on the tours. Three quarters of the tour groups now consisted of bearded men in ill-fitting dark suits. A few of them brought their wives and daughters, who were always dressed with conspicuous drab modesty in long-sleeved cotton turtlenecks and shapeless denim jumpers hemmed at midcalf or longer. Their hair was usually pulled back in a bun or covered by a cap not unlike those worn to bed by women in the 1700s. The women seemed awed by the mansion and impressed by the bus. They enjoyed the gift shop, but otherwise they didn't look like they were having a particularly good time.

The men, on the other hand, did a lot of laughing and joking and arm-punching. At least most of them did. Once in a while the tour group included an unattached man, and although most of these loners were nondescript, occasionally Jesse glimpsed a weird look in their eyes, like the one he saw down there now in the day's final group. The man kept his hands in his pockets and looked at the women sideways with an expression on his face like he just bit into a crab apple. Jesse had him pegged as a fanatic from the second he walked in the door. Once, a man just like that made a scene right there in the main hall, punching one of the women in the breast before anyone knew what was happening. Luckily, Mike and Rafe were there in a flash and threw the guy out. A prompt out-of-court settlement with a nondisclosure clause precluded any threat of adverse publicity. But ever since then, Jesse had beefed up security with hidden cameras and recorders and a team of security guards, one of whom is always assigned to each tour, pretending to be one of the group. Jesse wondered if the sour apple man might actually be one of their own guards. If so, he was overacting.

After the compound gates were shut at 5 p.m. and he had a few minutes to himself, Jesse went for a walk in the garden behind the mansion. He strolled through the small apple orchard, where the trees were so young his head and shoulders were visible above them, making him feel like Paul Bunyan. Beyond the orchard was a meadow lined with woods, which he entered, grateful for a little solitude. He sat down on a fallen log, listening to the peaceful soughing of the wind in the trees.

Life had gotten way, way too complicated. He sometimes wished they could be back in The Orchard, when the only problems they had to deal with were a late frost or an outbreak of canker. Or back on the road in the crowded Bluebird, stopping in a small cash-strapped town, where a manageable group would gather under their tent to sing and listen to Goddard talk about apples and love. It seemed to Jesse that although Goddard still used the word "love" in every sermon, he wasn't really talking about love the way he used to, the beautiful kind of love that welcomes all souls into its embrace. He thought the Church of the Orchard had gotten out of hand. Goddard was not as involved as he should be in day-to-day decisions. He delegated too much, letting his staff of writers make not-so-subtle changes to his sermons, although they always said, "We're just tweaking it here and there." It seemed to Jesse there was more concern with ratings than with the kind of messages they used to preach when the Church was just the four of them. He wasn't sure if Goddard was even in control anymore, and if not, why Goddard went along with it. On days like this he half wished another tornado, or maybe a flood, would come along and sweep it all away, so they could start over again and this time get it right.

Jesse rubbed his hand on his beard, got up, and started walking back to the mansion. He felt disloyal to even be thinking like this. Surely there was still real love in the old man's heart. He must have a long-term plan, a vision, that he just wasn't sharing, and Jesse should just trust in Goddard as he had always done.

What else could he do?

* * *

One afternoon, after finishing the day's baking, Edie sat in front of the television, nursing Seth. Seth had been as much of a surprise to Edie as Ken and Barbie's little boy had been, maybe more so, because she had thought of herself as infertile when no more children had followed Irene. She knew exactly when and where Seth had been conceived—that October day on the yellow, shell-shaped bathroom rug—and even though she knew it was unfair to this baby and to her dead son, she couldn't help but consider Seth a replacement gift.

Thinking this didn't make her love him any less. He looked just like Alan, with the chocolate-colored eyes and smiling mouth that would make him as handsome when he grew up as he was adorable now.

It was so good to have a baby in the house again. She relished the familiar smell of baby powder, the music of the mobile that spun brightly colored birds above his crib, the way he cooed at her before he went to sleep. Most of all, she loved to sit like this, cuddling his warm little body close to her heart, nurturing him with her love as well as her milk.

She had tuned to a channel at random, just to have background noise. She ignored the commercials for plastic wrap, tomato soup, yet another gas-guzzling, unstable SUV.

The screen went black momentarily as the next show was cued. She looked down at her son, cradling his head in her free hand, while the nasal tones of a country and western song came on. She sighed. It was not her favorite style of popular music. She reached around in the sofa cushions for the remote, trying not to disturb Seth's concentration.

You can love with all your heart,
You can love because you're smart,
You can love because this good ol' man loves you-ou-ou.

"And now," said the announcer, "live from Nashville, Tennessee, it's the Church of the Orchard Hour, with the guitar-picking, banjo-plucking sounds of the Two-Tones, special guest Oliver North, and your host, the one, the only...Goddard!"

Edie looked up sharply at the screen, startled to see her father walk across the stage in a suit jacket the exact color of a Red Delicious apple. His shirt, tie and pants were dark green, his shoes were brown. His silver hair shone in a golden spotlight as he turned to wave to the audience, then he moved downstage and shook hands with the men sitting in the front row. He ignored the lone woman sitting there. In fact, when the camera panned across the wildly clapping audience, Edie saw only a handful of women's faces in the camera shot; each face wore a polite smile, but she thought their eyes looked wary.

Goddard held both hands up and the audience quieted down. "I am," he started to say, but he was interrupted by wild clapping. He grinned and waved his hands again. "I am, as always, so happy to see you all that I think my heart will burst open right here in Nashville, Tennessee, in the good old U.S. of A."

Again, the audience cheered and clapped. The Two-Tones, whom she recognized as Rafe on guitar and Mike on banjo, strummed a few bars of "I'm Proud to Be an American." So far, the show was more like a Nascar event than a church service.

After another round of applause, Goddard moved over to an apple-shaped podium and began to preach the way he had preached so many years ago from the plain pulpit of the white clapboard church amid the apple trees. But the text of his sermon had changed.

"My friends, my children, you have heard me for these many weeks tell you that love is the answer to all your questions, that love is essential for your happiness, that love is the key to your prosperity. And I still believe that's true with all my heart." More applause.

"BUT," he waggled one finger of his right hand. "But...there are some people in this world who make it awfully hard to hold that kind of love in our hearts." The camera switched to the nodding audience and back to Goddard.

"You all know the kind of people I mean."

"Yeah," shouted the audience.

"People who don't care about love!"

"Yeah!"

"People who take love and twist it and snap it like a piece of string!"

"Yeah!"

"People who turn love into something obscene and dirty!"

"Yeah!"

"People who take your love and throw it right back in your face like ungrateful offspring!"

Edie flinched. She had to remind herself that Goddard was staring into a TV camera, not directly into her eyes.

His voice rose with every sentence, and so did the voices of the audience. After the crescendo of their response, he pounded on the pulpit and shouted, "Behold!"

He pointed behind and to the right. A large screen descended at center stage. The studio lights went dim. An announcer who sounded just like Jesse said, "We'll be right back after this word from our sponsors."

A commercial for toilet paper came on, followed by one for mouthwash and one for deodorant. The screen went black again, then it showed a succession of images: Madonna, Angelina Jolie, Martha Stewart, Oprah Winfrey, Hillary Clinton. With each image, the studio audience shouted, "Not anymore."

The camera cut back to Goddard. His face was hard as he asked, "Can you see a pattern here? There is evil brewing in the world, an insidious evil so subtle you don't even see it coming, evil lying like a snake in the grass ready to strike, evil that wants to eat its way into your heart. My friends, this kind of evil will grasp you before you even know it. This is the evil"—he paused and looked at the camera so long that Edie felt he was staring right at her—"this is the *evil* that will make a mockery of a man's love."

Edie found the remote and switched off the TV. She felt sick to her stomach. She moved Seth onto her left shoulder and rubbed his warm little back. She had never seen such an expression on Goddard's face, never heard such poison in his words, not even on the day he had found her in bed with Alan and threw them both out of The Orchard. She knew the old man had been badly hurt by both of them, but she had hoped he would get over his anger—hoped he had gotten over it long ago, in fact—and she had hoped to have him knock on their door someday to resume a relationship.

He had disappeared the day of that violent tornado that had made national headlines. They'd seen the photos in the newspaper: the twisted trunks, the uprooted trees, the concrete slab, all that remained of Goddard's church. Both she and Alan had tried writing to him afterwards, hoping their letters would be forwarded to his new address, but they always came back stamped "addressee unknown."

What kind of church was he running now? What had happened to make him preach the kind of things she had just heard? Had the tornado that destroyed the orchard destroyed his mind as well?

When Alan came home from the restaurant that night, after they had put the baby to bed and were getting ready for bed themselves, she told him what she had seen and heard on the show.

Alan frowned but he was skeptical. "Sweetheart, it can't have been all that bad. Goddard was never like that."

"You didn't see him. You didn't hear him. You don't know." She stood in front of the dresser in her nightgown, brushing the long, wavy, hair that was now frosted with gray. "He was mean spirited. He was ugly. It felt as though he was talking about mother, and about us. It felt like he was talking to *me*."

Alan shook his head. "He was talking to a camera, my love. I'm sorry you got so upset, but it can't have anything to do with us after all these years. We were just kids. I'm sure he's forgiven us, and he's just gotten wrapped up in show business. He probably has to be so dramatic to keep his ratings up and make his sponsors happy."

"I hope that's all it is, but next week I want you to watch it to see for yourself."

They got into bed and turned out the lights, but the bedroom was never fully dark, not since the city had installed sodium lights on the Navesink River Bridge. The eerie orange glow shone through the drapes all night and made it hard for Edie to fall asleep.

She turned up the volume on the baby monitor on the night table. She and Alan lay together like spoons, with his arm around hers. He held her hand in his and they listened as Seth woke briefly, waiting to see if he was going to cry. Instead, he cooed himself back to sleep. Soon Alan was breathing like Seth, evenly and with a quiet, regular snore. She liked hearing it, liked feeling his body so close. She was beginning to feel lonely with only one child at home. She wanted a house full of babies and toddlers again. She wished Ken and Barbie and their little boy were living here instead of up in White Plains. She wished her girls were home, but they were visiting their grandmother. Edie couldn't travel with an infant, and she hated being so far away from her other children.

She put a pillow over her head to block out lights, but that didn't take away the uneasy feeling she'd had since watching that dreadful TV show. She got out of bed and tiptoed into the baby's room.

Seth slept on his back. Edie could see his tummy rise and fall with each breath. Her baby was fine. The night was still. If there were still town criers, then one would be roaming the brightly lit streets, calling, "Eleven o'clock and all is well." But Edie had a growing feeling that all was not well, and had not been for a long time.

When had she last felt truly relaxed and truly safe, except in her husband's arms? Not since AJ's accident, certainly—but before that? Not when they took over the restaurant and all the responsibility of ownership. Not during the lean years when babies came too quickly but jobs did not. Never during childbirth. Not sneaking around The Orchard, not even at The Grove, serene as it was, both too hidden in the woods and too open within the gates, with no locks on any doors. Certainly not during a childhood spent on the road.

Maybe the only time she ever felt really, truly safe was as a very, very little girl, on a windy day at Point Pleasant Beach, flying a sunny yellow kite.

* * *

While Edie was watching her son sleep, sunset was only an hour away at The Grove. The girls had spent the afternoon with Lucy, getting The Sanctuary ready for the coming-of-age ceremony the next day, the first they would celebrate since Irene's two years before. Lucy was inside, making sure the ancient structure was clean and prepared. She had put her granddaughters to work outside, picking up twigs and making sure the grounds were comfortable enough for sleeping under the stars. The weather was holding well, and tomorrow was going to be a fine night.

They were just about finished. Sheila, always fastidious, walked a short way down the path to rinse her hands in the creek. Irene was kneeling, making sure the double row of white stones that marked the edge of the path was straight and neat. She didn't want Petal to trip over anything tomorrow night. Anna stood up, brushed her hands on her shorts, and watched the play of orange light against the treetops as the sun began to set. She was the only one looking down toward rest of The Grove when the evening exploded.

A fireball rose over the trees, its edges curling over into black smoke. Irene jumped to her feet. Sheila ran back. Lucy was just emerging from the entrance to The Sanctuary when the night exploded a second time. She stood up, herded the girls together and ran with them deep into the woods behind The Sanctuary. They crouched behind an ancient fir. All three girls were shaking and crying, but Lucy spoke to Anna in a sharp whisper that allowed no questions and no arguments.

"You need to get help," she said. "Take your sisters and keep going down the hill to where the creek meets the river. Follow the riverbank east until you come to the ranger station. It's a couple of miles but you need to get there as fast as you can. If no one is there, break in and use the radio to call for help. Do you understand?"

Anna nodded. "But Nana Lucy, aren't you coming with us?"

"Not until I know what's happening back there. I'm responsible for those women, do you understand? Just as you are responsible for Sheila and Irene. Someone has to get help from outside, and no one else can do now that but you. *So do not follow me!* Promise you'll obey me, all of you."

They nodded. "We promise, Nana Lucy," Anna said.

Lucy gave each girl a hurried kiss. "I love you, always remember that. Now *go! Hurry!*" She pushed them away, waiting only until she was sure they were obeying her before she turned and ran as fast as she could back to her own sisters.

The Grove was on fire. Lucy could see the yellow glow through the firs, a mockery of the nearly full moon rising behind her. She knew every tree root on the path she had walked on for so many years, but there was smoke, and there were tears in her eyes, making her stumble, slowing her down. She caught her skirt on brambles and tore the fabric free. She fell twice, all the while hearing nightmare sounds, but not from the woodland creatures, who themselves were running away from the horror. The very air was traumatized by the sharp crack of gunshots, by screams, by the snap of flames. And by distant whoops of brutal joy as engines came alive and vehicles sped away.

She stumbled again, caught herself before she fell, and lurched into the clearing, wanting to shout with rage and despair though she could not breathe. She stood for a moment, doubled over, gasping.

Everything was on fire. Every cottage, the milking shed, the barn, even the sunflowers in the gardens. She smelled gasoline and gunpowder. Where were the women? There were twenty-one younger women living in The Grove. She ran from fire to fire, choking on the smoke, hair singed by the heat.

It was Star she found first, her beloved Star, and beyond her Petal, whose coming-of-age they would have celebrated, and Daphne who sheared the alpacas, and Isis who had taught Irene how to bake. One after another she found them, all twenty-one, all dead. Bludgeoned, shot, blown apart, bodies hacked like firewood. All the animals burned alive, the entire compound destroyed. Lucy fell to her knees and howled, a sound that made far-off wolves run away, hair rising on the back of their necks.

It was the end.

The end.

The end.

Anna, Sheila and Irene ran as fast as they could in the growing dark, following the path to the ranger station. It was empty but unlocked. They went inside and radioed for help as they'd promised. They were so exhausted they couldn't have made it back to The Grove even if they tried. Fearfully, they kept their promise to Nana Lucy and sat huddled together on the ranger's couch until the ranger and the RCMP arrived, but of course the police arrived too late. The girls were questioned by the ranger about what they were able to see and hear from the hillside, but they were not allowed to go back to the site. A female officer put them to bed near dawn, and in the morning made sure they were on the next plane East. By the time they were on their way home, the news was all over the CBC, and it stayed on the cable news channels as "breaking news" for a full 48 hours. Edie was frantic until she was reunited with her daughters, which took place at Newark Airport in a throng of video cameras and on-air personalities.

None of them would see Lucy again.

After all the crime scene people finished crawling over the site with ash-covered booties, taking photographs and putting samples in zip-lock bags for analysis and placing the dead in body bags, the police did a body count and realized Lucy was missing. They attempted a search, but the fire had spread out from The Grove, obliterating any trail. They assumed that she had tried to flee, but was consumed by the flames.

The charred debris was bulldozed flat. Nothing remained except a burned out clearing amid scorched Douglas firs. Even the roadside stand where they used to sell honey and vegetables and goat's milk soap was gone, torched by what the investigators assumed was a Molotov cocktail. Everyone agreed it was a lucky thing the lush woodland had been damp enough to keep the fire from spreading any further.

As time passed people forgot there had ever been a colony of women living there, although once in a while a hiker would claim to have seen a crazy old woman with pale blue hair skulking behind the trees.

* * *

When the joint RCMP and FBI investigation attributed the attack to a fanatical arm of the Church of the Orchard, a visibly shaken Goddard vehemently denied any connection with them. He insisted his sermons were not intended to incite violence. He swore his message was of love, and only love, for men and the women who love them. He condemned the violence as the depraved act of a few misguided souls.

Goddard's public relations staff moved into damage control mode from the moment the story broke through the capture and trial of the perpetrators, all of whom were eventually found guilty and sentenced to life imprisonment, pending appeal. Still, Goddard's advertising sponsors dissociated themselves from his TV show, which was then canceled. The Church of the Orchard lost most of its members.

Goddard canceled all tours, retreated into his mansion, and shut the gates behind him.

Mike and Rafe got jobs playing backup in a Nashville recording studio.

Jesse wept.

* * *

It would be many years before Anna and her sisters could sleep easy, until they stopped waking in the middle of the night, straining to hear whether the noise that terrified them was benign, simply the house settling, a book falling to the floor from a sleeping hand, the rumble of a locomotive hauling freight cars full of ordinary things like household appliances and new cars. They would have long talks about what happened, at home and with school counselors, trying to understand the depth of hatred that made men slaughter women they didn't even know, women who had never hurt them. They would wonder when the hatred began, when it might end; whether it would ever end; whether you had to move somehow into a parallel universe to escape it; whether even in a parallel universe it would be the norm, like Dorothy going all the way to Oz only to find that people there were just like people back home.

Although Anna knew that her parents and school counselors wanted her to forget that night, she thought about it often. She thought that even if you click your heels three times, and wake up in your own bed, there's no place like home because there *is* no place like home, not anymore, and maybe not ever again. Between AJ's accident and the destruction of The Grove, she now knew that home was never safe, peaceful, and truly happy, like that orchard their father used to tell about in bedtime stories. His tales were so vivid he had made it seem like a real place, but now Anna understood it had only been make believe. Because if The Grove wasn't that safe place, then surely no such haven had ever existed.

Anna dropped out of college and moved back home to Highlands. On one of her frequent bad nights, she got out of bed, put on her bathrobe, and shut the bedroom door behind her as quietly as she

233

could. She knew her mother rarely slept through the night anymore, either, but she wanted to be by herself for a while. She tiptoed down the hall and into the kitchen. She picked an apple out of the bowl on the counter and tossed it absently from hand to hand. She stopped and bit into the apple, a red Gala, but was oblivious to its cool, sweet crunch. She stared out the window at the Navesink River and the huge dark bulk of the ocean beyond the narrow strip of barrier island. The orange lights on the bridge shone down into the water; she could see its current running fast toward the sea. Tide going out, she thought. What would it be like to let a boat carry her along on the tide, around Sandy Hook and into the wide ocean? How far would the tide take her? Would it be possible to drift from sea to sea, never touching land, never seeing people?

Of course not.

She took another bite of apple, but she wasn't really hungry, so she set it down on the counter and rubbed her eyes with the heel of her hands. The only way she would get any sleep tonight would be to take one of the sleeping pills that had been prescribed for her right after— she held her breath, willing the image not to come: *the night exploding into screams.* But the scene played in her head like a movie she couldn't shut off, a symptom of post-traumatic stress disorder, the doctor had told her. Perfectly normal, under the circumstances. How comforting.

Anna hurried into the bathroom, opened the medicine cabinet, and grabbed the pill bottle with shaking hands. She took a pill with a slurp of water from the faucet and held the sides of the sink until her hands were steadier. When she could, she wiped her mouth and shut the medicine cabinet. Her face in the mirror looked gaunt. She could see it reflected in the full-length mirror on the back of the bathroom door. The two mirrors tossed her back and forth like the apple she'd been holding, back and forth, back and forth. She was receding into the glass, each image getting smaller and smaller, disappearing into a silver-lined wormhole taking her back to that exploding night and beyond to every nightmare she'd ever heard of: girls' faces devoured by acid in

Afghanistan, girls whose genitals were mutilated in Egypt, girls with bound feet in China, girls dying in the holds of slavers, girls raped in every battle that men had gloried in, for as long as there had been men and battles.

She turned out the bathroom light and went back to bed. She lay on her side, holding a pillow to her chest, and stared at the window, waiting for sleep. Something odd about the light against the blinds made her open them.

From here, the artificial orange glow of the bridge lights was less apparent. She could even see a star or two. She opened the blinds all the way. There, framed in the upper half of the window, was the full moon, but only a sliver of bright light shone from one side. The face of the moon was almost completely eclipsed by the Earth's shadow.

Anna shivered and wrapped her alpaca-wool blanket more tightly around her shoulders. She saw the sliver of brightness narrow to a line, and then wink out completely. The face of the moon was now the rusty brown of dried blood, dark and duller than the skin of an apple.

CPSIA information can be obtained
at www.ICGtesting.com
Printed in the USA
JSHW020928251120
9810JS00005B/12